Once, Upon an Island

Other Books by
Laury A. Egan

FICTION
Jenny Kidd
Fog and Other Stories
The Outcast Oracle
Fabulous! An Opera Buffa
A Bittersweet Tale
The Ungodly Hour
The Swimmer
Turnabout
Wave in D Minor
Doublecrossed

POETRY
Snow, Shadows, a Stranger
Beneath the Lion's Paw
The Sea & Beyond
Presence & Absence

LAURY A. EGAN

Once, Upon an Island

Heliotrope Books

New York

ISBN 978-1-956474-08-4

Copy edited by Karla Linn Merrifield and Beverly Jean Harris

Cover design by Laury A. Egan,
with technical assistance from Vicki DeVico and Naomi Rosenblatt

Cover photograph: "Pelican Cove, St. Croix," by Jill Dedinsky

Typeset Design by Heliotrope Books

Prologue

Islands are places where you discover who you are even if your unconscious intention is to avoid self-discovery. At first, you bask in the hot sun, in the turquoise sea riffed with aquamarine, beneath undulating fans of green palm trees. The rum daiquiris taste delightful, everyone and everything is fun. But, eventually, the shorelines become walls into which you collide, and the romantic magnetism of your tropical paradise turns into claustrophobic confrontation. Then, if you don't escape, the gentle trade winds gain force, casting you upon a sharp reef, where you will be slowly broken apart.

Those who yearn for "Bali Hai" are often people seeking geographical circumcision and miles of ocean to disconnect them from their mainland lives—people who are running away from their pasts, desperate to shed the bindings and responsibilities of their previous existences. Dreamers, misanthropes, drunks, widows and widowers, depressives, small-time cons, loners, hedonists, and lost souls of every variety, including those who are still mostly innocent, as I was, at age sixteen, when I visited St. Croix in August 1966. Regardless of my youthful years, I possessed secrets—some I wished to keep from others and some from myself.

Once, upon an island…

1966

Day 1

The taxi sped along Prince Street and skidded to a swaying halt in front of the Pink Fancy, a small hotel with astonishingly bright bubble-gum-colored walls. After my mother and I stepped onto the sidewalk, the driver quickly disgorged our belongings from the cab's trunk, placed them at our feet, and hopped in the driver's seat. His car emitted a cloud of blue exhaust and took off.

The air was humid, a thick blend of salt from the nearby ocean and the perfume of flowers and vegetation intensified by an early morning shower that had greeted us upon our arrival on St. Croix. Despite my modest New Jersey tan, the afternoon sun sizzled the skin on my face. For a moment, the heat and the lush fragrances induced a dizzy, dream-like state, as if I had entered a tropical greenhouse. Even my eyes seemed fogged with condensation.

I pushed my sunglasses up on my head and stared with dismay at the steep stone steps beyond the open street-side gate and then at my mother. Our American Tourister suitcases—my large flat one, Mother's fold-over whopper, and her squat cosmetics case—stood between us, a matched trio in blue, each festooned with scarlet ribbons so we could spot them on the Pan Am carousel as they shouldered with other luggage.

At the airport, I had accepted my role as designated porter, though the taxi driver hurried to assist, probably to beat out the competition. My mother, Evelyn, had deigned to carry her aluminum case stuffed with sketchbooks, tubes of acrylic paints, oil pastels, drawing pencils, erasers, and canvas boards. This concession was unusual for her, but the contents were precious. She was planning a month of artistic production, which was the reason we were on the island. I had packed my prized Nikon F camera into a red TWA flight bag—both presents from my father—as well as rolls of Kodacolor and Tri-X film, books, a trip diary, and a private journal.

With the bag slung over my shoulder, I stood, blinking in the sunlight, overwhelmed by the glare and heat. No assistance was in sight, so I took a deep breath, and was about to grab the handle of my heavy suitcase, when my mother suddenly deposited her arts case in front of me and then straightened her navy-and-white dress.

"I'll see if there is any service, Olivia."

I started to say, "Wait," because I didn't wish to be left alone, but she was already marching up the stairs to the entrance.

After she left, I surveyed the Pink Fancy. The place seemed respectable, although a tall, wrought-iron fence surrounded the lower part of the building. On the next block, a well-kept house was protected by a similar fence. Why? Because the neighborhood also contained local residents? I swiveled around to stare across the street at a row of ramshackle dwellings, their tin roofs glazed with orange rust and sections of fluorescent green. Similar to the Crucian cars, many of which were haphazardly patched with fenders, trunks, and hoods of various colors, these homes featured a slapdash mixture of paints, such as on the structure opposite, whose woodwork was green, gold, and brown. A porch clung to the house, the deck tilting perilously. Wicker chairs and tables were strewn across its surface, and an old black woman with frizzy gray hair and her ancient dog with a similar hairdo sat together on the top step, watching me.

Wishing I could disappear, I turned away and looked upward at the clear blue sky. The sun was rounding the curve of a white cumulous cloud and now burst free, shooting intense sun on my head like a merciless spotlight. I muttered to myself, but I was stuck—unable to leave our possessions and unable to escape the old woman's scrutiny, whose curiosity had undoubtedly been snared by the sight of my glamorous mother. The lady was probably comparing my mother to me and wondering how the teenage fool standing on the steps of the hotel, her blond hair nearly on fire in the heat, could be the daughter of such a beautiful creature—a question I entertained during periods of doubt about my attractiveness, doubts that occurred whenever I glimpsed myself in a mirror, which I avoided except when necessary. At least in the last few years, I'd graduated from being a miserable, puffy mess into a taller, slimmer version, though at the moment, I felt extremely self-conscious. I pulled my suit jacket closed to hide as much of my body as possible, a habit I'd developed during that painful pre-teen period, a time made worse by my mother's criticism and her humiliating attempts to disguise my flaws in flowing dresses that she deemed "pretty" but weren't, and by cramming my feet into narrow pointed shoes that were agony to wear. Even after I emerged from this awkward stage, Mother preferred I remain unseen, having solidified her opinion regarding my inferiority and grown accustomed to my place in her shadow.

I leaned over my suitcase and fiddled with its tricolor I.D. tag, acting as if I had a purpose for loitering in the heat. This bit of silly behavior could only be justified for a few seconds—how long can someone stare at one's name and address? Once again, I considered hefting my suitcase up the steps, but I couldn't abandon the others on the street, and besides, Mother's bag felt like it was packed with bricks instead of clothes. Mine wasn't much lighter.

I straightened. Sweat slid down my face and wormed under the high collar of my ivory blouse. Risking a glance behind me, I saw that the old woman and her dog had retreated into their house. She peered at me through a window before dropping a wildly patterned curtain that blocked the view of the dim interior. I faced the hotel's entrance again, sure my face was scarlet as the prickle of annoyance mixed with my physical discomfort. My mother had probably stopped to smoke a cigarette—a habit that was a source of constant conflict, one that was especially irritating now because I was broiling in my yellow linen suit, which she had forced me to wear while she chose a cool sleeveless dress for herself. I swiped at the perspiration on my forehead, and as each minute passed, I felt more wilted and light-headed.

What was taking Mother so long? Even with a smoking break, she was seldom this slow. Usually, she rushed to the head of any line, parting crowds like a trim sailing vessel through waves, naturally assuming deference was her due—a *grande-dame* attitude was embedded in her personality, though it was overlaid with charm and social grace. Her good looks also provided an additional attractive veneer: violet-blue eyes, straight nose, a neat cap of curly dark hair arising from a widow's peak, a perfect figure, and shapely legs, the sight of which, on first viewing, had caused my reserved father to run his car up on the curb. He loved to tell that story to his male friends, a story he seemed to think was funny because a pilot should never lose control at the helm. I'd listened to him repeat this anecdote several times and watched as men grinned, slapped Dad on the back, and commented that Evelyn should have been a Hollywood movie star. Even at age fifty, she was a commanding beauty.

I was not in her league, not by miles, and never would be. My best features were my straight blond hair, inherited from my father, whose mother had been Swedish, and large brown eyes, passed down from my paternal grandfather. The fact that I hadn't inherited my mother's physical attributes was a source of embarrassment for her, which oozed to the surface at odd moments despite her meager efforts to hide her opinion. On the other hand, I wasn't much competition, which balanced her disappointment. However, even minor competition offended Mother, and as the only other female on her playing field, I was left as the primary target for judgment and criticism.

Shifting weight from one foot to the other, exasperation breaking out with perspiration, I pondered once again whether to lug the well-named "luggage" up the steps or hold the fort, but Mother's instruction had been tacit: stay. On the other hand, she often expected me to carry things for her, like a personal bearer, because I was strong like my father and, at sixteen, already five-foot-eight inches tall and regrettably still growing. While my size often proved useful—toting groceries, for example—at the same time, it also seemed to be an affront to my petite mother, who scarcely surpassed five feet. In her mind, I consumed too much of her space, an opinion she illustrated by moving me out of her path with an elbow or complaining, "Olivia, you're always underfoot." Nor was she pleased that I looked down on her, which I did, literally and sometimes figuratively. Regardless of the size and strength difference between us, ours was a hammer and nail relationship, with me usually playing the role of the nail, though Mother portrayed herself as a put-upon, all-suffering parent burdened with an imperfect child. As I had overheard her say to her friends, mother-daughter dynamics were difficult during the girl's teenage years. In other words, our failures were my fault.

As I sweltered on the steps, going round and round with my internal ping-pong conversation, I realized that this trip spent in my mother's company might bring us closer, or it might rip apart the fragile threads binding us together. I didn't know which would occur, but I decided two things: I would no longer allow my mother to define or control me, and I needed to stop tormenting myself over the loss of my little brother, Simon. The perfect, favorite child.

Up to now, I'd failed at both.

Finally, my mother appeared on the landing above. A few feet behind her was a very handsome man in his forties, with burnished bronze skin, green eyes lit with friendliness, and wavy, copper-blond hair parted at the left and angled back above a high forehead. His cheerful smile was instantly disarming. No doubt this gorgeous guy was the reason for Mother's tardiness.

He bounded down the stairs, his brown leather sandals making scarcely a sound, and offered his hand. Giving mine a firm shake, he said, "Hi, I'm Travis McVay."

"Olivia Livingston," I replied, though my voice sounded muffled. Either the sun or his radiant personality had melted my brain.

"Let me get those." He nodded at the two heavy suitcases.

Before I could respond, he gripped the handles of my suitcase and my mother's huge fold-over bag. I stood there, observing his crisp white shirt with sleeves rolled neatly above the elbows, his khaki shorts, and his flawless tan, and thought he was one of the best-looking men I'd seen in a long time.

As Travis struggled to carry the suitcases up the steps, he looked back and whispered, "Some people know how to travel light."

Perhaps I was imagining it, but his expression hinted at a small collusion, though this was conveyed with amusement rather than disapproval of my mother, who remained standing above us. I hauled her cosmetic case and aluminum portfolio to the top level, chiding myself for being so critical and vowing, for the millionth time, to be nice.

The Pink Fancy was arranged around an irregular L-shaped aqua swimming pool, whose sparkling water made me want to dive in, yellow suit and all. I resisted the impulse and looked to my right, where a gallery area was shaded by a dark blue scalloped awning. White plastic chairs, chaises, and tables were scattered on the gallery's wooden deck; along the back, between apartment doors, ran a cabinet holding a box stereo and a collection of records and books. At the left, a stone wall hemmed in a large garden, which overflowed with red, pink, and yellow hibiscus. Across from the pool's entrance was a small office fronted by a half-door below, fitted at center with a shelf, and vertically folded white shutters above.

Travis removed three keys from a pegboard inside the office and gestured to a red Coca-Cola machine by the door. "We use an honor system. Just mark down what you take." He indicated a clipboard hanging next to the keys. "And the same goes for snacks. Come in the office and help yourself to potato chips or nuts—whatever."

Coca-Cola was my favorite. Glancing again at the pool, I was eager to ditch my hot clothes in favor of my bathing suit. The image of lounging on one of the floating rafts, soda in hand, was enticing.

With us in tow, Travis carried the heavy suitcases to the last door on the left of the gallery. "The apartment next to you is Flattery, which is usually empty." He chuckled at his joke. "The others are Frivolity, Felicity, and Fertility." Travis laughed again. "I give that one to newlyweds for obvious reasons." He pulled the keys from his pocket. "You're here, in Fantasy."

"Better Fantasy for an artist," my mother said, smiling.

"I thought so, too," replied Travis, who apparently was familiar with my mother's artistic intentions, probably because she had requested space to work. "And just so you know the hotel's layout, that's Little Joy." He pointed to a stand-alone unit looking down on the pool, one reached via a cement path flanked by flowering plants and a short series of stone steps. Below Little Joy, a recessed area contained two more chaises, a round table with a sky-blue umbrella, and four chairs. A small bar and sink, sheltered by a short awning, were next to the office.

"Beyond it are three other units and, past those, on the left, is Upper Joy." Travis chuckled again. "I live there. Appropriate for a carefree fellow, don't you think?"

Mother raised a well-shaped eyebrow and laughed.

As Travis was unlocking the door, I noticed the scent of lemon on the sun-warmed wood. Presumably, the deck was scoured with lemon juice and water, the lemons provided by a fruit-laden tree growing by our corner of the building within a brown railing that led to the hotel's laundry.

The apartment's living room contained an open cabinet stocked with glasses and a few cooking items, a small refrigerator, and a hot plate, all facing a couch, bookcase, coffee table, and two chairs.

Mother laid her straw handbag on the table. "I believe this will make an excellent studio."

"I'm glad, Mrs. Livingston," Travis replied.

"Oh, please call me Evelyn."

The way my mother said her name sounded different to my ears, experienced as I was in parsing nuances and tone shifts in order to analyze changes in her mercurial personality. She could have introduced herself earlier as Evelyn, but perhaps she hadn't wished to permit this familiarity during the initial exchange with Travis. She maintained a firm set of rules regarding social etiquette, or at least they were firm for everyone else.

"Let me show you the bedroom." Travis brought our suitcases inside and switched on an overhead light above two twin beds, a dresser, and a makeup table with chair. An air conditioner rumbled in one of the windows, creating a welcome chill. Unlike me, Mother detested air conditioning. Unlike me, she was always cool. I knew she would turn it off.

"Here's the bathroom," he said, "and closet."

Travis then crossed the bedroom and unlocked a glass door leading to a long open porch. A half wall ran along its outside perimeter, allowing a view of the blue-green ocean in the distance, the nearby houses, and some palm trees swaying in a drowsy breeze. On the far end, two right-angled walls of white louvered shutters created an alcove for a single bed and lamp. Four chairs and a plastic-topped dining table were placed in the middle of the floor. A second glass door led into the living area.

I decided to claim the porch as my sleeping quarters, even though the main bedroom might be cooler, depending on the AC situation. Privacy and separation from my mother weighed more heavily than the heat, which I assumed would ease when the sun went down. I placed my flight bag and pocketbook on the bed.

Standing by the edge of the balcony, my mother said, "The view is lovely, Travis." She gazed at him briefly, which made me wonder if it was really the view that captivated her. Then, she leaned over to survey the street and houses below. "Very pretty but this is not an appropriate place for you to sleep at night, Olivia. Or to leave any valuables."

I was about to protest, but Travis agreed.

"We haven't had trouble with theft, but we caution visitors to be careful about their belongings." He gave my mother an engaging smile.

Mother glanced at me, conveying her belief I fit that category—one of her belongings. "Quite so. I don't like the look of that." She pointed to a metal pipe designed to transport water from the roof to a large container at street level; both the downspout and container were set beyond the wrought-iron fence. "Someone could climb up from the cistern without much trouble."

Arguing was futile. "Fine," I said.

She tucked her mouth to one side, usually a signal of disapproval. Apparently, she decided I wasn't being insolent or that this was not the time for a reprimand, because her lips rearranged into a smile, one aimed at Travis. Together, they returned to the living room. I stood in the doorway and watched as she opened her purse to remove a lighter and cigarette. She lit up, found an ashtray, and moved it to the coffee table.

"Your hotel is a treasure," Mother announced to Travis. Her voice, usually crisp like a northerner's, had reverted to her original sugared South Carolinian accent. This transformation mostly occurred after a few drinks, which made me wonder if she was as intoxicated with Travis as I was. "I'm quite sure Olivia and I will have a marvelous time here."

Was my mother flirting with him? If so, I couldn't recall another occasion when she had behaved like this despite numerous opportunities. Because my father was frequently in Europe, flying for TWA, and Mother often entertained without him, she could have taken advantage of his absence with one of their male friends. To my knowledge, however, neither parent had been unfaithful, though I'd heard my mother accuse Dad of having affairs, which he angrily denied.

"I hope your stay meets expectations," Travis said. "I'll do my best to make it so."

"Thank you. I'm sure you will."

There was an awkward moment of silence. Then, he tapped a telephone on the desk. "Local connections only, I'm afraid. If you need to call the States, come to the office." He scanned the room, checking that everything was in its place, and then outstretched his arm to include me. "You and Olivia may have plans, but if you don't, perhaps you'd like to go to the Club Comanche? They have excellent Indian curry, local fish, and West Indian lobsters."

My mother treated him to a big smile. "Sounds lovely! We would be delighted."

For once Mother was correct. I was delighted. Taking my eyes off Travis was proving as difficult for me as for my mother. He seemed to possess a guileless pleasure in life and in other people. Despite his handsome looks, the man didn't appear vain or conceited—quite the opposite. Travis blew like the trade winds, cool and easy.

"Great! Shall we leave a little before seven?" he asked. "It's a short walk."

My mother agreed with enthusiasm.

"Evelyn, here is the main gate key. We allow one per unit and lock the street entrance at midnight—either I do or my night man does. The gate is open before then. And Olivia, here is your apartment key."

"I don't think she'll need her own key," my mother interjected.

"I might. You're planning to be sketching in town, aren't you?" I took the key from Travis.

"Well, yes, I suppose," she said.

Travis gave me an amused look and departed, closing the door behind him. Not wishing to extend the conversation with my mother, I walked into the bedroom, moved my suitcase to the floor near the porch door, and rifled through my clothes to find my blue tank bathing suit, sandals, and a tube of Coppertone oil, whose dark scent equated with sexy in my imagination. I hurried into the bathroom to change, excited by the prospect of the pool and perhaps another interaction with Travis. From experience, I knew Mother would unpack her clothes and art supplies first and was less likely to swim until late afternoon when the sun was lower, if at all. She was not a fan of tanning, nor was she especially interested in getting her coiffed hair wet.

When I returned to the front room, the air was awash in a cloud of cigarette smoke. Mother was sitting, perfect legs perfectly crossed, on an end chair.

"Olivia?"

I didn't slow my transit toward the door, so she exhaled a long breath, which added to the air-borne morass. Her smoking behavior was manipulative, designed for subtle control. When she said, "Just let me finish this cigarette," everyone was required to wait for her. To focus attention, the flame of the lighter, the outpouring of smoke, drew all eyes. The implication was now clear: until her cigarette was extinguished, she expected me to remain in the room.

She coughed, then said, "Where are you—"

"Swimming." Ignoring her, I opened the door and fled to fresh air and freedom.

Living with my mother in such tight quarters—and with her smoke, which aggravated my allergies—would be trying. I intended to wander around Christiansted, to read on the porch, and to swim and sunbathe. The big draw to being near the pool was Travis, who, at the moment, was standing in the gallery area by the stereo. A jazz record was playing.

"Les Brown and His Band of Renown," he explained before I asked.

I nodded. My mother liked Glenn Miller and Eddy Duchin as well as the pianist Carmen Cavallaro, so I was somewhat familiar with Big Band music. "I listen to Broadway mostly."

Travis fanned a handful of record jackets, including *Kiss Me, Kate.* "You can play whatever you want."

"Thanks. In fact, I rather like what you have on. Les Brown, was it?"

"Yeah." He chuckled. "You have good taste."

Standing beside him, I realized he was only an inch or two taller than I was, though his sweeping gestures and expansive personality made him appear larger. As "Sentimental Journey" began, I felt warmed by the sun and by Travis's high-voltage smile.

When he returned to his office, I headed to the shallow end of the pool, laid a towel on a nearby chaise, twisted a rubber band around my shoulder-length hair, and walked to the steps. Suddenly ill at ease, I didn't want to turn to see if Travis was watching. Without hesitation, I plunged into the water. As I swam under the surface, my body cooled instantly, and the magical sensation of near weightlessness overcame me. Below, on the turquoise floor, white chains of light danced, reflections from the sun striking tiny waves on the surface.

The only sound was the faint vibration of the band's drums, though if someone shouted, I could certainly hear a raised voice. If my mother called, I would pretend to be deaf, at least for a moment or two.

I crossed part of the pool underwater and felt sleek and powerful. Like my father, I was a natural athlete, and having lived by the ocean since birth, I had learned to swim at an early age and now owned a drawer-full of medals in freestyle, sidestroke, and breaststroke.

Reluctantly, I crested to the surface to breathe, thinking I should unpack my snorkel and mask to use in the pool, although I was worried this might look childish. From what I'd read in the guidebook, St. Croix had fantastic reefs, and Buck Island Reef National Monument was reputedly an underwater spectacular, so I could always say that I was practicing. The more I thought about it, however, the more I realized I was acting as if an omnipotent behavior judge was perched on my shoulder, scrutinizing every move. Funny how the judge resembled my mother. Next visit to the pool I'd bring the snorkel and mask.

After this decision, I felt happier. I reminded myself that some of my frustration with my mother was unreasonable, that I might be inclined toward making false assumptions about her disapproval. Facing the office, I observed Travis speaking on the telephone and recalled my pledge to adopt his tolerant attitude. Tonight, at dinner, I would be well-behaved even if my mother acted in an imperious manner, though it was doubtful this would happen, not with Travis present. In social situations, she was adept at charming anyone she wished; I had studied her and was determined to pull off a fine impersonation.

For half an hour, I lazed on a yellow and blue canvas raft. When I became hungry, I stepped out of the pool and checked what snacks were available, settling on peanut-butter sandwich crackers and a Coke. Practicing my new-found nice self,

I brought my mother the same. She was sitting in the bedroom with her sketchbook and drawing the view of the houses and banana trees through the window.

"Why, thank you, Olivia."

"You're welcome." I studied her sketch. "Hey, I like that."

She looked surprised by my compliment and then smiled.

—

My mother smoked and worked and smoked. I lay on the porch bed and began reading a book on our school's summer list, William Golding's *Lord of the Flies*, which I thought might be suitable fare. The novel was dark—a story about a troupe of English schoolboys cast upon a deserted island. Although I had never been in dire straits like the character Piggy, I sympathized with how ill at ease he felt with others. His cruel treatment by the boys did not bode well; in fact, page one began with an ominous tone. I also found the character of Simon upsetting because he reminded me of my deceased younger brother and shared his name.

After twenty pages, I surmised one of the book's purposes was to illustrate how humans behave when the structures of society are removed. This led me to wonder why people were attracted to life on islands—Travis, for example. Why had he chosen to come to St. Croix? If my mother didn't ask him this evening, I would.

—

With instruction from my mother, the clothing fanatic, I dressed in a plaid Madras skirt, blue blouse, and white sandals, adding, of my own volition, a navy-and-green bead necklace. While combing my hair, I noticed my face was tinged with a light sunburn from the afternoon swim. The color looked good, and I felt almost presentable for a change, though my official dresser had not yet cleared me for take-off.

"Don't forget your sweater, Olivia." She gave me a quick appraisal before turning her attention to her favorite companion, a table-top mirror, which reflected a beautiful woman clipping on pink jeweled earrings the same color as her dress. Mother always matched.

From my suitcase, I dutifully removed a white cardigan, though it was too hot to wear. My mother believed that a lady should always carry a garment to cover her arms. She did not say why. Personally, I thought this sounded silly, something from the Victorian era that my grandmother might decree. But I supposed one might become chilly or need protection against mosquitoes. Mother opted for an ivory linen shawl draped loosely over her sleeveless dress.

We met Travis by the steps. He wore a summer-weight blue blazer with brass buttons, tan pants, and a starched, open-collared, white shirt. I glanced at my mother and noticed she was smiling at him. Obviously, Travis met her clothing prerequisites and more.

The Club Comanche—a hotel and restaurant—was situated on Strand Street, one turn off Prince Street. Travis explained the place was originally built in 1756 as a townhouse and that Alexander Hamilton had roamed the area during his youth before moving to the mainland. We climbed the stairs to the dining room. Three sides were open except for brown half walls. Wood columns supported the raftered ceiling, where rotating fans kept the place cool and made the tabletop candles flicker. I felt like I was in a large treehouse.

We were shown to a table overlooking Strand Street. On Travis's recommendation, we ordered two frozen lime daiquiris—Mother gave the okay for me to have one. Travis requested a beer.

"Now, I want you to see some of our West Indian lobsters. Follow me." He led us into the bustling, steamy kitchen, greeted the chef and several cooks, and walked to an enormous glass tank, where twenty or more lobsters grappled with each other. Their shells were olive green with yellow spots and their legs striped with blue, purple, and yellow—far more colorful than our drab, dark brownish-green New Jersey and Maine varieties.

"Notice they don't have large pincer claws. The tail meat is what's eaten," Travis said.

Although I hated the idea of killing these beautiful sea creatures, I loved lobster. At least I wouldn't witness the tank-to-boiling-water maneuver.

We returned to the table. Our daiquiris looked like magic potions in the soft candlelight—frosty green, with condensation rolling down the bulbous glasses.

"To artistic endeavors," Travis toasted, clinking glasses with us.

The daiquiri was both tart and sweet and so icy cold that it hurt my throat as I swallowed. I loved it and knew I'd want another, though my mother might not approve. At holidays and during our European travels, wine had been acceptable, but no more than one glass; now, however, I was sixteen, and perhaps the quota would be expanded. After all, the waiter wasn't fussing about my age as he would in America, so I assumed that despite it being a U.S. Virgin Island, St. Croix was more lackadaisical about serving liquor to teenagers. Whether Mother would agree with this permissiveness probably depended on her own alcoholic intake.

Everyone ordered conch chowder and lobsters. When the soup arrived, I was pleased to add another notch on my culinary belt. While the conch was somewhat rubbery, it tasted much like cherrystone clams and was served in a tomato base similar to Manhattan-style chowder but with a greater infusion of herbs and heftier chunks of meat and potato.

"This is wonderful!" my mother exclaimed.

Travis beamed, as if he had concocted the soup himself. "Sometimes conch is served with cream or in a stew."

As we finished our first course, the waiter passed by and Travis raised his chin. Within minutes, another round of drinks appeared. My mother gave me a warning look, implying that a second drink was my limit for the evening, but she said nothing.

"So, why did you come to St. Croix and buy a hotel?" she asked Travis.

He laughed. His laughter was distinctive: a small pause, then almost a reverse bark, like a jolly hiccup. It was contagious, and Mother and I shared in his amusement, though we had no idea what was so funny about the question.

"Evelyn, it's best not to ask anyone what he or she did before arriving here. Americans, Brits, Europeans, South Americans come for many reasons. But it's fair to say that many wish to maintain a state of amnesia about their past lives and to live with fewer rules and regulations." He chuckled and raised his glass. "And, of course, we also like the cheap liquor."

"Well, might I ask where you're from?" my mother persisted.

Travis sighed but smiled. "I grew up north of Baltimore. I've been on St. Croix for ten years. Owned the Pink Fancy for the last six."

I was wondering—as I was sure my mother was—how he could afford to buy a hotel and what he had done in his years prior to leaving America. Somehow, I doubted he would tell us.

Travis acknowledged my mother's artistic intentions and asked why she had chosen this specific island. My mother explained about her connection to the A. H. Riise Gallery on St. Thomas and that she had been advised St. Croix was less spoiled by tourism.

"I'll also exhibit some landscapes and local studies in New York City."

"Wow! Sounds like you're doing well," Travis said.

Mother lowered her eyes, doing an imitation of modesty.

"Well, I've been very fortunate. Some of my better paintings have been purchased by museums and private collections."

One museum and a small one at that. Collections? Mostly Mother's wealthy friends. I'd heard this spiel countless times, and though she was an extremely accomplished artist and deserving of admiration and greater recognition, I always squirmed when she tried to promote herself.

Travis leaned toward her as if eager to catch every word. "Will you show me your drawings every few days, Evelyn?"

She gave him a coquettish smile. "With pleasure. I'd be delighted to do so. Thank you for your interest."

They were flirting with each other and made no effort to disguise their behavior. Except for making a few comments, I sat there in uncomfortable silence and let my mind wander, assisted by the effect of the daiquiris, which also seemed to affect my mother. She was slurring her words a little, her speech had once again migrated to her native Charleston, and her eyes were too bright.

The lobster was delicious, served with sweet drawn butter, a mound of yellow saffron rice, and grilled tomatoes garnished with fresh mint. The cheerful colors, the candlelight, and Travis's company added to my enjoyment.

After we finished the main course, my mother excused herself to go to the ladies' room. Travis turned to me. "Are you having fun, Olivia?"

"Yes," I replied, happy to speak to him alone. "It was a lovely dinner. Thank you." I sounded like my mother and shuddered at the thought.

"My pleasure. I think you'll enjoy St. Croix. Maybe we can arrange an excursion to Buck Island or Pelican Cove."

"I'd like that. I brought a snorkel and mask."

"Excellent! And I have a selection of flippers in the office. You can try them on tomorrow morning." He finished his beer, wiped his mouth with a napkin, and asked if I wanted-ed another daiquiri. "Quick, before Evelyn comes back."

Travis gave me a mischievous grin.

I nodded, and as if the waiter had a sixth sense, he cruised by and received the signal from Travis. When my mother returned, nose powdered and lipstick freshly applied, round three had landed.

"Oh, dear," she said. "I think Olivia has had enough."

My mother seemed worse off than I was, perhaps because I outweighed her by thirty pounds. "I'm okay. Besides, this is a special evening, isn't it?"

She couldn't argue with that. Travis's face creased in a smile, and they talked about nearby buildings that would be good artistic subjects, the exchange shifting from a three-way to a two-way conversation. Usually, this exclusion would be upsetting, but tonight a pleasant mellowness had overtaken me. The evening air was warm and, together with the effects of the early morning departure and the alcohol, made me sleepy. I rested my chin on my hand and observed the people passing below. Then, I sat up. A blond-headed boy about my age was coming down Strand Street. He wore a navy blue shirt and trousers, but in the near darkness, I couldn't see his face. Within a few seconds, he vanished.

My cheeks flushed and I felt hot. *Simon.* My brother's straight hair had been cut long like the boy's, with a fringe of bangs sweeping across his forehead. The color was the same straw-yellow as mine. He even walked like Simon did—a slight hunch forward as if this might enable him to reach his destination faster.

My hands tensed on the arms of my chair. I desperately wanted to run after the boy to be sure he wasn't my brother. But what could I say that would allow me to leave? Mother and Travis were discussing the check. I couldn't bolt from the table, and besides, the boy was gone.

After the bill was sorted, we descended the stairs. At street level, no one was visible in either direction. I followed behind Travis and my mother, aware that I was a little high from the drinks. Perhaps the boy had been a hallucination of some kind? Yes. He couldn't be my brother. Not Simon.

At the Pink Fancy, Travis invited my mother for a brandy, explaining again that his apartment was above the pool, at the end of the path.

She appeared to weigh the offer, then said, "Olivia, will you be all right by yourself?"

Her question was really a statement. In other words, don't spoil her fun. I thought about my father in Rome with the airlines. Had Mother considered him once all evening?

"Yes." I felt rejected, but asking to tag along would be a mistake. "I'll read for a bit."

She opened our door and instructed me to turn the lock after she left. I thanked Travis and bid him goodnight.

"And tomorrow, flippers!" he said, grinning.

—

I turned on a living room lamp so my mother wouldn't crash into furniture upon her return, when she would probably be in an even more inebriated state. Both my parents tended to overindulge at parties, so I was familiar with the scene. At least there would be no arguments tonight, so long as I kept my mouth shut or, better yet, feigned sleep. After changing into cotton pajamas, I removed my small journal from the TWA bag, a journal I was careful to hide at home so my mother wouldn't read it. I lit a stub of a candle and brought it to the porch, where I sat and wrote about our arrival on St. Croix and about Travis. Then, as I often did, I turned to the journal's first page. My initial entry, written in tiny script in January 1958, was etched in my memory: a conversation overheard between my mother and my brother, Simon.

"Mommy, do you love me best?"

"Of course I do. I've told you many times."

"More than Olivia?"

"Yes, darling, more than Olivia."

Tears formed in my eyes, and I gritted my teeth. Crying was something I detested because it revealed vulnerability, which was like waving a red cape in front of my mother. She wasn't here, but it would be my foul luck to have her return and find me weeping. I tried to distract myself with other thoughts yet kept thinking about Mother's preference for Simon. I had never confronted her about what I'd heard. I was too afraid of the answer. But I knew, had always known, that she loved him more since the day he was born and certainly after his death in 1958.

The memory of that spring night when Simon died was grooved in my mind like a worn record. I opened the journal to my sketch of the dock and scanned some of the long entries about the accident. My descriptions of the event were thorough where I could remember what occurred; other parts were hazy or missing entirely, especially the ending. Reading about my feelings at the time, which I'd recorded, and afterward, which I'd also documented, still filled me with despair even after the hundreds of times I'd pored over my accounts. The process had become a compulsion and a torture; one that didn't really reduce the pain, only kept me engaged with Simon and with my guilt.

My brother and I had been restless for adventure, so I suggested we sneak out of the house to try night fishing for winter flounder. Simon was seven, a year younger than me, but more fearless and physically daring. Because I wished to seem brave, I often suggested escapades that appealed to him yet secretly scared me, such as this one. Simon was immediately enthusiastic, so I couldn't back down and reveal my fear of the dark.

During the afternoon, we prepared for the adventure in the garage. We tied three fish hooks to the line on my father's pole—winter flounders were small, and several would often bite at the same time. After readying the pole, Simon took a trowel into the garden and filled a bag with bloodworms, nasty little buggers that often nipped while being hooked. Meanwhile, I rode my bicycle to the store and purchased two cans of cat food—a tip Dad had passed on: puncture a can several times, fasten a long string around the tin, and dunk the cat food a few yards downstream from the hooks like chum.

Throughout dinner that evening, Simon kept jiggling in his seat. Mother asked him to sit still. He did but hardly ate anything. This should have alerted her that something was afoot because my brother always had a big appetite. However, she was planning a party for Saturday, when my father would return from a flight, and her brain was in organizational mode.

Simon and I watched television, then turned into our individual bedrooms, which were across the hall from each other, in a separate wing from the master bedroom. Our parents had presumably chosen the house because of this arrangement, so they could pretend their two children didn't exist after bedtime. This worked both ways: to our advantage when we were doing something we shouldn't, to our disadvantage when we had nightmares and were frightened. And both of us had many bad dreams, usually ignited by overhearing our parents argue in the living room. Because I was older, Simon came to me for comfort. I had no one.

We met in the laundry room after Mother went to bed. I wore jeans, a black turtleneck and wool sweater, and slip-on Keds sneakers; Simon was also dressed in dark clothes and had added a navy windbreaker. Together, we crept out the side door.

The night was clear and cool, with only a few clouds stretched thin along the horizon and underscoring the April moon, which was a nick shy of full. Its white light poured over the purple lilacs that grew along the slate path near the back door. The evening dew saturated the flowers so their scent was sweet and their petals glistened. I slowed to take in the smell because I could never resist it but then hurried on because my brother was walking quickly toward the garage. We entered and, using an awl and a hammer, I punched holes in the cat food cans and then replaced them in the paper bag, which I carried along with the tackle box. Simon grabbed the fishing pole and another bag containing the worms.

"I hope we catch something," Simon whispered.

"Me too, but I hope it's not us who get caught."

He laughed and we exited the garage and crossed into the woods. The moon cast dark shadows beneath the newly budding trees, and the humus soil underfoot was soft. Simon and I often played in the forest, seeing how close we could sneak up on each other without snapping a twig. I usually won at this game because Simon was too boisterous.

We scurried through the trees, along the winding path, past a grove of mountain laurel, their shiny green leaves slick with moonlight. I loved to read within the enclosure of these bushes during the day; tonight, their huddling shapes were suggestive of evil creatures, ogres that might rise up and carry us off. Every small gust of wind blew images of lurking monsters into my mind, and once planted there, their ferocious faces expanded larger and larger until I finally stopped and squeezed my eyes shut, willing myself not to be a coward. Simon kept going, oblivious, but he had never possessed much imagination. All he cared about was reaching the river to fish.

"Hurry up, Olivia!" he called in a loud whisper.

I couldn't let Simon think I was afraid. This outing had been my plan, and I was older and responsible for my brother. I opened my eyes and ran after him, staring at Simon's yellow head as it bobbed through the woods. If I concentrated on him, maybe I could ignore the blackness that seemed to tighten its grasp around me.

Eventually, the forest thinned, and we came upon the high bluff overlooking the river, a thin peninsula of land, and beyond that, the Atlantic Ocean. On the cliff, the treetops were withered by the wind off the sea, which always blew harder here than at our house. I shivered in my sweater and wished I had worn a jacket like Simon.

The moon hung over the black water. I looked away from the ocean and saw Simon sliding down the cliff at breakneck speed. This wasn't unusual. He loved to do somersaults and handstands and balance on fences. One morning, he told Dad that he planned to become a mountain climber or maybe a scuba diver like Lloyd Bridges in *Sea Hunt*, a show he adored. Anxious that he might hurt himself, I shouted at him to be careful, but he kept going.

At the bottom of the bluff lay a beach that partly disappeared during extreme high tides. Many years before, someone had built a narrow wooden dock, accessible by eight steps and extending from above the flood line out into the water. The walkway was decaying, and some of the boards were missing or rotten. The only vertical pilings that rose above the dock's platform were at the end, part of a square area where boats could tie up. Because there were no railings, the passage from the steps along the length of the dock required care. Simon waited by the stairs, then asked me to set down the toolbox, which I did. From within its tiered enclosure, he took two handfuls of sinkers—various weights and shapes from triangular to teardrop—and thrust them in his jeans' pockets before adding a Swiss Army knife into the pouch of his windbreaker.

"I have two Cokes in here, Olivia." He patted his chest and grinned. "Now, I'll take the pole, and you take the cat food and tie the string to the piling on the right."

While the river was usually swift, tonight it was gushing. I was thinking the tide would carry away the cat food and the trick might not work, when Simon dashed up the steps and began jumping over rotten boards. He was going fast, too fast. Even with the moonlight, it was difficult to see which planks were sound and which were not. I ran after him.

—

I closed the journal. My hands were trembling. For an instant, I considered ripping the pages from the book and burning them in the candle flame, but I knew the images and thoughts would persist regardless. I blew out the candle and lay on the bed, wishing to be erased by the darkness. Although I was afraid to fall asleep, certain of having bad dreams, exhaustion overcame me.

—

Blackness. Tree branches and bushes claw at my arms. Leaves slap my face. Running, I blast through the forest, to the cliff above the river. The ocean spreads before me, a cold wind blows, freezing my eyes. My heart is knocking in my chest. I see my brother and bound up the steps onto the dock after him. Terrified, I shout, "Stop! Simon, don't!" But he doesn't hear me or thinks I'm playing a game. Simon laughs. Laughs louder. I rush halfway down the dock toward my brother and hear a loud crack like a gun shot. My foot plunges through a wooden plank, and my sneaker slips off. A huge nail gouges my ankle. Hot blood drips into the river. I try to stand but can't. "Simon! Simon!" I yell.

I awoke, soaked with perspiration, and sat on the edge of the bed, out of breath, my body shuddering from the aftershocks of the dream. Probably I'd been calling out loud to Simon. I often did, though at home my parents were too far away to hear. Frightened that my mother had returned, I peeked into the bedroom and the living area. I was alone. While relieved she hadn't witnessed the nightmare, it was almost 12:30 a.m. according to my travel clock. Why was she so late? In the bathroom, I washed my face to cool my fevered skin, noting how upset I looked, then closed the door to the porch and turned on the air conditioner, which Mother had switched off earlier. Selecting the bed nearest the porch, I laid down, still unnerved by the dream, by the boy on the street, and by being in a strange place.

About half an hour later, the apartment door opened. I pretended to be asleep. The last thing I wanted to hear was an explanation of what she'd been doing with Travis. Plus, I felt too distressed to risk a conversation with my mother, especially after she had been drinking daiquiris and an unknown quantity of brandy.

Day 2

Sunlight slanted through the white wooden shutters. I felt frazzled, though not from an alcoholic hangover. My mother, however, would probably have a doozy. She lay on her back, snoring, which she would vigorously deny doing. On the basis of past experiences, I suspected she was unlikely to rise soon, so I slipped out of bed, grabbed some clothes, and escaped into the bathroom to brush my teeth and get dressed. A peek in the mirror revealed how dispirited I still felt. I'd seen that look before, often. As Mother would say, "If you frown so much, Olivia, those lines will set on your face permanently."

Because Dad had given me some money for the trip, I could afford to buy breakfast. I slid my camera's strap over my shoulder, placed my wallet in my back pocket, and left the apartment. A maid was removing bed linens and towels from an adjacent room. She was young and pretty, with glowing skin the color of dark plum.

"Good morning," I said.

"Good morning to you, Miss," she replied in a melodic voice.

I hurried across the gallery, down the steps, and turned right. During the taxi ride from the airport, the driver had detoured to show us the town. The largest shops were on King Street and on several neighboring streets that ran toward the harbor, but it was too early for them to be open. I felt a little guilty not sharing this first exploration of Christiansted with my mother, but I was hungry. After walking past several intriguing jewelry and clothing stores, I came across Fort Christiansvaern, a red building constructed by the Danes in 1749. From my reading, I remembered it was built to protect the port from attack, administer customs' duties, and garrison soldiers. Convicts were imprisoned in the basement, where they were often abused, but so, too, were slaves, who were probably treated worse.

I strolled around the fort's perimeter and composed several photographs, then continued away from the water until I found a small café that sold baked goods. I bought sweet rolls and tins of orange juice for me and my mother and then sat outside, wearing my sunglasses because the sun was already fierce and because they concealed my eyes from observers passing in the street. Someone once said eyes were windows into the soul; if so, better block the view.

As I ate a roll, I thought about the dream and about the blond-haired boy, who had triggered the journal reading and the nightmare. Could I find him? Was he a resident or a guest at a hotel in town? It was also possible he had taken a taxi or had driven from one of the beach resorts outside of Christiansted. Or perhaps he didn't exist at all. Perhaps he was an illusion sparked by the character of Simon in *Lord of the Flies*.

These circular thoughts renewed my concern, making me desperate to locate this boy and verify he didn't look at all like Simon. And that he wasn't my brother.

I finished my breakfast, returned to the harbor, and wandered around to see if I could find him. I looked in the lobby and bar of several hotels such as King Christian, facing the wharf; King's Alley Hotel, also on the waterfront; the Comanche; and Hotel Caravelle, on Queen Cross Street. After spending forty-five minutes checking these establishments, I returned to the Pink Fancy. My mother would fret about me—though she hadn't last night—and, besides, it was getting hot.

When I entered the pool area, my mother was on a white chaise, lying in grand style like Cleopatra on a barge. A cloud of smoke circled above her head, and she was sipping coffee probably made on our hot plate.

"Well, there you are," she said.

Did this statement contain a subtle reprimand or was it only a casual comment? I walked over to her, surprised she didn't look worse for the alcoholic wear. In fact, her makeup was immaculate, and she was wearing a sunny yellow dress that gave her a youthful appearance. I handed her a roll and orange juice.

"Thank you." She opened the tin and took a sip. "Glad you took initiative to find breakfast, but I don't want you walking around town by yourself."

After she said this, my mother gazed over my shoulder and smiled. Travis approached and greeted us.

"I'm sure Olivia will be careful," he said.

I appreciated his tactful support and wished him good morning.

"Of course she will." Mother looked away as she said this, as if she thought the opposite.

I sat on a chair a few feet from the smoldering volcano that was my mother and explained where I had been and how many interesting stores lined King Street. This was a safe topic of conversation, one that unfailingly interested her.

"We should check out the shops in a little while." She pinched off a small piece of the roll and ate it, one hand below her mouth to catch crumbs.

I agreed, somewhat confident we might manage this without strife, unless it came to clothes.

Travis glanced at Mother, perhaps noticing the slight tension. "Olivia, let's see about those flippers."

I followed him to his office and stood outside while he pulled out various sizes and colors from a large wicker basket. After trying them on, I settled on a blue pair.

In my absence, Mother had disappeared into the apartment for her sunglasses, purse, and a new pack of cigarettes. After I carried the flippers to my side of the bedroom, we headed out for our shopping expedition, saying goodbye to Travis and setting off down Prince Street. At King Street, we turned and descended toward the wharf along walkways shaded by the buildings' overhanging second stories. We passed through a series of arcades, some whitewashed, some painted pastel colors. My mother reported that much of the construction was composed of cut coral, molasses mortar, or Danish bricks brought as ballast on the trading ships during the 1700s. I had read the same information; like her, I was a thorough researcher whenever we traveled.

"I love all the shutters," my mother said. "And the red-tile hipped roofs."

I hadn't known what a "hipped" roof was, but I did now: four slanted sections joined to form a horizontal peak at the top.

We perused shops such as C. & M. Caron's, a high-end jewelry, perfume, china, crystal, and accessories store owned by the family of actress Leslie Caron. Of more interest was Cavanagh's, an emporium featuring international goods from forty-four countries. As we entered, I smelled dry straw from the pocketbooks, suitcases, and hats on display, though a selection of exotic Thai silks snagged my immediate attention. These fabrics were very appealing—woven plaids of harmonic colors such as yellow, orange, chartreuse, and olive or, my favorite, blue, purple, lavender, and green.

"Look at these." I ran my fingers along the smooth material.

My mother loved the scarves, shawls, and bolts of cloth as much as I did. I settled on a rectangular scarf in the blue-purple palette; she selected one with warm colors. Then, we moved on to the polished cotton dresses, which were a magnet for both of us. Even though dresses aren't usually my favorite items of clothing, a scoop-necked, sleeveless dress shone with turquoise, green, and white flowers. I tried it on, feeling self-conscious when I had to re-enter the showroom so my mother could see how it fit: amazingly well. In fact, I thought I looked like someone else. Maybe my glamorous mother?

"Oh, Olivia! How beautiful...and such great colors!" This was high praise from the high chieftain of haute couture.

Standing there in front of her and catching the eyes of some nearby shoppers, I realized they were regarding me with admiration, though the dress was spectacular and probably the cause of their stares. I returned to the changing room, placed the dress on its hanger, and slipped on a white blouse. Its front panel, collar, and cuffs were embroidered with white thread. The material was starched yet delicate; the salesgirl explained that the fabric would soften to the consistency of a handkerchief after one washing in cold water.

Mother wandered to some hat trees nestled in a corner. From one of the wooden pegs, she grabbed a pink, floppy-brimmed, straw hat festooned with purple and green ribbons. She modeled it in the mirror, then took a matching hat and stuck it on my head.

"Perfect!" she announced. "We can be twins."

I was not a "hat" girl, even less the type to wear ribbons, as my mother knew, and the idea of being her twin made me queasy. Feeling embarrassed, I felt my face warm and quickly replaced the floppy hat with a more sober model, one with a flat, downturned brim. After scrutinizing it, Mother agreed it was more "me."

I liked the hat, but shopping for clothes with my mother brought out my stubbornness. "No, I don't think so."

"Well, whatever you want, Olivia." She couldn't resist an almost imperceptible sniff, but she didn't protest my decision, perhaps realizing my unadorned head would be less compelling than her hatted and beribboned one.

While Mother tried on several dresses, I walked to the perfume counter and smelled Travis's scent, which I identified as

St. John's West Indian Lime Cologne. Its bottle was encased in open-weave wicker with the pale green liquid peeking through. I decided to buy a bottle as a gift for my father, hesitating only because my mother might think of Travis when Dad wore it, but then again, I would, too.

We bought the dress, the scarf, and the white embroidered blouse for me; the lime cologne for my father; and a rather "swanky" emerald dress (as she described it), straw hat, scarf, and pink shawl for my mother. The goods were inserted in orange paper bags decorated with a lively white line drawing of the shop's exterior. Mother wore her hat, cementing her tourist credentials.

After visits to The Copenhagen, Ltd. and several establishments on Company Street, I noticed perspiration had caused the orange ink on the bags to stain our fingers.

"Uh-oh. We look like orangutans," I said, displaying my hand, "with orange palms."

She examined hers, found the same inky ailment, and laughed. "I hope this washes off."

Our shopping now complete, we stopped for lunch, first scouring our hands in the restaurant's bathroom. At the table, we ordered turkey club sandwiches. I kept watch for the blond boy and considered mentioning him to my mother, but I had learned long ago not to talk about Simon, to hide odd thoughts, and to avoid making emotional admissions. No point in loading her gun so she could take potshots at me. Even so, after we finished our meal and Mother still seemed to be in such a rare good mood, I couldn't help myself.

"The other night I saw this boy—"

She set her glass of iced tea on the table and frowned. "What boy?"

Did she already know what I was about to say? I lowered my voice. "A boy who looks like Simon."

"Oh, for god's sake, Olivia." She folded her napkin with an angry snap.

"But he might be—"

"Don't be ridiculous," Mother hissed under her breath, as if I'd uttered a string of obscenities. After giving me an angry glance, she thrust her hand in the air for the waiter.

I started to apologize, but didn't. Although I knew the unspoken rules about Simon, I really hadn't said anything wrong. "Never mind."

Mother pressed her lips together and paid the check.

—

Afterward, as we walked toward the Pink Fancy, Mother seemed to forget the exchange over lunch and suggested we take a swim, to which I readily agreed, thinking it might reset the unpleasantness. Two blocks from the hotel, she slowed at a tattered house with pink bougainvillea hanging from flowerboxes and commented that it would make a fine subject. We continued on to the hotel, climbed its steps, and, once inside our rooms, hung up our new purchases. Then, Mother laid out a pair of shorts and a blouse.

"Aren't we going swimming?" I asked.

"I've changed my mind, Olivia. We'll do that another time. I'm sure you'll find someone to play with."

I stood there, stunned, as she dressed, seized her sketchbook, and hurried out the door to pursue her newest artistic quarry.

"Someone to play with?" I blew out an angry breath, folded my arms, and paced around the bedroom, trying to work off my irritation. What did she think? That I was nine years old? I felt like I'd been smacked in the face as delayed punishment for mentioning Simon's name. Yet why had my mother been friendly and offered to go swimming? I shook my head and slumped on the bed, muttering to myself until my annoyance transformed into more familiar emotions: disappointment and sadness.

I needed to do something other than collapse into depression. I stood, walked into the bathroom, and removed my clothes. My blue tank swimsuit was still damp, but I scooted it up my body and slipped the straps over my shoulders. I grabbed my book, flippers, snorkel, and mask and went outside. No one was around, so I approached the stereo and removed *Kiss Me, Kate* from its sleeve. The recording, starring Alfred Drake and Patricia Morison, was one I owned and loved. I also added the Les Brown record to the stack.

Standing by the pool, listening to "Why Can't You Behave," I thought—as I always did—that it should be my mother's theme written about me. I sat for a few minutes until my favorite song came on: "So in Love." A bout of nostalgia settled over me—not that I'd ever been in love. I'd had a few crushes, none eliciting any grand passion or reciprocal interest. Looking to the future, I tried to imagine being in a serious relationship or marriage and having a family, but I couldn't conjure such a picture. All I foresaw were more years feeling as I did now: lonely. No one was close. Not my parents or other relatives or school friends. I felt different, was different.

Dejected, I sat on the pool's second step, jammed the blue flippers on my feet, and fitted the facemask on my head and the snorkel's mouthpiece in my mouth. As I knifed into the cool water, I felt instantly better. The flippers provided easy power as I swam the length of the pool, arms at my side, moving like a human torpedo. Most likely I looked foolish, but the sensation was exhilarating. I switched off my stern self-monitor and allowed myself to be a child rather than a teenager.

When the last song of *Kiss Me, Kate* began, I returned to the steps and removed my mask, snorkel, and flippers. As I did so, I noticed a woman in her late forties, or perhaps fifty, sitting on the chaise several feet from the pool, in the curved alcove below Little Joy. She was reading a folded newspaper and was dressed in a black-and-white floral-print bathing suit. Her hair was gathered within a pink dotted-Swiss kerchief, though some silver and black curls escaped from the scarf's enclosure and fell on either side of her forehead. Her skin was tanned a deep mahogany, probably a result of recent sunbathing. The woman's slender arms and legs were graceful, yet her torso was thick—a figure others might describe as matronly. I didn't think of her in those terms because she exuded an exotic sensuality that was immediately apparent, though I couldn't explain why.

As I climbed the few steps out of the pool, the woman looked up. She wore dark green wrap-around sunglasses, so her eyes weren't visible, but something told me they would be mesmerizing.

Although I usually avoid beginning conversations, I said, "Hello," aware that I was dripping water, my hair was an uncombed mess, and I held equipment more suitable for ocean swimming.

"Good afternoon," she replied. "You must be our newest resident." Her voice was resonant, accented.

I smiled. "I suppose so. My mother and I are here for four weeks. She's an artist."

This amused the woman for some reason. Her chuckle was rich and creamy like melted chocolate. "I see. How lovely!" She removed her sunglasses to reveal luminous, grayish-blue eyes. Her gaze was direct but uncritical, appraising yet strangely empathetic. The French actress Simone Signoret sprang to mind. A few months earlier, I'd seen her for the first time in *Ship of Fools*. This woman spoke with the same musical cadence and faint sibilant lisp, though this may have derived from her native language, which I didn't believe was French.

"And what is your name?" she asked.

"Oh, sorry," I said, aware that I had been staring at the woman. "Olivia Livingston."

She considered this for a moment and then said, "Olivia

suits you." She placed the newspaper on the adjacent table. "My name is Sofiya Florián." An air of pensive sadness seemed to surround her.

"Nice to meet you." I reached for my towel and wiped my wet hands, then offered her my right. Her grasp was gentle but not tentative. "Have you been at the Pink Fancy long?"

"About a month. I'm staying up there." She pointed to the apartment above the pool, to the right of the path. "Little Joy, which I suspect is not meant to be ironic, but for me it's quite apt." Sofiya laughed. "I plan to live here until I find a job and a place to rent."

"So you're not a visitor?"

"I am a visitor everywhere." Her smile was enigmatic.

This was a sentiment I understood. Suddenly, it occurred to me that Sofiya Florián was the person I was supposed to meet at this time, in this place. I had no idea why or for what purpose.

Sofiya continued. "I was born in a village near Prague."

I nodded, intrigued. "I don't think I've ever met anyone from there. But Florián is not—"

"Yes, actually, it is a Czech name. However, my husband was...German." She said the last word with reluctance. "You are an American, yes?"

I nodded again. "From New Jersey, on the coast."

"So you love the water." She laughed. "I can see that you swim like a dolphin. Perhaps you possess a fluid spirit."

Was Sofiya some kind of gypsy? Yet she appeared to be quite thoughtful, devoid of fortune-teller theatrics. I didn't know how to respond because I'd never experienced such a startling exchange. Without asking permission to join her, I pulled over a chair and sat, covering my legs with the towel.

"I like being invisible," I admitted, surprising myself. "Although it sounds silly, being in the ocean or even a pool allows me to disappear. Kind of ridiculous."

"Not ridiculous at all." Sofiya held my glance, her

expression intent, almost searching. "I understand completely. You're wise to wish to disappear—at least some of the time. The world is often harsh. It targets the sensitive people."

She was speaking about me, but I suspected she was also referring to herself, employing an uncommon familiarity after such a brief conversation. Although I was usually shy, Sofiya's perceptiveness had stripped away my reticence. "Travis said not to ask people about their reasons for coming to an island, but—"

"I know only a little of his story. Travis is very private, as are many people who live here." She sighed. "As for me, I came to St. Croix without thinking about it. Without planning to do so."

I cocked my head. "What do you mean?"

"When my ship arrived in port, I felt drawn to the island. I had never been here before, and there was no reason to choose to stay, yet I respect instincts when they're strong. I disembarked, and after visiting several places in Christiansted, I decided on the Pink Fancy because it's more home than hotel. Thus, Olivia, I have washed upon these shores, a displaced person." Sofiya reflected on this, her eyes darkening, as if she had plummeted from dazzling sunlight into deepest shade. In a quieter voice, she added, "Maybe I have been one since I was young." She paused, observing me with unusual care. "Perhaps you are a displaced person, too."

I studied her wide-set eyes, broad cheekbones, strong chin, and full lips painted with a lustrous pink lipstick. She was not a standard beauty like my mother, but there was a churning intensity underneath the surface calm, whether the product of lifelong anguish or vestiges of youthful physicality.

"Yes, you're probably right. I do feel displaced," I replied. "I don't feel like I belong anywhere, to anyone." I hesitated, amazed by my openness. "Well, maybe I did once, for a little while. A long time ago."

Leaning forward slightly, animated by our conversation, Sofiya listened to my admission, then relaxed against the back of the chaise. "I believe we understand each other, Olivia." She smiled, as if we were old friends. "But we will talk more about this soon. Would you like that?"

"Yes, Mrs. Florián."

"Ah, please. Sofiya is better. I am no longer a 'Mrs. Florián.'"

She didn't elaborate on this remark, which whetted my curiosity to learn more about her. I noted that Sofiya wore no wedding band. Was she widowed, divorced, separated? Did she have children? I wanted to ask yet didn't wish to be impolite.

Sofiya considered me for a moment. "This may be somewhat forward, since we just met," she began, "but if you're free the day after tomorrow for lunch, would you and your mother like to come for Hungarian goulash...prepared by a Czech?" Sofiya replaced her sunglasses, perhaps dropping a veil between us or protecting herself in case I rejected the offer.

I laughed, then realized I didn't want to share my new friend, but I had no excuse not to include my mother—it was only proper for her to meet Sofiya. "I'll ask. Mother is working on a portfolio, so I'm not sure she's free. I'd like to come even if she can't, if that's okay?"

"Yes, of course. I'll prepare enough for both of you. Let me know about her tomorrow. It's fine to knock on the door. Now, I must go and cook my dinner." She tucked the newspaper under her arm and rose. Gently, she touched my shoulder, smiled, and climbed the path to her apartment.

I stood. In a daze, I carried my things to the cabinet, turned off the stereo, and walked into Fantasy, feeling quite fantastic. For some inexplicable reason, I sensed an understanding with this mysterious Czechoslovakian woman despite our differences in age—probably thirty-five years—and in our backgrounds. Was I imagining this connection? Had Sofiya perceived it, too?

The mixture of curiosity, excitement, and eagerness was oddly thrilling, as if I had witnessed a brilliant comet shooting across the sky, arriving from a far-distant galaxy. I wanted to learn about her life, and at the same time—unusual in my experience—I wished to share my thoughts.

—

I changed into a polo shirt and shorts and settled on the porch bed with my book until my mother arrived, carrying a bag of groceries. We stored some items in the refrigerator, then she placed her sketchbook on the porch table and sat in a chair. Her face was pink with heat and a slight sunburn, but she was also invigorated by her new drawings, which she spread out for me to see. Mother's ability to capture a scene was exceptional—she could draw better than any of her very talented painter friends. The displayed pages included numerous details, with lines connected to color notations such as "yellow ochre" or "alizarin crimson." I knew these names from the tubes of oil paints at home, though she planned to work with oil pastels, pencils, and acrylics on St. Croix because oils wouldn't dry before transportation to New Jersey or to the gallery on St. Thomas.

"Some of these studies can be finished into final drawings," Mother remarked.

I hesitated, remembering her earlier behavior, but meeting Sofiya had wiped some of the negativity away. "And many are great as they are. These sketches have real energy."

She stared at me. "Really?"

I nodded. "Maybe it's because of the medium, the new place, and the subjects."

"The light, clouds, architecture, and people are inspiring." She flipped through the pages, as if reconsidering her work. Then, she showed me a drawing of the house we'd seen earlier. "It's still rough, but I'm pleased with it."

I admired its composition, the colors.

Mother leaned back in her chair. "Would you like to get us a Coke, Olivia? With a slice of lime? I bought both and a few things for tomorrow's breakfast."

"Okay." From the freezer section, I pried ice cubes out of a tray, added them to glasses along with lime wedges and soda. When I returned to the porch, my mother was gazing over the distant rooftops.

"Perhaps I'll do an acrylic painting of this view. The white shutters and the buildings. I like the red roof across the street."

"With the ocean in the background?"

"Good idea, yes!"

I decided to forget about our earlier disconnection and hoped the tone of the present conversation would mark a change in our relationship, a small thaw, though I was still suspicious.

She sipped some soda. "By the way, Travis invited us for dinner tonight. At eight. A restaurant called the Stone Balloon. He says the place is a lot of fun."

—

The Stone Balloon was situated on Queen Cross Street. Travis led the way past the bar and an intimate club area, which contained card tables, captain's chairs, bookcases, and shaded ceiling lights that haloed the room with a golden aura. A few people were playing backgammon and chess. Cards and board games were also available, as well as a selection of magazines and newspapers. Mother commented on how friendly the atmosphere was, a sentiment I seconded, as we followed Travis outside into a candlelit courtyard. A big mango tree stood in the center, with banana and pomegranate trees and flowering shrubs surrounding it. Wooden tables and more captain's chairs were scattered about wherever the vegetation allowed. A Frank Sinatra recording was being piped through loudspeakers.

Our table was so rickety that Travis pulled out a matchbook. "I always come prepared because all of the tables are on uneven ground." He wedged the matchbook under one of the legs, tested the steadiness, and shrugged. "Good enough. We'll be tipsier than the table pretty soon."

The evening was warm, and the enclosure was sheltered from the sea breeze, so I was glad to be in slacks and a short-sleeve blouse rather than dressier clothes—Mother had finally come to her senses and agreed that carrying a sweater was unnecessary. As I scanned the laughing people around me, the magnificent trees, and the spots of yellow flickering lights, I thought the restaurant was magical, a place Dad would like. I started to say this and stopped. He might be an unmentionable man in the present situation, whatever the situation was. Two dinner invitations in a row from Travis exceeded hospitality and extended into territory that made me nervous. Even with no experience of romance, I could tell my mother and Travis were fascinated with each other. Their eyes were not lit just by candlelight.

Despite their attraction, both made an effort to include me in the conversation, Travis especially, though Mother tossed topics my way, her charitable mood continuing from our earlier artistic exchange. After banana daiquiris arrived, with a beer for Travis, we ordered salads, which came first, and then the main course landed, served on square mahogany plates: big charcoal-grilled sirloins and potatoes topped with hefty dollops of sour cream. Everyone dug in.

A few minutes later, I broke the silence. "Travis, I met Sofiya Florián today. What do you know about her?"

My mother arched her left brow. "Who is this, Travis?"

"Well, Sofiya's an interesting woman. A Czechoslovakian. She's been here for a month and is applying for administrative positions at several hotels and beach resorts."

"How old is she?"

"Oh, around your age, Evelyn."

Mother took a quick swallow of her drink, clearly displeased Travis hadn't described Sofiya as closer to "their" age. My guess was that he was several years younger than my mother.

"Well, does this woman have experience doing that kind of thing?" My mother fluttered her fingers in a dismissive gesture. "I mean…being a manager or whatever?"

"I didn't have any experience when I bought the Pink Fancy." Travis shrugged. "Sofiya seems very capable. Speaks fluent French, German, English, and Czech. A little Italian and Russian."

My mother hadn't been able to manage more than *bonjour* and *merci* during our recent trip to Paris, so I thought this linguistic expertise should impress her. It certainly impressed me. For each foreign country we visited—and we were frequent travelers due to our free TWA passes—I'd struggled to learn some of the language, believing this showed respect, an effort encouraged by my father, an international pilot, who was conversational in most of the Romance languages.

She speared a piece of steak. "Oh, well, I suppose one learns many languages living in Europe," she replied in an offhand manner.

I gave Mother a sharp look and stifled a rebuttal. "I liked Sofiya a lot."

Chewing her meat, she noted my reaction with a tiny twitch of her lips, then addressed Travis, as if I had suddenly vaporized from the table. "Is this woman married?"

"A widow, I believe." To me, he said, "If you ask her, maybe Sofiya will tell you about her war experiences. You might learn a little about the Nazis."

"Terrible people," my mother muttered, taking a swallow of her drink.

I faced her. Though I didn't want to mention Sofiya's invitation, having Travis present as a buffer might be helpful. "As a matter of fact, Mother, she's asked us for lunch the day after tomorrow. Goulash."

"Goulash? In this heat? Oh, dear god, no. That's too rich and heavy for me." My mother pursed her lips.

"And, Evelyn, don't forget we're going to the sugar plantation that afternoon," Travis reminded her.

"Oh, yes, that's right. Travis says there is a fabulous old mill with ruins that might be wonderful to draw. I assumed you would come along, Olivia, but since you have a luncheon date…"

I noted how swiftly they discouraged me from accompanying them. This intensified my suspicions about the nature of their relationship and hurt my feelings, but the prospect of spending time with Sofiya alone outweighed those reactions.

"Dear, please make my excuses to this Mrs.—" Mother began.

"Florián."

"Yes. I'm sure we'll meet your Mrs. Florián in the morning—just to be certain that she's…well—"

"Suitable?" I made no attempt to disguise my irritation.

Noticing my tone, Travis intervened. "Sofiya is a really fine person, Evelyn. Olivia will have a lovely time."

After the first daiquiri, I switched to Coca-Cola with lime. Travis and my mother had two more rounds, their hilarity increasing as the evening passed. I loved Travis's stories about funny island characters and his engaging chronicles of St. Croix life. Mother and I kept prompting him to continue, which he did, his face shining with good cheer and humor.

"You said running a hotel was a new experience," I said. "What did you do before you came to St. Croix?"

"Me?" He grinned. "Can't you guess?"

I shook my head.

He lifted his chin, as if to show off his good looks, and patted his chest. "I was a film star, of course."

"Oh, Travis!" Mother exclaimed.

"Hey? Don't think I'm handsome enough?" He looked askance at her, barely suppressing laughter.

"You are and you know it," she said.

This bit of flirtation sent both of them reaching for their drinks. I continued to eat my steak.

Travis finished a bite of potato and turned to me. "So, other than swimming, what are you planning to do here?"

"Maybe a little photography."

"Yes, Olivia is showing promise," Mother said. "She's in the high school camera club."

"That's great! Have you learned how to develop film?"

I nodded. "I'm not very good yet, but Dad plans to build me a darkroom."

"It's a nice hobby," my mother added.

"Actually, I'm considering it as a career," I said, to correct her dismissive attitude. "Maybe combined with journalism. I like to write, too."

"Well, we'll see." My mother smiled at Travis. "Olivia is young yet. We're hoping she'll follow a serious profession… law or business. Something along those lines. She's very smart. Top of her class."

Travis—bless him—made a face and burst out laughing. "I guess wartime photographers didn't know they were entering such a frivolous field."

I grinned. My mother frowned but probably realized this didn't look attractive and lightened her expression. "You're right, Travis, but at Olivia's age, goals change quickly. We will support her regardless of her choice."

This amused Travis. "You sound like Mrs. DeStasio. My high school guidance counselor."

Mother didn't like being teased. "I only meant to say that…oh, never mind." She removed her blue cigarette case and fingered a cigarette.

Travis reached in a pocket for his brass lighter. He flicked it into flame and lit Mother's waiting cigarette. She inhaled and blew smoke above our heads, then focused on Travis, who managed a charming smile, which elicited one from her. The unpleasantness of a moment ago had disappeared. To my mind, Travis had the skills of a diplomat.

We continued eating and drinking, and the two of them talked while I scanned the restaurant, noting all the happy faces illuminated by candlelight. Then, I attacked the last section of my steak, as did Travis with his. My mother, however, rested her knife and fork diagonally across the plate, a signal she was finished, though, as usual, a quarter of her food remained. I kept chewing, expecting what came next. Another cigarette. This time she exhaled smoke in my direction. I knew she'd done it deliberately.

I half-closed my eyes, sneezed, and gave up on my food.

Glancing at me, as if newly aware of my presence, she said, "Olivia, why don't you see if anyone wants to play backgammon?"

In other words, "Run along. Immediately."

I had been enjoying myself. Had I totally misread the light-hearted exchanges the three of us had just shared, all of which had included me? For once, I believed I'd achieved modest success. Yet, as often happened, I hadn't accurately determined my mother's mood. I now realized she was itching to be alone with Travis. I grabbed my Coke and went inside to the game room.

No one seemed available for a pick-up match, which was fine because I was too shy to ask. I sat in a chair by the window and gazed on the small street, wishing Sofiya were present so we could continue our conversation. As couples strolled past, I felt increasingly more miserable, especially because I was in a rare talkative mood. I sipped my soda and then noticed a taxi drive by. The blond boy was in the back seat! Beside him sat an older woman, a brunette in a black dress, though my impression of her was a blur.

I came to my feet, hesitated for a second, and rushed out

the door. The taxi had accelerated and was probably too far away for me to catch on foot, but I could still see the boy through the rear window. Was he with his mother? An older sister? A girlfriend? On the chance the cab would stop at a hotel or house, I ran after the car, though my dress sandals impeded my speed. The taillights blinked red several times as the driver braked for people in the road, but then the cab turned and disappeared.

After two blocks, I stopped, out of breath and frustrated, and replayed the boy's profile. His hair had been smooth and fairly long, the correct color and texture; his nose was arrow-straight like my mother's. Simon had such a nose. In fact, adding eight years to make Simon fifteen, this boy could be that age or he might be older, a young man. Sometimes estimating the correct age of a teenager was difficult.

The still night air was dense with humidity, as if it had collected in the confines of the narrow street and intensified. The heavy steak lurched in my stomach, and for a moment, I thought I might be sick. Moving to the side of the road, I waited until the nausea passed, then walked slowly to the restaurant, thinking my head felt exactly like a stone balloon.

My Coke had been removed by the waiter. In the courtyard, my mother and Travis were sitting close together, his arm around her shoulder. Their faces were enlivened by alcohol and attraction. I returned to the game room, grabbed a deck of cards, slumped into a corner chair, and began playing solitaire.

—

After half an hour, Travis and my mother appeared beside my table, arm in arm, laughing.

"Come on, Olivia. It's time to go," my mother said as she walked past me.

I tossed the cards onto the table—it was another losing

hand like the bigger one I'd been dealt. For a second, I stared at the mess before gathering the cards in a neat pile and replacing the deck in the box. By the time I raised myself from the chair, my mother and Travis were through the door and on the street, walking together like lovers, their heads almost touching as they spoke to each other.

It had been years since I'd seen my parents behave in such a fashion. I knew Dad would be furious about this affair, if it was that, but was I responsible for telling him about my suppositions? If I didn't, was I being disloyal to him? If I did, was I being disloyal to my mother, who was presuming an alliance with me that didn't exist? Even if I decided I should be honest with Dad, I couldn't remember when he was returning home or precisely where he was. Usually, he flew the New York/Rome route, but while he was overseas, there was no direct way to contact him. If Dad phoned us, which he probably would do at some point, the call would come into the office and most likely wouldn't be private, either because Travis would notify my mother first, or Travis would be present if I answered before her.

Frustrated, I kicked a loose stone and watched it skitter across the lane and bang into a flower pot. I was tired of being impaled on one of the sharp horns of our family triangle, an inherently unstable structure and definitely not equilateral. And I was weary from the quarrels in which Mother accused Dad of infidelity, insisting that during the many days he spent away from home, he was busy rubbing shoulders with beautiful stewardesses and female airport personnel. What did he do on those evenings by himself in hotel rooms, she asked? Mother claimed he wasn't sleeping alone. Was she now evening the score?

When we reached the Pink Fancy, Mother asked me to go inside the apartment, which I did. Annoyed and hot, I switched on the air conditioner, donned my pajamas, brushed my teeth, and climbed into bed, but was unable to sleep. Two hours later, I heard the front door open and the click of her cigarette lighter. Why had it taken her this long to say good night to Travis and what had they been doing?

"I'll be right in, Olivia," she called from the living room, as if she knew I was awake.

I wouldn't say a word about Travis. There was a slim chance they were only friends, and I had misconstrued their behavior because I was too inexperienced to decipher the relationship.

I turned toward the wall and told myself not to be so innocent. A minute later, Mother flipped on the light, ignoring my feigned sleep. Smoke floated to my side of the room. Wherever I was, it seemed to find me. I coughed.

"Ah, so you're up." My mother tossed her high-heeled shoes in the closet.

"I am now."

She grunted in response. I heard her unzip her dress, the metal hangers clang, the closet door close, and the air conditioner button click. The machine ceased its weary drone. "Well, I hope you had a nice time tonight."

"Yes, I did."

"The Stone Balloon was great. I wish we had a restaurant like it at home, don't you?"

And presumably a dinner companion like Travis. I clenched my jaw in irritation. "Yeah."

Mother tamped the cigarette in the ashtray by her bed, opened the window, and walked to the bathroom. I hurried to switch off the light, hoping that darkness would discourage further conversation. By the time my mother returned from slathering cold cream on her face, I was once again facing away from her. She exhaled loudly, as if to manifest displeasure, but went to bed without a word.

—

A strong wind blows through the trees, scissoring the blue sky between the green fronds, creating strange sky shapes that change with the breeze. I'm in a jungle, lost in the dense tangle of vegetation. The humidity is so dense it's almost rain. Strange noises ripple through the air: monkeys' screeches, lions' growls, birds' cries, the buzz of insects. Frantic to find safety, I run, squeezing between bamboo and rubber trees, tripping on vines, falling, running. Brutish, half-naked children wave spears, chase me, and shout threats. I sprint faster. The vibrant colors bleach to muted tones, and everything is silent. My ears pop as if I were descending in an airplane. Slowly, they fill with undifferentiated sound, like being underwater, which is where I am now—in a swiftly moving, frigid river, unable to breathe. The current clutches me in its powerful grip, swirling downward into the depths. Then, as suddenly as I dropped into the river, I'm tossed on the ground, in the yellow gravel driveway in front of our house. The light has turned dusky—a creamy orange with charcoal clouds hovering above the trees. Almost instantly, it becomes night, the house transforms into a black unlit mass except for the gold light emanating from the living room. I walk closer to the window. My mother and Simon are sitting on the sofa.

"Mommy, do you love me best?"

"Yes, darling, more than Olivia."

The scene shatters into hundreds of kaleidoscopic fragments. I smell lilacs, sweet and sickening. The slate path stretches before me, pointing a gray finger into the forest. From inside the house, Simon bursts through the door and runs past. I take to my heels and follow him into the dark woods. Leaves slash against leaves; their slithery sounds blend with the shrieking pitch of the wind. I call to Simon to wait, but he's in a hurry, his voice tinged with hysteria. Finally, we explode out of the forest, and the sky, river, and ocean unfold before us. A steep bluff lies at our feet. My head spins. The stars twirl above, as if my eyes are rotating in their sockets. I have to stop Simon, but my brother dashes down the cliff, holding the fishing pole. I tumble over the edge. Tall, spiky weeds like monster's fingers grab at my legs. Before I stand, Simon leaps forward and charges up the steps. Panic squeezes my heart as I watch his blond head. Ahead of him, the black river rushes furiously.

I cry out: "Simon! No!"

My brother approaches the end of the dock. I climb the stairs and lurch forward. My foot plunges through a board. A sharp nail thrusts into my ankle. Pain. Blood. I scream his name again.

"Olivia! Whatever is the matter?"

I jerked awake, thrusting backward on the pillows. My mother loomed over me, a dark form in a dim room. I jumped to my feet and hurried into the bathroom.

"You were having a dream," she called from the other side of the door.

I cursed silently. I had been afraid of shouting in my sleep, afraid my mother would hear. "It's okay. I'm fine."

I ran cold water and splashed my face, trying to stop the dream's reverberations. I waited until the shaking subsided and my breathing eased. After a swipe of the towel, I opened the door. My mother was lying in bed, the light off, but she was staring at me. What was she thinking? I was fairly sure I had yelled "Simon" in my sleep, in which case that's who was on her mind. Simon. The one she loved more.

Day 3

After my rocky night, I rose, feeling brittle as glass and just as transparent. My verbal outburst during the nightmare had revealed grief and pain, emotions that provoked my mother and left me vulnerable. At this very moment, she might be sharpening her arsenal of spears in the living room because I had dared to utter Simon's name, even in my sleep. When I walked into the front room, feeling like one word of criticism might shatter me, Mother was smudging a pencil line with an eraser. A lit cigarette rested in an ashtray.

"Remember, we have the guided tour of Salt River this morning. Better get dressed, Olivia," she said, not looking up from her drawing. "And bring your camera to take some reference pictures for me."

My mother hadn't made eye contact at all. Would this be the extent of her negative reaction? If so, I was getting off lightly. Hopefully, as the morning progressed, with the guide present, the tension would disappear. Relieved, I rummaged around for orange juice and a Kaiser roll. I took these to the bedroom and threw on clothes while eating, trying to ignore her peremptory attitude about taking the photographs. When I was ready, I placed my travel journal and film inside my red TWA bag, my camera strap on my shoulder, and then hung around by the door while my mother carefully packed her supplies, washed her hands, and applied some red lipstick.

As we left the apartment, I said, "I need to tell Sofiya about lunch tomorrow."

My mother sighed with annoyance. Though she had kept me waiting, she was now in a hurry.

"You should meet her," I added, trying to keep up with Mother, who had moved into full-speed-ahead mode.

"All right, Olivia." She came to an abrupt halt by the office. "But only for a minute. The guide will be here at ten."

I climbed the steps to Sofiya's apartment, my pulse quickening, and knocked on the door. She appeared in a sleeveless blue and pink dress, its mandarin collar edged in cobalt blue. Her silver and black hair was swept up in a French twist; some shorter locks curled over her ears and near her temples.

She gave me a cheerful smile. "Good morning. How are you?"

"I'm fine." This was now true. Sofiya's welcoming expression made me feel like the world had righted on its axis. "If you would still like me to come to lunch, I can."

"That's wonderful!" Sofiya stepped outside and smiled at my mother, who waited by the pool. "And your mother?"

This prompted Mother to introduce herself. "Good morning, Mrs. Florián. I'm Evelyn Livingston."

"Hello, Mrs. Livingston."

I thought it was rude of my mother not to shake hands with Sofiya and meet her properly face to face. While this was irritating, I was secretly pleased Sofiya hadn't asked my mother to call her by her first name, as she had done with me.

"Thank you for inviting Olivia to lunch."

"It will be my pleasure. And will you be joining us?"

"No, I'm afraid not. I'm going to the market to sketch, and then later Travis and I are driving to a sugar plantation and the grocery store."

Sofiya glanced at me. Was she speculating as to why I hadn't been included in their plans? Had she observed any romantic transactions between Travis and my mother? Sofiya's apartment overlooked the pool, the office, and the path to his residence.

She returned her attention to my mother. "Another time, perhaps. Oh, and may I offer Olivia a glass of wine with lunch?"

"If Olivia would like one, that's fine." She flashed her hand in a brusque wave and walked toward the hotel steps.

Sofiya's eyes narrowed slightly. Perhaps my mother's impolite behavior hadn't gone unnoticed. In contrast, when she addressed me, her smile brightened. "About one?"

"I'll be here," I said. "I can't wait to try your goulash."

—

The guide, a Mr. Thomas, was an older fellow, of mixed white and black ancestry, who told us he was distantly related to the slave, Queen Mary, who helped instigate the October 1878 "Fireburn" rebellion against plantation owners, during which many acres of sugar fields were burned.

"Queen Mary was imprisoned in Denmark but died here," he said. "Crucians honor her as a heroine."

Mr. Thomas showed us to his small car and politely opened the doors for both of us. Mother sat in back, with her sketchbook and pencil box, while I chose the front seat, preferring the better view and a few feet of welcome distance from my mother.

We drove about five miles west from Christiansted, stopping at Salt River Bay, where Columbus and his sailors landed on November 14, 1493. According to Mr. Thomas, when the Spaniards were returning to their ships in a longboat, they encountered a canoe with the war-like Caribs and their Taino slaves on board. The two groups skirmished, and one Carib and one sailor died. He said St. Croix probably was the only place where Columbus set foot on what was to become United States soil.

Mr. Thomas escorted us through Fort Salé, a French earthworks fortification built about 1617. I took a few photographs, though there wasn't much to document, and then followed him to an area he described as a ceremonial ball court, which had been originally encircled by carved stones. He explained that an excavation by Gudmund Hatt in 1923 resulted in the removal of many of the ancient stones and significant artifacts to the Danish National Museum. Next, we stopped at a burial ground on a hill amid a forest of trees. Mr. Thomas handed me a battered spoon and suggested I do a shallow dig. He and Mother left because she wanted to draw the view, so I knelt and began scraping in the dirt, feeling a little foolish until I hit something hard. Probably a rock, I thought, but I decided to gently uncover whatever it was. Almost immediately, a rim appeared. Excited, I kept removing dirt, using my fingers to avoid scratching the pot, and, slowly, a half bowl emerged: it was reddish-brown and undecorated, without a lip or base or cracks, perfectly smooth and round. The outside was slightly blackened, no doubt from a cooking fire. I searched nearby for the other half but couldn't find it.

When Mr. Thomas and Mother returned, they were astonished by the bowl. He said island archaeology was a hobby of his.

"You've found a cooking pot, Olivia. Perhaps made before Columbus's visit. The bowl isn't painted like earlier Saladoid vessels, and there are no incised decorations such as on later Ostinoid-Taino pots."

"How old do you think it is?" I asked.

He stroked his chin and frowned slightly. "Probably it was created between 800 and 1200 A.D."

"You're kidding! It was only a few inches from the surface."

"Well, the earth may have eroded, or maybe an early excavator left the pot because it was broken," Mr. Thomas replied.

"So the bowl could be over a thousand years old," Mother said, finally doing the math.

Mr. Thomas nodded and related more history, saying the

Tainos—or Arawaks—had been the dominant population from 650 A.D. to a few years before Columbus's arrival, when the Caribs had enslaved them, killing many.

I placed the pot in my flight bag, and the three of us walked to the car. We continued along the North Shore Drive to Cane Bay, where Mr. Thomas told us the "Wall" was located, a mecca for skin-divers. Here, the Puerto Rican Trench extended outward, eventually reaching depths of over 28,000 feet. I took some photographs of the magnificent sea, which shifted from a stunning purplish-blue to creamy aqua, and of the rugged terrain, with its undulating green surfaces patched with darker shadows from the overhead clouds racing across the brilliant blue sky. Afterward, we drove to Davis Bay and then reversed course for home. Mother jotted notations on her various sketches, while Mr. Thomas and I observed the rapidly changing weather.

"Rain?" I asked.

Mr. Thomas studied the sky. "Looks like it. And soon."

A short while later, torrential sheets of water fell with astonishing swiftness, obliterating the view through the windshield. Mr. Thomas was forced to pull off the road, where we sat for ten minutes, uncomfortably hot, the noise on the car's roof deafening. The deluge finally quit as suddenly as it began, and we rolled down the windows and proceeded eastward, making a stop at the market to buy sandwiches for lunch and potato salad and barbequed ribs for dinner.

When we arrived at the hotel, I showed the bowl to Travis, who was enthusiastic about how beautifully formed it was. I knocked on Sofiya's door, but there was no answer. Mother and I ate a late lunch, and I spent the rest of the afternoon in the pool and then on one of the chaises until Sofiya climbed up the steps, grocery bags in her arms.

"Whew," she cried. "I hate those stairs."

I came to my feet, rushed to help her with a bag, and followed Sofiya into her apartment.

"Thank you, Olivia. Now, let me put everything away, and I'll be with you shortly."

I left to fetch my flight bag, and when Sofiya joined me outside, dressed in her bathing suit, I showed her my archaeological find, explaining its origin.

She held the pot with care, turning it in her hands. "I can't believe you found this! Look at the perfect curve of the bowl."

"I know. I wonder what else is buried there." I replaced the pot in my bag, closed the zipper, and faced Sofiya. "I want to apologize for my mother. She was rude this morning. Not meeting you at the door and then hurrying off."

"She was in a rush. It's okay."

"Even so, I didn't like it," I said. "Her behavior had nothing to do with you. Anyone I like...well, she doesn't. And any subject I'm interested in is automatically criticized or judged unimportant."

Sofiya smiled. "A classic power struggle, perhaps?"

"I guess so, but it's hard to deal with her. Sometimes, she can be so nice, but I never know what to expect."

"It must be difficult, Olivia."

I realized I'd been complaining and apologized. After that, we chatted about good beaches to visit and swam in the pool until Sofiya announced she needed to complete a job application. "I'll see you tomorrow at one, if not before."

An hour later, Mother and I ate the ribs and potato salad and then played gin rummy. Her cigarette smoke made my eyes smart, but I won by a little, which often happened lately. Although my mother was a crafty player, I was beginning to catch on to some of her tricks. Too bad I wasn't as successful in winning the power struggle that Sofiya had mentioned.

When my mother left to have a drink with Travis, I made no comment, though I was upset about what the two were doing and not happy to be alone. I lay on the bed, feeling restless without a television or radio for amusement, and leafed through a magazine, which only took a few minutes to finish.

After reading ten pages of *Lord of the Flies*, I turned off the light and hoped the book wouldn't inspire more frightening dreams about Simon.

Day 4

The next morning, Mother and I walked to Christiansted's outdoor market. I brought my camera, and Mother selected her smallest notebook in order to be discreet if she sketched anyone. She needn't have bothered because the place was swarming with people who paid no attention to us. Of special amusement were some of the tourists decked out in loud tee shirts, straw hats, and golf wear—a few had cardigans over their shoulders, with the sleeves tied around their necks, which made me hot looking at them. Overall, I was surprised how easily recognizable Americans were by their dress and manner. Knowing I could also be identified as such was disquieting because I didn't think of myself as a tourist, although, of course, I was, and probably the Crucians viewed me that way. My assumption of being different made me wonder why I wished to lose my national identity while traveling, why I wanted to be invisible and anonymous. Maybe this arose out of a need to observe people and their culture without disrupting it with my presence.

As we strolled through the crowd, I noticed one woman wearing a sunhat stuck with pins featuring sayings like "Jesus Loves Me," a pink enamel cross (in case her religiosity had been missed), and a plastic "Welcome to Disneyland" pin next to a pair of miniature Mickey Mouse ears. I touched my mother's arm and thrust my chin in the direction of the hat owner, causing my mother to make a face. She mimed that I should take a photograph, which I did—only of the hat.

The local vendors were mostly Crucians, though tanned Caucasians were sprinkled in the mix. The sellers stood behind tables painted lime green or lemon yellow upon which lay bolts of bright island fabrics and clothes. Others sat next to stacked wooden crates as they hawked fruits and vegetables. Still others owned glass cases displaying seashells, handmade jewelry, jellies and jams, and artwork depicting nearby locales—none of the paintings as accomplished as my mother's. Many of the women were dressed in loose cotton shifts imprinted with boisterous designs showcasing flowers, leaves, and geometric patterns, drawn as if done with heated wax crayons. A matching strip of material was often used to tie their hair or as a bandana wrapped across their brow. From the look on my mother's face, I could tell she was thrilled with the people, colors, shapes, and light pouring over the entire scene. I was, too.

While she circled the outskirts and stopped to begin a study, I stood, smelling barbequed chicken crackling on a grill, some pungent spices, a mixture of colognes and sweat. Once I felt calm and centered in this bustling place, I removed the cap from my camera lens and strolled over to one local woman wearing a beautiful tunic illustrated with white palm trees scattered on a jade green background. She was selling fruit and vegetables and gave me a friendly smile, revealing large teeth, several of which were missing.

"And how are you this fine day, Miss?" she asked.

"I am well, thank you," I replied. "Could you please tell me about some of your fruit?"

"Ah, well, Miss, we have very tasty papayas and mangos. Breadfruit—very nice grilled on an open fire. Melons—all good. And bananas."

The bananas were small, sold in a bunch that had been hacked off. I bought a cluster, which the woman placed in a bag. After I slipped its handles over my arm, I asked if I could take her portrait, remembering my father's comment: "if you photograph people, they are giving you the gift of their images, so be respectful."

She laughed and touched my hand. "Oh, dear, no one ever asks. They just snap pictures like I am a big old tree or something." The woman gave me a long look and chuckled. "For you, I agree." She leaned away and struck a pose. "How is this?"

I smiled, set the exposure, moved the camera to a vertical position, focused, and clicked the shutter. After moving a step back, I shot a second image of her, including the fruits and vegetables at the bottom. "Thank you!"

"You are most welcome. My, what a polite young lady! You come back and see me soon."

As I moved on, music began to play. A man with bongos and another with two steel drums set in tandem were joined by a third fellow playing maracas. The sounds were inexpressibly joyful, the notes whirring above the crowd, the maracas punctuating the melody like cheerful crickets, and the bongos tapping like thudding heartbeats.

Next, I came across a display of shells arranged on a thatched mat. They were lightly oiled to enhance their lustrous hues and glistened in the sunlight. Some of these specimens I knew from studying my shell book: sunrise tellins, cowries, moon snails, and scallops, but one was a mottled orange and yellow, its wing extended in an odd shape. The vendor explained that it was a rooster-tail conch. I purchased it and then asked if he would allow me to photograph his collection. The man agreed and I stepped in as close as the lens' minimum focal distance would allow, about eighteen inches, and made detailed images.

After replacing the lens cap, I looked up and saw Mother on the opposite side of the market. She was squinting and drawing, her fingers holding the sketchbook, a pencil, and a lit cigarette, whose white smoke circled her head. It occurred to me that being an artist in a crowded place was much easier

than being a photographer. She could delete anyone or anything that impeded her view, whereas I had difficulty avoiding bodies, heads, and waving hands. Several images had
probably been ruined by people cutting in front of me just as
I depressed the shutter.

Despite these obstacles, I was in the zone, that rapturous
place where everything appears magnified and glowing, where
the viewfinder encompasses the world. Almost unconsciously, I adjusted exposure, focused the lens, and determined the
most interesting composition and cropping.

I finished exposing a roll of Kodacolor, ducked under an
arcade to block the sun, unwound the film, and inserted a roll
of Tri-X film—I intended to take black-and-white pictures of
St. Croix for a school project. The sun had risen in the sky,
and the temperature was in the high 80s, sizzling hot despite
a light sea breeze. After shooting more of the vendors and
locals, I exposed all but four frames and rejoined my mother,
who scarcely noticed me because she was so intent on the
lively activity before her eyes.

"I'm going to the hotel for a swim," I told her.

"Did you take enough photographs?"

I shrugged. "I think so. By the way, I saw a photo shop.
Once I have a few more rolls to develop, I'll drop them off."

"Oh...good..."

Mother had answered me, but when her brain was dialed
into visual mode, her speech became halting and occasionally unintelligible. Long ago I'd realized that talking with my
mother in these situations was futile. I sighed and left for the
Pink Fancy.

—

Predictably, my mother had turned off the air conditioner. I
switched it on and stood in front of it to cool my face and
arms. Then, after drinking some cold water, I shed my sticky

clothes, donned my bathing suit, grabbed a towel, and hurried outside to the gallery. An older couple sat under the awning reading newspapers, and, to my pleasant surprise, Sofiya was swimming in the pool, wearing a blue scarf on her head. As I walked down the steps, she turned and waved. Within seconds, I was underwater, feeling the rush. I surfaced a few feet from her.

"Ah, so here is my dolphin friend," she said, chuckling.

"Yes." I smoothed back my hair and smiled.

"A successful visit to the market?"

I nodded. "Mother is still sketching, but she'll be here in a little while."

"For her afternoon with Travis."

"Yeah. A sugar mill first and then lunch."

"I'm sure they'll have a lovely time." From the merry twinkle in her eye, it seemed Sofiya had calculated the lay of the land between Travis and my mother. "So, where's your father? Will he be visiting while you're here?"

"Dad is a pilot and could be in Europe or on his way to New York. It's tough to keep track, but no, he's not planning a trip to St. Croix."

"I see. And you, are you close to him?"

I shrugged. "Dad's easier to be around than she is, though he's not home often."

She regarded me intently but remained silent, letting my statement hang in the air. I realized my comment hadn't been an enthusiastic endorsement of my father and certainly not of my mother.

"Well, we'll talk more later. Now, I must prepare a salad. If you finish your swim and are ready early, come over then."

Sofiya began a stately breaststroke toward the steps and rose from the water; as she toweled off, Travis bounded down the path from his apartment. He looked sporty in a starched blue-and-white-striped shirt, white shorts, and brown Top-Siders. After saying hello to Sofiya, he grinned at me.

"How are you doing, Olivia?"

I swam closer to him. "Fine. Mother should arrive soon."

"Good. Thanks."

He turned and walked to his office, folded back the shutters, opened the bottom half door, and went inside to make a phone call. When Mother appeared, looking hot and bedraggled and saw Travis inside, she put a finger to her lips, indicating I shouldn't alert him to her presence. Then she scurried into our rooms. I knew she would step out looking like a fashion plate, and, a half hour later, she did: white slacks, red-and-white boat-neck blouse, navy espadrilles, gold earrings in the shape of anchors, and a gold charm bracelet.

I opted to remain in the water while Travis and my mother greeted each other and exchanged a few words. He called to one of the maids, who was squeezing lemons into a bucket of water, and told her he would be away for the afternoon, and no new guests were due to arrive. Resembling King and Queen for a Day, the twosome waved goodbye and headed for Prince Street, with Travis carrying my mother's sketchbook.

The afternoon spread before me with delightful promise. I dashed into our apartment, showered, and selected my new embroidered blouse and a pair of pale blue Bermuda shorts. After combing my hair carefully, I risked a peek at the mirror and then smiled.

—

Sofiya answered the door promptly and invited me in. Excluding a small bathroom across from the entrance, the apartment was a single rectangular room decorated with several island-themed watercolors on the walls. At the far end were twin beds covered in navy and gold paisley spreads; at the foot of one bed was a battered steamer trunk, its surface plastered with airline and shipping stickers. Two easy chairs faced each other mid-way, and, near us, an oblong table with four chairs was placed adjacent to the built-in kitchenette, where a large covered pot was on the stove. The tang of sauerkraut and a dill-like aroma wafted through the apartment, undissipated by the window air conditioner, which, fortunately, was on full blast.

For a moment, I stood next to Sofiya, conscious of being several inches taller, yet also sensing how thoroughly her presence seemed to dominate the room. She suggested I sit in one of the comfortable armchairs.

"Can I help you?" I asked.

"No, that's okay. This is a very simple meal. A salad, bread, and a Szegediner goulash. A lot of paprika, potatoes… well, you'll see." She began uncorking a bottle of red wine. "A French burgundy. One thing nice about St. Croix is the tax-free liquor. As they say, here the luxuries are cheap and the necessities are expensive." After removing the cork, she hesitated before pouring.

"Yes, I'd like some, thank you," I said, taking a seat.

Sofiya poured the dark ruby wine, handed me a glass, and took the seat opposite. I sipped the burgundy. It was heavy and acidic, but I liked it and told her so.

"It may not be a perfect accompaniment to goulash or suitable for a hot day, but I was in the mood for it," she said, smiling. "Now, Olivia, I know very little about you except that your mother is an artist and your father is a pilot. Do you have brothers and sisters?"

"No."

"Ah, an only child?"

I exhaled slowly. "Not exactly. I had a younger brother." I reached for my glass of wine. "His name was Simon."

Sofiya nodded as a prompt.

"I'm sorry, but I would rather not talk about him."

She studied me but let the subject drop. I asked if she had any children.

"No, I don't. Probably for the best, all things considered."

Sofiya turned quiet, leaving another enigmatic statement hovering in the air. I hurried to cover the awkwardness by describing where we lived in New Jersey and my favorite classes—English, French, and art. I also mentioned that I had traveled through Europe and Scandinavia because my father flew for TWA.

"Occasionally, we're bumped from a flight, but usually we've been fortunate." I considered for a second. "Actually, I am very lucky to have the chance to see so many places. No one else I know has, at least no teenagers."

Sofiya sipped her wine. "Travel is extremely important. A way to learn about others. To learn about yourself."

"I guess I'm worldly wise for my age, because of all of our trips, though I don't think I'm experienced like some of my school classmates."

"Why do you say that?"

"I'm not sure exactly. You were probably more sophisticated at sixteen than I am."

"Sophisticated?" She laughed. "No. Far from it. I was a provincial girl who lived in a rural area. Stuck cleaning horse and cow stalls, feeding chickens, drawing water from the well. But I knew this was not what I wished to do later in life, so I worked very hard in school and read every book I could find, including those my grandmother gave me in English. I dreamed of visiting Paris, Rome, London, and New York, yet before the war, I had only been to Prague once with my father—a city about fifty miles away."

"I guess I meant sophisticated...like in romance."

"Not at your age." A faint sadness seemed to pass over her face, and just as quickly, the mood disappeared. She swallowed some burgundy. "Ah, yes. One other thing I know about you. You're serious about photography."

"Yes, I am," I said, noting that she'd changed the subject. "How did you know?"

"You were carrying your Nikon camera yesterday. When you introduced me to your mother."

"Oh, yes, that's right. Well, if I'm good enough, I hope to study journalism. Maybe become a professional photographer and a reporter."

"A worthy occupation. An important one. Significant truths are captured on film, and important information published in newspapers. Sadly, many people ignore what they read and don't heed warnings."

"What do you mean?"

Sofiya looked down at her glass. "Oh, it's just that no one wants to hear bad news, I suppose."

"What kind of bad news?" I thought about Travis's suggestion that I ask Sofiya about the war. "Are you talking about Hitler?"

She gave her head a small shake, as if she didn't want to answer my question, and was silent for a moment. "Yes, I am."

"Did journalists warn about him?"

She nodded. "They did. In articles and editorials." Sofiya drank more wine, gazed at the ceiling, and finally focused on me again. "If the leaders—if everyone—had believed the reports and acted during the days when Hitler was consolidating power, a tragic disaster could have been averted and millions of lives saved. But, foolishly, Britain, France, and America, my country and others, downplayed the dangers. And how many Jews read his alarming pronouncements and ignored the peril?" She shook her head again. "Olivia, the Nazis were the most horrible people to ever walk the earth."

I took this in and studied her, trying to gauge if she wanted to continue the conversation. Sofiya seemed reluctant to speak about the subject, yet she had responded as if willing to tell her story.

"I feel sort of stupid admitting this, but I don't know a lot about the war. We don't study it until senior year." As gently as I could, I asked, "How was it to live in Czechoslovakia then?"

Sofiya smiled at my admission, but then she grew more serious. "Well, in late 1938, the Germans began invading my country. I was twenty-one, almost twenty-two. As I told you, we lived on a farm. Outside of a small village." She exhaled a long breath. "We knew the Nazis were coming, but we could do little to stop them. Many of our local men formed resistance brigades. Not to fight directly—we didn't have enough people or guns. Instead, we ambushed the Germans at night, blew up trains and supplies, destroyed bridges."

"We? Did you help?"

"Yes, I did. I didn't use dynamite or anything, but I carried messages and food in pouches to our fighters. Through the fields at night." She placed her elbow on the chair's arm and rested her chin in her hand.

"That must have been really dangerous. Were you scared you'd be caught?"

Sofiya raised her head, her expression darkening. "Yes, it was risky. Even being seen in the wrong place at the wrong time wasn't good. The Nazis posted sentries and would shoot at any noise, any movement. If they had too much schnapps, they fired at nothing at all." She contemplated her wine, then took a sip. "Yes, I was scared. The Germans were vicious. You have no idea how awful they were. Czechs who were captured...they were tortured to reveal names of other partisans, where they lived, who their families were. If the Nazis discovered identities, they would come in the night and murder everyone." Her voice, which had been low but steady, now quivered with emotion. "Even women and children... and the animals."

I sensed there was more. If all of those people had been killed, what had happened to Sofiya and her family? Although I'd hoped to learn about her country and about the war, I hadn't expected to hear such a tragic story. I gripped my glass, afraid to drink, afraid to move, and waited, my mind bristling with questions.

"I'm not sure you want to hear the rest, Olivia. Or should."

"Do you want to tell me?"

Sofiya observed me closely with her grayish-blue eyes, which seemed almost black in the dim afternoon light. "I don't usually talk about my history...but I will. With you." She reached for the bottle, poured us more burgundy, though I had scarcely touched mine, and set the bottle on the table. "My family was very unlucky. In October of 1941, my younger brother was arrested with explosives in his knapsack."

"My god, what was he going to do?"

"I'm not sure, but I think he and some other members of the Resistance were planning to blow up a train. One carrying German troops." Sofiya stiffened slightly, as if to brace herself. "The morning after his capture, the Nazis lined him up against a wall with several others and shot all of them." She let out an uneasy breath, and with it, her face seemed to collapse with the weight of her memories.

"Oh, Sofiya, no! How old was he?"

"Tomáš was only eighteen. A lovely, kind boy." As she said this, a chasm opened between us, pushing Sofiya into the past while I remained anchored in the present. She kept speaking, but her tone sounded flat.

"The situation grew even worse. Although my brother hadn't confessed his name, one of the other prisoners knew him and told the Germans who he was and where he lived. You must understand the situation. Some Czechs were loyal to the cause. Others feared the Nazis and provided information." Her eyes flashed with anger. "Because of that coward, the brutes came after my parents. They burned our house and barn. Everything."

I gasped. "Did you and your parents escape?"

Sofiya fell back against her chair, her energy taxed by the momentary outburst. An uneasy silence stretched between us. While I desperately wanted to fill the uncomfortable emptiness, my question still hovered in the air.

When she finally spoke, she didn't look at me. "My father was killed. The Germans hung him from the oak tree in our yard. They used the rope from the swing he made for me when I was little." Her face softened. "The oak tree was at the top of a small hill. Sometimes, in the evening, my father would push me on the swing. I would go higher and higher, laughing so hard that he would laugh, too. I remember telling him I was flying." The memory caused her to smile, but her smile immediately evaporated. "I found him after the soldiers left. It's a sight I will never, ever forget." Sofiya paused, then added, her voice raw with pain, "Even my little black dog..." Turning her attention on me again, she said, "What did a poor, defenseless animal do to deserve being shot?" Her body shuddered.

"I'm so sorry, Sofiya."

She took in my response and nodded.

"And...your mother?"

"Oh, my dear, dear mother." Her chin dropped onto her chest. After a sigh, she replied, "I'm not sure. All I know is that the day after the Nazis murdered my father, they found her, hiding in a hay loft. Probably a neighbor woman, who was friendly with my family—or so we thought—had informed on my mother."

I leaned forward. "That's terrible!"

"It was. I don't know if my mother was shot or sent to a prison camp. I never learned her fate."

I tried to imagine how Sofiya felt and couldn't. "If I lost my mother, I don't know what I would do," I murmured, half to myself.

We both drank some wine. Finally, she said, in a soft voice, "It is a very deep wound. One that will never heal."

I was unable to speak. I had never known anyone who had suffered such a devastating experience. After swallowing hard, I whispered, "Your father, brother, and your mother—all gone?"

Sofiya held my gaze. In those seconds, it seemed that a curtain was briefly drawn open, exposing her anguish, which still burned with searing heat. Phrases of sympathy flew through my mind, all of them inadequate. I sat there, stunned, realizing what a sheltered, safe life I'd lived except for Simon's death. All my carping about my mother suddenly seemed stupid and childish.

"Yes, within a few weeks." Sofiya exhaled an uneasy breath. "To be honest, Olivia, there have been many times when I wished I'd died in our house. I've asked myself over and over, was I fortunate to survive?" Her shoulders lifted in a small shrug. "I don't know. If I hadn't been in the forest when the Germans came, I would have been killed. You might say photography saved my life."

"Really? How?"

"I was delivering a roll of film."

"To the Resistance?"

"Yes. One of my jobs was to document anything of military interest. I was given a Russian FED camera but received little instruction."

"Really? Did you have to get close to the Nazis to take the pictures?"

"Often. The camera came with a one hundred millimeter lens. It enlarged a little—"

"But not enough."

"No. And the lens required a lot of light."

"So you had to photograph during the day?"

She nodded. "Most of the time."

With my experience, it was easy to imagine how dangerous her work had been. I visualized scenes of forests and fields, shooting photos behind trees and rocks, trying to keep my hands from shaking. "So if you could see the soldiers...they could probably see you."

"Yes, unless I was really well hidden." As she discussed some of the pictures she'd taken, Sofiya's agitation seemed to lessen, perhaps because she was more comfortable relating technical details than her personal story. "In truth, I wasn't very skillful. Not like you, I'm sure." She was quiet for a moment and then finished her wine and placed the glass on the table. "But now, I need to heat the bread for lunch."

Rising from her chair, she walked into the kitchen area, wrapped a baguette in foil, slipped it inside the oven, and stood there, facing away from me.

"That was very brave of you," I said. "Taking photographs. I don't think I could have done it."

She turned and leaned against the counter. "You never know if you have courage—whether you will fight back or surrender—until you must make a choice. Sometimes you don't think, you just act." After considering this statement, she added, "And sometimes you think and then do the wrong thing."

Her hands curled around the countertop, holding it to steady herself. Although I was curious about what she meant, I sensed Sofiya didn't wish to say more. I waited, in case she would explain, but when she didn't, I asked if any other members of her family survived the Nazis' massacre. "Cousins or—"

"Only my fiancé, Dano. For a short time. But that is another story. One I will tell you later." She unclenched her grip on the counter and shook herself. "Enough of this talk about the war. It is too sad for such a lovely day and such lovely company. The goulash is ready. Time to eat."

I wasn't prepared for this abrupt end to the conversation, which I hadn't handled very well. I should have expressed more care and concern. I cursed my shyness, my inability to say how much Sofiya's story had upset me. As she moved large bowls beside the cooking pot, I went to stand beside her.

"I'm so sorry about what happened." I turned and put my arms around her shoulders. Sofiya felt solid and substantial, and yet I could sense her fragility.

When we drew apart, she smiled, but her eyes had filled with tears. "Thank you, Olivia."

I was unsure what to do. Sensing my confusion, Sofiya briskly wiped her wet cheeks and walked to the refrigerator to remove two salads. She dressed both and set them on the table. After stirring the goulash, she began ladling it into bowls.

"I hope you like this," she said. "The recipe is from my father's mother, though the ingredients vary depending on what is available." She handed me a bowl, keeping her focus on the food. "And would you light the candles?"

Even though it was early afternoon, the room was somewhat dark because the windows faced north and west. After doing as she asked, I blew out the match and took a large swallow of the burgundy. As I did, Sofiya reached for a dish towel, dried her eyes more thoroughly, and cleared her throat. Then, opening the oven door, she removed the baguette using pot holders and tugged off the foil. Using a large knife, Sofiya sliced the bread and brought it to the table, where we took seats across from each other.

"More wine, yes?" she asked.

When I agreed, Sofiya refilled our glasses.

I felt strange about holding a normal conversation after having heard that her entire family had been murdered by the Nazis. But then she smiled and lifted her glass as a toast.

"To life," she said.

I clicked my glass against hers, took a sip of wine, and picked up a large spoon, imitating her. The goulash was spicy, with frankfurters, sauerkraut, apples, onions, and potatoes.

"Wow! This is excellent. Could I have the recipe?"

Sofiya laughed at my enthusiasm. "In anticipation of that request, I've already written it out." She handed me a sheet of Pink Fancy stationery. On a pink bar across the top, the hotel's name was set in ornate, circus-style, white lettering. In contrast, Sofiya's handwriting was lean and unembellished.

The spaces between the words and lines were generous, and the "i" dots were placed directly over their stems, giving the impression of a calm and deliberate personality.

"The secret is using caraway seeds and a high-quality sweet paprika—I brought some with me," she explained.

We continued eating until our spoons scraped the bottom of the bowls, then we headed to the stove for seconds. Afterward, I asked Sofiya how she had learned languages. She told me that a schoolmaster had recognized her facility and taught her some German and French in return for instruction in English, which Sofiya knew because her grandmother had been British. "Just before the German invasion, my grandmother fled to England, using her British passport. She died some years ago."

"How did she meet your grandfather?"

"He managed a small hotel in Prague, where she stayed while visiting. They fell in love and married. Because her family owned a farm in Kent, and he had grown up on a farm, they decided to leave the city, return to his village, and buy a place where they could raise cows, goats, pigs, and chickens. He died in 1936 of tuberculosis."

I was uncertain whether to comment on the death of her grandparents but decided to avoid returning to her family tragedy. "Your accent isn't quite British, is it?"

"Kind of a blend—you're right. I worked in post-war Berlin for the American army."

"How did you get from Czechoslovakia to Germany?" I asked. "And what did you do in Berlin?"

"That's complicated." Sofiya raised her hands. "Another time, perhaps."

I felt like I had stubbed my toe. I smiled, to cover my reaction. "Yes, Travis wouldn't approve of all these revelations of past histories."

Sofiya chuckled. "No, he certainly wouldn't."

I ate some sauerkraut and a chunk of apple.

"He's a very handsome man."

"Travis is an unusual mix of good looks and charm."

"Like my mother."

Sofiya placed her chin on her hand. "They are well matched, except, of course, that your mother is married."

"An exception that seems to be forgotten at the moment," I said, with some bitterness, before chiding myself that my suspicions might be unfounded. "I wonder why Travis is so private."

"Well, I suspect it has to do with events before he arrived on St. Croix."

I pulled apart a piece of baguette. "In America?"

She nodded and swallowed some wine. "I dislike spreading rumors, especially those heard from third parties."

"Please tell me, Sofiya. My mother is spending so much time with Travis, and yet we—I—know nothing about him."

After a brief hesitation, she began. "Soon after I arrived here, Travis recommended I contact a friend of his from the States—for advice about jobs on the island. During our conversation, the man started chatting about Travis, and though I didn't ask, he said that Travis's wife and daughter had been killed in an automobile accident."

"Oh, no!"

"I'm not sure this friend knew the full circumstances of what occurred, though perhaps he did, so this story may be the truth or partially incorrect. At any rate, he implied the deaths were caused because someone had been drinking at a party and lost control of the car. The man said Travis was thrown clear and survived with only broken bones."

I looked at her, surprised.

"Needless to say, I couldn't inquire about the details because it was a business interview," Sofiya said, "so we may never know the actual facts. Except that Travis, if this account is true, must live with the consequences."

"What if his wife was driving?" I suggested.

"That's possible."

"Was Travis ever charged with anything?"

She shrugged.

"Do you think he came to St. Croix...to escape?"

"Islands are good for that." Sofiya sat very still, seeming to reflect on this remark. Then, she dismissed it with a small wave. "But I have no idea. All I know is that I like Travis very much. If he made a single, tragic mistake, if this story is accurate and he caused the accident, it's very sad." After eating a bite of potato, she added, almost in an offhand manner, "Many of us do things that scar our lives forever."

Her comment made me think about my suggestion to go night fishing with Simon, a decision I would always regret. Had Travis made a similar misjudgment? Had Sofiya?

Sofiya drew her fork through her salad and lifted a piece of lettuce. "So, do you have someone special?"

"You mean a boyfriend?"

She nodded.

"No, I don't." I felt embarrassed making this admission. "I don't have many friends, either. Although I'm more comfortable with adults than with kids my age, I feel pretty inept with people."

Sofiya set down her fork and sighed. "Oh, Olivia! I don't think you're inept at all. You have a very appealing manner."

"Copied from my mother."

"Perhaps, to some extent. That's how we're socialized. But you're a separate individual and a very exceptional one. You'll surprise yourself. Soon, I think."

"I'm not so sure about that."

"Because you aren't extroverted like your mother?" Sofiya laughed. "Not everyone can command center stage. The most interesting people, in my opinion, are those who are more reflective. When I was young, I was very shy. Even now I tend to be reserved. Maybe, like me, you are a private person, yes?"

I nodded. My face warmed, and I reached for my wine. "What about you? Did you have a relationship when you were my age?"

"Not a serious one until I was twenty-two. That's when Dano and I met."

"What was he like?"

She gazed out the window. The sun had rotated to the west and was beginning to shine into the apartment, bisecting her face vertically, half in light, half in shadow, reminding me of a comedy/tragedy mask.

"Dano was slender, rather tall. Dark hair."

"Was he handsome?"

"Yes, I suppose so. Of course, I thought him quite dashing," she said, with a dry chuckle. "A mischievous young man who loved adventure."

"What sort of adventure?"

She began to answer, then abruptly stopped and shook her head.

It was obvious the subject had aroused painful memories. "I'm sorry, Sofiya, I don't mean to be so curious."

"No need to apologize." She stood, drew the curtain to block the sunlight, and returned to her chair. After scooping up another bite of goulash, she continued. "People like us have often observed more than we can fully absorb, either because the information is too painful or because we aren't ready to comprehend what we've witnessed. Or we have no safe place to explore how we feel. Sometimes it takes years to sort through the various compartments where we've hidden our thoughts and feelings," she said softly. "Eventually, perhaps you'll be able to make sense of your experiences—if that's ever possible."

"Have you been able to do that?"

She smiled and shook her head.

I puzzled over what she meant. "Do you think we're alike?"

"In some ways, yes, though an outsider might not think

so. I was an introspective child, an observer. You are as well. And you're wiser than most girls your age and many adults."

"Which you are, too."

"I'm not so sure about that," Sofiya said, laughing. "But it's my belief, Olivia, that you will grow even wiser later in life. Think of yourself this way—you are old, though young."

I met her eyes, which were lit with sympathy. Her gentleness and caring surprised me. I sensed she read every emotion with stunning clarity, an unfamiliar experience that made me want to run away, but also the opposite: to stay in this apartment with this kind woman and, most frightening, divulge long-held painful secrets.

Worried that I was blushing, I focused on my goulash and ate a piece of potato. "I wish I'd known you when you were my age."

"Ah, well, no doubt we would have been devoted friends. But you probably wouldn't have enjoyed life on a farm, and my mother could be difficult, though it pains me to say a word against the dear woman. Admittedly, I wasn't always a perfect child."

"So you had difficulties with your mother, too?"

Sofiya nodded. "That's why I understand how you feel."

"I wish my mother and I got on better. It bothers me a lot."

"I can see that it does," she said. "However, have confidence that one day all will be resolved between you. It might be many years before you arrive at an understanding. But, as I said, and remember this—you are old, though young. Your mother may be young, though old. At some point, a balance will occur. When it does, your relationship will be a source of strength and mutual respect."

"Probably on my deathbed...or hers."

Sofiya's face clouded. "Why do you say your deathbed before your mother's?"

I shrugged, suddenly aware that I had said this and the order felt correct. "I don't know. Mother seems so powerful."

"*Formidable?*" Sofiya pronounced the word in French, then gave me a sad smile. "And by comparison you are weaker? No, I don't think that's true, although I don't know your mother. But she is not who concerns me."

Being placed before my mother was a rare occurrence. Speechless, I waited for Sofiya to explain.

"You're far stronger than you realize, which is probably why your mother feels threatened. If she didn't, she wouldn't attempt to control you so much."

I shifted in my chair, trying not to appear embarrassed by Sofiya's attention, which I was. A quiet thrill shot through me because I felt recognized. "Do you really believe that?"

"I do. My guess is your mother passed through her younger years with ease, without having to deal with any difficult issues."

"Because she's so beautiful?"

"I'm sure her appearance helped a lot. It gave her social confidence and attracted people, if nothing else."

"She has no idea how I feel being her unglamorous daughter."

"Oh, my dear. Yes, your mother is a great beauty, no question, but you aren't in her shadow either in looks or intelligence. In fact, Travis remarked this morning how smart and pretty you are."

"He did?"

Sofiya smiled and wiped her lips with a napkin. "Ask him."

I laughed. "I could never do that."

"No, I don't blame you." Sofiya chuckled. "But believe me, Travis is a fine judge of women." She squeezed my hand and stood. "Now, how about some ice cream after that heavy meal?"

—

I helped Sofiya with the dishes. By the time I reluctantly left, it was late afternoon. My brain was swirling with new perspectives and complicated emotions. I rushed to find my journal and pen and sat on the porch to document our dialogue, but first I needed to describe my mother's rude behavior yesterday when introduced to Sofiya. As I wrote about this exchange, a surge of anger caused me to hold my pen tighter, pressing harder into the paper.

When I finished this account, the tension had slowly eased. A light breeze blew off the turquoise-green ocean, and a nearby banana tree waved its long leaves. I thought of Sofiya's kind face, of her deep chuckle, and felt eager to savor our afternoon by describing it, despite the tragedies she had shared.

I turned the journal's page in order to keep my mother's section separate from Sofiya's, as if it might contaminate what I was about to write. In a miniscule script, I noted details about our afternoon, worried that my private thoughts would be discovered by my mother, yet happy to extend my engagement with Sofiya. My pen seemed to fly, words spilling as they seldom did. Excitement mixed with exhilaration as I described the surprising intimacy that had arisen between us. Even when I wrote about her painful wartime experiences, I felt a strong urge to record everything swiftly, though my delight transformed into grief as I imagined lying beside her in the fields, camera in hand, or standing by the oak tree, staring at her father's body.

When I'd finished, I realized I'd done a lousy job of showing Sofiya how much I cared, despite my wish to comfort her. She, on the other hand, had been generous with her sympathy.

I closed the journal. I was exhausted, as if I had been bleeding but to good purpose, purging some pain in the process. I then made entries in my travel diary, depicting the sounds, colors, smells, and sights of the market; praising my mother's drawings; and listing what we ate during last night's dinner at the Stone Balloon, neglecting to mention how spurned I'd felt. The comments were uniformly positive, though should I ever require information about the island, my notes would be useful in addition to my photographs. I placed the diary on the table by my bed, knowing Mother would see it, and fairly sure she would read it. With luck, she would conclude this was the only diary I kept.

Afterward, I remained on the porch with my book until my mother arrived, her gait unsteady and a bag of groceries in her arms. I rescued the bag and began placing eggs, orange juice, lunchmeat, milk, and butter in the refrigerator.

"You should have been there, Olivia. We had a fantastic grilled dolphin at lunch. Or, rather, it was a dolphin-fish or dorado."

Wine or some kind of alcohol had also accompanied the meal. She yawned, covering her mouth.

"Think I deserve a nap." She headed toward the bedroom, swayed a little, and steadied herself on the door frame.

"The goulash was excellent, by the way," I called after her.

"Oh, yes. That's nice."

I heard the bedsprings on the mattress creak and finished storing bread, crackers, chips, and coffee in the cupboard. Unsure what to do next, I returned to the porch. Through the glass door, I saw that Mother was already asleep, or rather, passed out. It was 7:25 p.m. and there had been no discussion about dinner, though I wasn't hungry. In all likelihood, my mother wouldn't wake for an hour or two, because when she did nap, she slept almost as soundly as at night. I scribbled a note: *Will return soon.* I didn't say where I was going because I had no idea.

With the key, wallet, and a roll of film in my pocket, my camera slung over my shoulder, I walked into town, hoping the blond boy might cross my path. Since he had been in the vicinity of Club Comanche and the Stone Balloon, I headed along Strand Street.

On the way, I wondered if I should relate the story about Travis's car accident to my mother. He might have already confided in her, though he seemed more intent on having fun and showing her the island rather than discussing anything serious. However, if her insobriety was any indication, Travis must have been driving in a somewhat drunken condition during their afternoon outing. Was this a habit of his? Admittedly, my father—and sometimes my mother—were behind the wheel when they shouldn't be. In my parents' social set, this was a commonplace behavior. Examined in this light, the accident could have also happened to us. But what if Travis had been at fault and had been charged? Had he fled the country to avoid responsibility? St. Croix was a U.S. territory, but could the American authorities come after him, if they discovered where he was? Was Travis McVay his real name? I shook my head, reproaching myself for conjuring unproven notions about a man I liked.

I arrived at Club Comanche and climbed the stairs in order to take a peek in the restaurant in case the boy was eating there. He wasn't. I ventured to the Hotel Caravelle and approached the man behind the desk.

"Excuse me, sir, but is a teenager about my age, with blond hair, in residence? I saw someone near here, in the street the other night, and he looked like a friend from home."

The man replied, "No, I don't think so."

I thanked him, then wandered around a pool and past an old sugar mill to a waterside bar. Calypso music poured into the night, the beat infectious and exuberant. I surveyed the crowd and the dancers, mostly whites with whites, blacks with blacks, though some couples were mixed—an unusual sight for me. I didn't harbor any bias, but when a Crucian man in a gold Banlon shirt caught my eye and lifted his chin, as if asking me to dance, I smiled and hurried out the door. I was alone, in an unfamiliar place, and the man appeared a bit inebriated and old, over thirty. Black or white, I would have refused. However, my mother, a native Southerner, would have been vehemently offended by his approach and might have made a stinker of a scene. She held contradictory views on race: in favor of equal treatment and respect in theory; but on a personal level, she was prejudiced, especially after a few drinks in like-minded company.

The loud music faded as I returned to the street. Apprehensive, I checked behind me twice, but no one was following. The sun was beginning to set, and longer shadows collected between the buildings, changing cheerful small lanes into more ominous streets. I increased my pace, growing more anxious. My mother wouldn't be pleased to know I was roaming Christiansted at this hour, yet I really wanted to find the boy who looked like Simon, to photograph and document his existence. In the failing light, taking a picture would be problematic but not impossible with a slow shutter speed and a wide-open aperture, both of which I had already adjusted in anticipation.

I didn't understand why I was so preoccupied with him. Was he a product of my overwrought imagination, a phantom who had broken through from the sphere of my nightmares? In which case, did this make me delusional? I asked after the blond boy at two more hotels, but none of the desk personnel recognized his description. This left me with the previously considered possibilities: he was staying at a privately rented apartment or at a resort outside of Christiansted, hence his use of a taxi. Whatever the case, I needed to quit searching for someone who might not be real.

The harbor was peaceful except for a sailboat owner tossing a sail bag into a dinghy and another scrubbing a boat's deck. A breeze stirred the thick heat left over from a hot day and dried my damp forehead. I sat on a bench and observed the moon rising over the horizon, casting its liquid silver over the ocean. The nearby island, Protestant Cay, was transforming into a black silhouette except for the area around its hotel, where the sprinkling of lights were reminiscent of yellow fireflies. I stared at the scene surrounding the wharf, turning now and then to check the fort and sidewalks, and wished

Sofiya were sitting beside me. It would be so pleasant to share the beautiful evening with someone, especially her.

As the moon ascended higher in the sky, sadness—tinged with fear—washed over me. I shut my eyes, and the terrible slide show began again: images of the dark forest, the steep cliff, the wooden dock, and then there was Simon. Simon running to its end, the violent river, falling...falling.

"No," I whispered.

Realizing I had spoken aloud, I opened my eyes and was relieved no one had heard me.

"You have to stop this, Olivia," I said to myself. But I had uttered these sentiments before, each time I slipped out of the house alone, late at night, and forced myself to walk through the dark, frightening woods to gaze down on the river from the bluff. How many sojourns had I made without my parents' knowledge? Twenty or more? Spring nights, when the purple lilacs were in bloom, were the hardest times for me to remain in bed.

Shaken and upset, I drew in a breath and slowly came to my feet. I walked to King Street, all the while anxious someone was behind me. Was it the boy? I tried to focus on the shops, a few of which were open; others were closed but lit with interior lights. As I noticed the reflections of my blond hair in the windows, I kept being reminded of my brother. I should go back to the hotel. Maybe have a last swim in the pool, maybe see Sofiya or Travis, who would make me laugh.

But at the intersection of King and Queen Cross Street, I remembered the route the taxi driver had taken before disappearing. Enticed by visions of Simon, I strolled for a few more blocks, but soon the neighborhood changed, with shacks outnumbering the newer homes, and fewer lights illuminating the darkness. Suddenly, a gang of male teenagers appeared a block away. They were jeering at one another, their voices loud and raucous, and all were obviously drunk. Afraid, I clutched my camera against my side and began walking rapidly to the Stone Balloon.

Near the restaurant, more people were on the street, so I felt safer. I peered inside the entrance and saw two college-age boys playing chess and a group of people milling about the bar, glasses in hand, laughing and talking. In my current mood, this conviviality made me feel more isolated and lonely. I considered asking for a table, but I didn't want to dine alone. However, I passed through the game room to the exterior restaurant and inspected the clientele. The boy wasn't there. I returned to the street, wondering what I would have done if he had been sitting at a table. Introduce myself? I shook my head at my foolishness.

A half block from the Stone Balloon, I sensed someone behind me again and turned to look. The road was empty except for a couple heading into town. Even so, my anxiety increased, and I rushed down Strand to Prince Street. When I reached the Pink Fancy, I mounted the steps, pausing once to catch my breath. At the top, I saw my mother and Travis standing by his office, illuminated by a spotlight. They were kissing.

I froze. My fingers clutched the Nikon, and I stood there, appalled and fascinated, suspended in time, unable to go forward and interrupt them or to retreat into the street. Almost without thinking, I removed the lens cap from the camera, focused, and squeezed the shutter. The sound was loud in the still air, but Travis and my mother were too intent on each other to notice. After taking another photograph, I remained by the corner of the building, frustrated that their whispered conversation was inaudible but somewhat glad it was. Above their entwined figures, Sofiya's light shone. Could she see or hear them?

My mother finally separated from Travis, trailing her fingers along his arm for a few seconds before walking to our apartment. Travis watched her leave, then closed and padlocked the office door, withdrew a cigarette, flicked a lighter, and headed in my direction. Almost immediately he noticed me standing in the darkness.

"Olivia?"

I stepped into the light, hoping he would think I had just arrived.

"Yeah. Hi, Travis."

"My goodness, it's late for you to be out by yourself."

"I guess I lost track of time. Mother fell asleep earlier, and I decided to explore Christiansted."

Travis exhaled a plume of smoke. "Well, it's not the best idea to do that. After dark, I mean, and alone. Your mother was concerned." He pointed to the cigarette as if someone else was smoking it. "By the way, I've given up this bad habit, except for one before bed."

I moved closer, unsure whether to confront him with what I'd witnessed or to pretend I hadn't. "I wish my mother would stop smoking," I said, unable to avoid mentioning her.

"Well, I'm sure she wishes she could," he replied. "Now, Evelyn was looking for you, so maybe you'd better go in."

I nodded and told him goodnight. When I tried the door to our apartment, it was locked. Hmm, I thought: Mother's locked into Fantasy. I removed the key from my pocket, opened the door, and cautiously stepped inside. Mother was sitting on the couch, staring at me. The cigarette smoke did not dim the fire in her eyes.

"Where have you been?" she demanded.

"I went for a walk in town."

"You did? You know that isn't acceptable."

"So Travis just told me."

Mother blinked when I said his name but didn't respond. I carried my camera and wallet into the bedroom, placing both on the top of the dresser, wanting to be away from the smoke and from what appeared to be a brewing argument. The air felt as though a storm were consolidating forces, the atmospheric pressure dropping, the sudden stillness unnatural.

Except for a triangle of light on the floor, created by the living room lamp, the room was dark. I was about to change into my pajamas when my mother walked in and flipped on the overhead light. I squinted and asked her to turn it off.

"No, I won't. We need to have a discussion about your behavior this evening."

"*My* behavior?"

She inhaled, held the smoke in her lungs, and blew it out slowly. "I've had a long day. I fell asleep for a little while. What's wrong with that?"

I snorted. "That's not what I was referring to, as you well know."

Her chin jerked back. "You may not speak to me in this fashion, Olivia! I am your mother."

"Being my mother doesn't give you the privilege of being so thoughtless. I deserve some consideration...like telling me what our plans were for dinner."

She stubbed out her cigarette after another puff. "Oh, please. I'm sure you ate enough at lunch. Goulash, was it?" Her face prickled with disgust. "With your new pal?"

Now I was angry. "It's a good thing I have Sofiya because you've been too busy with Travis to spend any time with me." I considered sitting on the bed but preferred to maintain the advantage of my height. "And, in case you wish to know, her company was very welcome."

My mother tightened her arms across her chest, as if trying to contain her rage. "Travis and I are just good friends. It's pleasant to have male companionship now and then."

"Except when it's my father's?"

She opened her mouth to refute my implied accusation, then changed her mind. "Let's stick to the matter at hand. Your roaming around Christiansted."

"Why is that the only matter at hand, Mother? Because you don't want to admit what's going on with Travis? Is that it?" She gave me an icy glance, and I continued. "What am I supposed to say to Dad if he calls and asks how everything is? Should I lie and say you're staying in every night, that we're getting on brilliantly? Should I?"

"You don't know what you're talking about."

"About Travis or about us? As a matter of fact, I have firsthand knowledge of both."

Her frown deepened into a scowl, corrupting her beautiful features. "You're crazy."

"I might be, but I'm not blind. And I have proof." I pointed to my camera.

Mother stood there, her hands tucked into fists. Then she lunged for the Nikon. I tried to block her, but she was closer to the camera and knocked it off the dresser. It landed on the floor, lens first, and I heard a sickening crack of glass. Furious, I pushed my mother aside and kneeled, gently grasping the camera in my fingers. The lens cap had popped off, and the outer UV filter was shattered. I unscrewed the filter and saw that the lens glass was also cracked. My hands shaking, I removed the lens to check the slanted mirror. Miraculously, it appeared undamaged. Without another lens, however, the body was useless.

My mother was silent. I shot her a look of outrage, staggered to my feet, and carried the lens, filter, and camera onto the porch. After throwing the filter into the wastebasket, I sat at the table, replaced the lens, and unwound the black-and-white film until the sprocket pin released, then opened the back, pulled out the spool of exposed film, and placed it in my pocket. I checked that the shutter curtain wasn't jammed and the film advance lever was working properly and laid the Nikon down. Trying to control my fury, I folded my arms on the table and rested my forehead on top, but all I wanted to do was tear my mother apart or snap every pencil, brush, and pastel stick she owned.

In the background, I heard my mother return to the living room, her lighter click, and footsteps approaching the other door to the porch. Would she apologize? She who was never in the wrong? I waited, my jaws tight.

"We can go to St. Thomas and buy a new one. If they don't sell them here."

I raised my head, glared at her, and pointed to the Nikon. "Dad gave me this camera. What you did was unforgivable."

I thought she would forget the earlier part of our conversation, that the shameful breaking of my lens would have expended her aggression, but she wasn't finished.

"I've been considering this for some time, Olivia, as your behavior has become more insolent and hostile toward me. When we return home, I will make an appointment for you to see a counselor."

I exhaled sharply. "What? For me? You just smashed my camera!"

"Yes, for you. We can't continue like this." Her eyes seemed opaque, unreadable.

"Why is everything always my fault? What about your role in our relationship?" She didn't answer. "Ah, so you don't understand your role? As a loving parent? But, of course, you're probably unfamiliar with that term. You haven't cared for me since—"

Mother did not wish to hear the rest. "I refuse to be criticized—"

"But it's okay for you to constantly criticize me, isn't it?"

"Your father and I will discuss the matter and make the appropriate decision."

"You mean *you* will! He won't agree to it."

"Steven already believes you're disturbed."

"That's a lie, and you know it. Dad knows how you treat me, and he doesn't like it."

"That's nonsense."

"No, it isn't." I stood and faced her. "I've had it with you and your sham good-mother act—good until we're alone, and then I get it in the neck. Besides, Dad won't be happy that you broke the lens he bought—the only one I have."

"I said I'd buy another one. He'll never know the difference."

"But I will and he will if I tell him." I gripped the edge of the table. "And if you can't be nicer to me, I'll give him the pictures I took of you and Travis kissing."

Mother's face reddened. "You wouldn't! That's blackmail!"

"It's up to you what I do."

She drew herself up to her full height. "Oh, if only you had been the one—"

"What? If only I had been the one—what?"

Her face drained of color. She turned and stalked off the porch.

I followed her into the living room. "Finish it for once, will you?" I demanded. "Say it!"

She gave me a twisted smile, as if she had bested me, then drank some water from a glass, switched off the room light, and entered the bedroom.

Dazed, I returned to the porch and slumped on the bed. Was I relieved my mother hadn't completed her sentence? Or was I upset that once again she hadn't admitted her true feelings about Simon and about me? Her words to my brother, "Yes, darling, more than Olivia," ricocheted in my brain. I could force her to say, "If only you had died and Simon had lived," but I was too afraid to hear the truth.

I wouldn't share a room with her tonight. I pulled down the blue bedspread and crawled inside the sheets, daring my mother to tell me I wasn't allowed to sleep outside. As I gazed at the rooftops and the few silver stars, tears fell from my eyes. I cried silently, but a few minutes later, through the partly opened door, I heard my mother sobbing.

Day 5

I leaned on the porch railing. Birds were chatting in the trees. The seaplane flying to St. Thomas, the Goose, revved its engines, and in the other room, Mother rattled pans, preparing her breakfast. Hungry as I was, the thought of sharing a meal with her was repugnant. When I heard her finally leave the apartment, I entered the bedroom and placed the camera on my suitcase, then checked the living area. Mother's sketchbook and supplies were missing, so it was likely she wouldn't return for some time. I ate two bananas and a slice of bread and drank a glass of orange juice, then slipped into my bathing suit, unsure whether I could tolerate being in public.

The day stretched before me without any plans. I wanted to see Sofiya, though not to confess what had happened with my mother. A thank-you note was in order, however, so I removed a sheet of Pink Fancy stationery and an envelope from the desk drawer and wrote a few lines about the goulash and how much I enjoyed her company. I paused at the bottom of the page, unsure how to end the letter. "Yours truly" or "Most sincerely" sounded stiff. I wrote "Love, Olivia."

After sliding the letter into the envelope, I found the conch wrapped in white tissue. With both in hand, I walked to Little Joy and left the envelope and shell on her steps. I returned to the apartment as the maid—Rosita—arrived to clean. She was from St. Kitts. She began dusting while I cleaned my dishes. A minute later, there was a knock on the door. As I opened it, I felt a burst of hopeful anticipation.

Sofiya stood there, holding the shell. "Good morning, Olivia. Thank you so much for your thoughtful note...and for this beautiful shell. I've never seen one like it."

"Hi. I bought it at the market. It's a rooster-tail conch," I replied. "And you're welcome. Thank you for lunch yesterday."

She smiled. "My great pleasure."

Suddenly, I felt better. Sofiya's comforting presence soothed the raw soreness from last night.

"I was wondering if you might like to come with me to Pelican Cove," she said. "It's a small club with a lovely beach and a coral reef very close to shore. Lots of fish. You could bring your mask and flippers."

"Sure! Sounds like fun."

"Good. I rented a car for job interviews, so I can drive us. Now, should you ask your mother's permission? Is she here?"

"No, she left to go sketching. I don't know when she'll return." I considered for a moment, balancing my usual dutifulness against my desire to spend the day with Sofiya. "But it's okay. I'll write her a note to tell her where I am."

"Travis has the number of the hotel if she needs to reach you."

We arranged to meet in fifteen minutes. I wrote a message to my mother, weighing whether to apologize or not. Although I didn't believe my actions were to blame for our argument, I took the high road and added, "I'm sorry for last night. Hope we can start over." I left the slip of paper on the coffee table and packed towels, my snorkeling equipment, flippers, wallet, book, private journal, and the exposed roll of black-and-white film into my TWA bag. Over my suit, I donned shorts and a white terry shirt and then asked Rosita to lock the door when she was finished. As I left, the gloom seemed to dissipate; seeing Sofiya waiting under the blue awning, the last gray cloud of unhappiness vanished entirely.

—

The car was a small Ford sedan, with the steering wheel on the left as in the United States, but on St. Croix, the driving was to the left also, British style. I had noticed this on the first day, in the taxi from the airport, and on our trip with Mr. Thomas, yet as we set off north from Christiansted, I was unnerved to be on the wrong side of the road, though Sofiya was an adept driver.

When we passed a large building, Sofiya said, "A murder occurred here not long ago. According to the newspapers, crime on the island is on the increase—more burglaries and assaults. I suppose we all need to be careful."

"I went out last night by myself. Guess I shouldn't have."

Sofiya glanced at me with mild alarm. "No, probably not." She turned her eyes back to the road. "Where was your mother?"

I rubbed my cheek, wishing I hadn't raised the subject. "She fell asleep after her day with Travis. I didn't have anything else to do so I walked into town." It was tempting to reveal the reason for my excursion—the search for Simon—but Sofiya might think I was disturbed, as my mother had insisted during our argument.

"I see. Well, best not to do that again, okay?"

I nodded.

In silence, we rode several miles to Pelican Cove Beach Club. Sofiya needed to concentrate on her driving, while I privately replayed how frightened I had been of the gang of kids and the dark streets. After we pulled into the parking lot, we unloaded our gear, bought beach passes, and walked past the restaurant and a few sea grape bushes, their rounded green leaves fluttering on pink stems. Near the water was a grove of coconut palms, whose trunks curved toward the ocean. Three brown pelicans were fishing beyond the reef.

We strolled along the white sand, past several thatched cabanas, each housing two chaises. Several kids were kicking an orange, blue, and white ball and shrieking whenever it fell into the water. Sofiya kept walking until we reached the last hut.

"Is this okay with you?" she asked. "I hate being close to too much activity."

"Children, you mean?"

She laughed. "Exactly."

I grinned at her and plunked my flight bag in the shade of the cabana. After we dragged our chaises into the sunlight and removed our street clothes, Sofiya began rubbing some oil on her skin. Her hands were graceful, long-fingered, with nails neatly trimmed and covered with clear polish.

"This is a blend of lemon juice and olive oil that I make myself," she said.

"It smells wonderful."

She handed me the plastic bottle. "Try some. Just keep in mind that you'll burn more easily."

I applied the mix on my arms and face, thinking I had noticed this scent on her before, along with a rich, spicy perfume. "What cologne do you wear?"

"Youth-Dew by Estée Lauder."

I decided to buy a bottle at Cavanagh's, to remember Sofiya when I returned home, the thought of which made me sad.

We lay in the hot sun, sharing humorous anecdotes. For the moment, I was content to luxuriate in the beneficent atmosphere. It felt good not to be embroiled in an argument or listening to a tirade.

After half an hour, I sat up. "Okay, I'm fried."

She laughed. "I think the water is calling, yes?"

"Yes." I grabbed my snorkel, mask, and flippers.

"Have you been swimming on a reef before?" she asked, removing her sunglasses. The area of her skin protected by the sunglasses was whiter, thus enhancing the size and color of her eyes.

"Only once. Two years ago on Bermuda."

"Well, this reef is in very shallow water. Be careful where you place your feet. Sea urchins."

"Black spiky things, right?"

Sofiya nodded. "Occasionally, their white skeletons can be found on the beaches. You might even find large ones about this big." She gestured with her fingers, creating an expanse about four inches across.

The sea was spectacularly beautiful. Modest waves were breaking offshore, forming white ruffles against very dark purplish-blue patches. Other sections were milky green or turquoise, depending on the depth, rocks, reefs, or shadows of the huge cumulous clouds skimming overhead. We waded in, laughing at how warm the water was. I wedged the flippers onto my feet, fitted the mask on my face and the snorkel in my mouth, and dove underwater.

Instantly, the world transformed into a myriad of dazzling colors. The nearby coral reef was split in two, with a trough about fifteen feet between. Both sections ran almost parallel to the beach but open-ended close to us, so that Sofiya could stand safely or swim without worrying about the reef, while I could enter the space and cruise along, turning to my left and right, examining the coral. As fish darted all around me, I tried to recall some of the names from the guide to tropical marine life that my father had purchased for our trip to Bermuda. I had studied the illustrations before leaving for St. Croix, to refresh my memory, and could identify several: a greenish-yellow sergeant major, with multiple vertical bars; a neon-blue angelfish, with trailing thin fins above and below its tail, the scales edged in yellow; and two large parrotfish with broad white horizontal stripes. Schools of small silvery moonfish flitted about, turning deftly, as if orchestrated by overhead strings in a marine marionette theater. The underwater silence was dense except for the sound of my respiration within the hollow tube of the snorkel.

After a few minutes, I raised my head and asked Sofiya if she would like to borrow my mask.

"Maybe later. You have fun." She was floating on her

back. "The hotel manager let me borrow one when I was here a few days ago."

I wanted to share the beauty with her, but Sofiya seemed content to relax. The magnetic underworld called, so I reset the mask and snorkel and swam along the reef, noting the various sizes of brain coral, the antler-shaped branches of staghorn and elkhorn coral, as well as purple and magenta sea fans undulating with the current. Near the sandy bottom, I came upon a gruff-looking reddish-brown grouper, one of the bigger fish, about fourteen inches in length. He noticed me but didn't seem threatened, nor was he particularly interested since I wasn't a designated member of his food chain. Next in the parade were several vibrantly colored triggerfish. Their bodies were gray to bluish green, with two blue curved lines on the sides of their heads, as if they were smiling, and dark shaky lines radiating from their eyes. I was enchanted. It was astonishing that this panorama could lie in chest-high water, unseen from the beach.

The glass on the mask clouded with condensation, giving the scene a dreamy impression of bright colors fading to muted hues within the same fish. I checked that the sand was free of obstacles and set my flippers down, tipping up the mask and snorkel. Sofiya had returned to the chaise and was reading a book, but when she noticed I had surfaced, she smiled and waved. She seemed like a good shepherd watching over me.

I returned her greeting and felt a happy glow, a unique connection between us. While I loved swimming on the reefs, which were mesmerizing, I was equally mesmerized by Sofiya and wished to be by her side, smelling the perfume and the blend of lemon and oil and absorbing her kindness. In fact, kindness was a quality I had never really considered before; it seemed the lightest emotion, and yet one that was substantial and profound, a fundamental underpinning of most lives but not of mine.

I replaced the mask and snorkel and entered the glittering sea again, pondering the nature of my feelings for her and wondering about the nature of love. Certainly, my parents cared about me, but even when Simon was alive, our family hadn't been happy. Not like the ones I saw on TV, though I knew those families weren't realistic. However, since my brother's death, when Dad was home, he was busier—playing golf, socializing with friends. Mother was different, too. More distant and critical, picking over any transgression I committed. I couldn't remember when either parent had said "I love you" to me, at least not since Simon's accident. They appended "Love, Mother" or "Love, Dad" to my birthday and Christmas cards, but these expressions seemed rote. Without my brother, we had become three individuals glued together by circumstances.

Even the trip to St. Croix had begun on a wrong note. My mother had decided to create a collection of drawings and paintings about the island, expecting Dad to stay in New Jersey with me, but when he was notified of a flight schedule change, my father refused to argue with the airlines. She was furious and complained that he left whenever he liked while she was always stuck with me. Overhearing that familiar sentiment, I was less than thrilled to be a forced tag-along on this venture, knowing my presence was unwanted, even resented. I now wondered if the affair with Travis had been fueled by my mother's anger at Dad about the trip. Or maybe it had to do with feeling older due to starting menopause, though all I knew about that was women had hot flashes and mood swings. Perhaps last night's unusual weeping episode had been a symptom of the change of life, but I suspected the crying jags were merely a new weapon in Mother's emotional bag of tricks.

Just then, a skinny needlefish came close, cutting through the water with precision. The fish was silvery white, almost transparent, except for a blue horizontal stripe and several dark gray vertical bars; its slender, sharp nose looked as if it could run me through. I couldn't recall whether needlefish were predatory but decided it was prudent to head in the opposite direction, down the trough to the beach.

I was also hungry. More significantly, I missed Sofiya, though I didn't understand why the feeling was so powerful. The time alone, swimming, had been my choice, but the separation seemed to intensify my desire to be with her, as if by delaying my return to the cabana, my excitement had compounded. I couldn't recall experiencing such a strange longing before, one mixed with vague uneasiness because my mood didn't seem quite normal. After slipping off my flippers, I hurried from the water.

Sofiya placed her paperback on her lap. "Ah, so you're finished for a while?"

I nodded, grabbing my towel. "I saw a large needlefish." I described what it looked like. "Wasn't sure whether they're safe or not. Do you have any idea?"

"Not really. I know the fish—they're pretty creepy. I always swim away from them."

I stood above Sofiya, smiling and self-conscious, then sat on my chaise and dried my feet. She observed me as I did this, her eyes trailing to my right foot.

"What happened, Olivia?"

I stared at the old, jagged scar running from my ankle to the sole of my foot. "It's nothing." I thrust my foot into the sand.

Her blue eyes fixed on mine. "Doesn't look like it was nothing."

"It's from eight years ago." My voice weakened, almost to a whisper. "An accident on a dock."

"Hmm," she said, "that must have hurt."

"I guess it did." Desperately, I wanted to change the subject. Desperately, I wanted to tell Sofiya everything. "I don't really remember."

"I see." She made no further comment. Finally, she asked if I wanted some lunch.

"Yes, I do. And, if you don't mind, could I treat you? I'd like to do that since you cooked the goulash and drove us here."

Sofiya chuckled. "That's fine, Olivia. Thank you."

—

We sat side by side on a bench, eating cheeseburgers. Sofiya spoke about her childhood and her duties on the farm—how she was afraid of the hens, who would peck at her hands when she tried to remove their eggs. When we stood to return to the cabana, she touched my shoulder.

"You're getting a bad sunburn."

"I am?"

"Yes, all that time in the water, facing down." She examined my legs. "They're not so bad."

After we arrived at our beach hut, Sofiya reached into her bag and handed me a tightly rolled white tee shirt. "Here, it's from Travis. He figured you'd get into trouble today."

"Travis?" Instantly, I was on the alert. "How did he know we were coming to Pelican Cove?" I refrained from saying what I feared: that Travis had pressured Sofiya into entertaining me so he and my mother could spend the day together. I held my breath for her reply.

Sofiya sensed my distress. "I mentioned to Travis where we were going. I do that when I leave town because there has been some unrest lately. Why, is something wrong?"

Annoyed at myself for overreacting, I shook my head. "Travis is really thoughtful to think of the shirt. I'll thank him."

Sofiya gave me a searching look. "Perhaps I am incorrect...and, of course, it is not my business, but are you upset with him?"

"No, not with Travis."

Sofiya straightened slightly. "With your mother?"

I stared at the water, wishing I could grab my snorkel and mask and disappear into the ocean. "I'm always upset with her. And she's always upset with me. That's a permanent condition. It's been like this for as long as I can remember."

"I'm sorry to hear that." Sofiya was silent for a moment, then spoke again. "Last night I saw your mother with Travis. And I noticed you standing by the steps."

I groaned. "You're right. I was there and watched what was going on. And stupidly, impulsively, I took two photographs of them. I shouldn't have done it."

"Did they see you?"

"No, and if I hadn't said anything to my mother later, my camera would still be in one piece."

Sofiya's eyes opened wide. "You mean she broke it?"

"Mother knocked it off the dresser. The lens and filter are shattered."

"Oh, Olivia!"

"And because I don't have another lens, it means I can't take any more photographs."

"That's a real shame. I know photography is important to you," she said. "I suppose the two of you had words?"

I laughed bitterly at this. "Words? We had paragraphs, entire pages. She didn't want me to come with her to St. Croix, and now she's upset I'm here because she wants to be alone with Travis. I'm worried that the romance with him will put me on the spot if Dad calls. The subject won't come up, but not telling him is a lie of omission. On the other hand, he may have been unfaithful to my mother. It's possible."

Sofiya considered what I'd said. "Olivia, people have affairs. It's a regrettable fact of life. If your mother could, I'm sure she would conceal what's going on with Travis, but sharing an apartment with you makes that impossible. As for inserting you in the middle of your parents' marital conflicts, if that's happened, well, again, it's hard to disguise major problems when you're all living together."

"I don't think my mother and Travis are trying very hard to hide what's going on," I said. "Maybe I've seen too much 'happy family' television and keep expecting her to act better." I slipped the tee shirt over my head and covered my bathing suit.

"I doubt she means to hurt you. When people are attracted to each other, they act out of impulse rather than weighing the situation rationally."

She was being reasonable, but I was angry. I dug my toe into the sand. "Well, you're probably right, but I'm sick of her." I glanced at Sofiya. "You wouldn't do something like this."

"I haven't, no, but..." She smiled. The smile didn't light her eyes.

I registered the change in her immediately. "But what?"

"Nothing really."

"I'm sorry. I didn't mean to—"

"It's okay. Now, I think it's time for another swim, don't you?"

I sensed she wished to vanish into the sea as I had wanted to do earlier. I brushed the sand off my mask and snorkel and followed her. Once we were standing in thigh-high water, Sofiya turned, laughed merrily, and splashed me. Unprepared for this display of youthfulness, I hesitated to splash back, but then I did. We giggled and sank into the water a few feet apart.

"Well, we are certainly behaving like grown-ups today, aren't we?" she said. This brought on another eruption of laughter.

—

The afternoon passed in a companionable way. I swam along both reefs and found a small, oblong sea urchin skeleton, which I brought to Sofiya.

"Nice," she said. "On more deserted beaches you'll find bigger ones."

"Could we go to a beach like that?"

Sofiya thought for a moment. "If we do, it would be best to include Travis and your mother. A group of people is safer than the two of us. Besides, Travis likes to spearfish. He can catch us lunch, which we could cook on the beach."

Although I wasn't thrilled with the idea of a party with my mother, having a picnic sounded exotic. "We should ask them."

"And speaking of your mother, she might have made dinner arrangements. Perhaps it's time to head back."

Observing the aquamarine colors of the ocean and the gold sunlight painted on the waves, I agreed, though I would have been content to remain in the cabana all night, talking with Sofiya. She seemed to share this mood and lingered, her eyes now covered with sunglasses, which made it more difficult to read her expression. At last, she sighed, slipped on her beach robe, and packed her things. I wrung out the wet tee shirt, folded it in one of my towels, and added my terry jacket over my swimsuit. We left in silence, reluctant to end a perfect day.

In the car, we didn't speak much. I was tired from swimming and hot from the sunburn that was beginning to hurt.

"Put some cream on after a shower," Sofiya suggested.

I promised I would, though my thoughts were once again on my mother and Travis, in anticipation of encountering both at the hotel. I knew I was inexperienced about male-female relationships, but I was positive my mother was sleeping with Travis, and equally positive I didn't think it was right. But what if my parents had decided to get a divorce before we left home and not told me? Was it okay then? In that case, why shouldn't my mother find a little joy? In a different way, wasn't I also searching for the happiness that was absent at home?

Sofiya parked the car on Prince Street, and we trudged up the steep hotel steps. Three people were in the pool, two holding plastic glasses containing some type of alcoholic drink, or so it appeared from their giddy behavior. I stopped at the juncture where Sofiya and I would part.

"Thank you," I whispered.

She gently patted my arm and headed to her apartment. I watched as she climbed to the door and unlocked it, then I shouldered my gear and walked to our end unit. Inside, Mother was sitting on the sofa, sketchbook propped against the table. She glanced at me and placed her pencil in a small box.

"You've had a lot of sun, haven't you?"

Her sympathetic tone surprised me. I'd been anticipating criticism for leaving without permission.

"Yeah. Sofiya gave me a tee shirt from Travis to wear, which helped, but not before I'd been snorkeling for a while."

"How was Pelican Cove?"

"Really beautiful." I explained about the parallel reefs, the coral, the fish, and the colors. "Maybe you'd like to go there? It's only a few miles from town."

"I might. Perhaps you would show me how to use a mask and snorkel?"

Her manner was friendly, engaging. I blinked, thinking my mother had been transformed into Sofiya. "Sure. You could practice here in the pool, although the water at Pelican Cove is calm and shallow."

"One or the other sounds good." She looked at her watch. "Shall we go to Café de Paris this evening?"

"That's fine."

I walked into the bedroom, astounded by my mother's pleasantness. After a shower and after applying some lotion, I dressed in blue-and-white seersucker slacks, a white blouse, and a thin navy leather belt. My hair was tangled, but after strenuous efforts with a brush and comb, it finally looked neat. The dreaded mirror reflected a face that appeared more relaxed.

When I returned to the living room, Mother handed me

a glass, saying she had made daiquiris using packets of mix and Cruzan Rum. I thanked her, and we sat together at the porch table.

"Would you like to come with me to St. Thomas tomorrow morning? I've finished a few pieces to show the Riise Gallery, to give them an idea what I'm doing."

I knew my mother had already written the manager on the advice of a friend who used to live on the island. "I'd like that."

"Fine. We'll take the seaplane. And when I called to schedule the appointment, I asked advice about where to buy Nikon lenses. The manager offered to make the purchases and have them at the store."

"But did you tell him—"

"Yes, Olivia. I said you needed a fifty millimeter Nikkor lens with an f/1.4 aperture. I checked that and the filter size, and though I'm no expert, it appears that your camera is working, so it doesn't need to be replaced." She drank some of her daiquiri.

I was surprised she knew enough to do this, but then recalled she'd used Dad's Nikon on occasion. "Thank you." And when she checked my camera, had she searched for the incriminating roll of film? The one hidden in my flight bag?

"I also asked him if he knew what other lenses were available for your camera, and he recommended a telephoto lens. I believe it's a one hundred thirty-five millimeter Nikkor?"

I had wanted this lens very much and was hoping Dad would buy it for Christmas. "Really? With that lens I can take photos of people from a distance, and they're less likely to notice. Maybe some of the pictures will help you in your work."

Mother nodded. "I'm glad I made the right choice."

I polished off my drink. "You did, thanks."

—

Café de Paris was in King's Alley. Its official host was Charlie, a friendly English Springer Spaniel, who greeted us. Mother and I sat underneath a yellow umbrella and ordered onion soup and lobster blinis: lobster meat cooked in a Béchamel sauce with sliced mushrooms, rolled in a crêpe, and sprinkled with Parmesan cheese. Mother found a French Chablis to accompany the meal, which we enjoyed, though I drank only one glass. After my day swimming and tanning, I was thirsty and preferred ice water.

To my amazement, our dinner passed without conflict. It was a relief to hang up our boxing gloves for a change. I listened as she described several completed drawings and was pleased when she inquired about Sofiya. As we left the restaurant, I thought it was one of the nicest evenings we'd spent together in a long time.

—

We read our books in the bedroom. Travis had loaned Mother a hardcover of Michener's *Hawaii*, which she struggled to hold since it was one thousand pages in length. I was halfway into *Lord of the Flies* and struggling because I kept inserting my brother into the character of Simon. In this section, Simon had found a hollowed pit under a thick mat of creepers and was lying alone within it. Although the book's Simon had a mop of black hair, a pointed chin, and was plagued by fainting spells, I pictured him as blond, broad-faced, and energetic. It was clear the character represented the author's perspective, as the boy warns the group, who are turning into savages, that there is no beast except the beast inside of them. This mild, kindly child was drawn in sharp contrast to the others, and in this aspect, my brother merged with the novel's Simon. The darkness of the story was becoming increasingly more ominous, so when my mother asked to turn off the light, I willingly agreed.

Day 6

The next morning, we rose early for our 8:40 flight to Charlotte Amalie in St. Thomas. With her usual care, Mother was turned out in a cream dress belted at the waist, a wooden-bead necklace, and ivory espadrilles. Her curly hair, damp from a shower and the humidity, lay close to her head but looked fashionable. My long, straight hair, by contrast, felt thick and heavy, causing me to consider having it cut so it wouldn't take hours to dry. However, permission probably wouldn't be granted because Mother deemed this length appropriate for girls. I wore last night's outfit and was instructed to add the seersucker suit jacket, which I refused to do, citing the heat. I placed my camera, wallet, film, and travel journal in my TWA bag.

As we walked along Prince Street toward the ocean, I volunteered to carry my mother's portfolio, for which she was grateful. At the Antilles Air Boats office, we purchased tickets and observed the peculiar Grumman Goose perched on its ramp, nose aimed at the water. The body was white with a red and gold stripe running horizontally and up the plane's tail. Two engines were mounted on the high-set wings, and a man in a khaki jumpsuit stood on top, doing some sort of maintenance, while another loaded cargo via movable steps parked by an open hatch door.

"Too bad Maureen O'Hara isn't here this morning," my mother told me.

I gave her a quizzical look.

"You know, the actress. Red hair? Starred with John Wayne in *Rio Grande*? Travis said she's dating the owner, Charles Blair."

My mother was fond of celebrities, but I couldn't recall O'Hara and was more interested in the seaplane, which I planned to describe to my father.

I was allowed to keep my flight bag, but the portfolio case was stowed before we boarded because it was policy to secure larger loose cargo. Scanning the weather-beaten plane, I hoped the seats were fitted with strong seatbelts for the ten passengers.

We sat mid-way down the aisle. The cockpit was partly exposed, with a view of the windshield, the dashboard instruments, and the pilot, who was in the process of completing the pre-flight check.

I leaned over to my mother. "Guess what. Someone's missing up front."

"Oh my god! No co-pilot?"

"Dad would have a fit."

Just then, a passenger was told to go forward and was shown to the seat beside the pilot. They began chatting about the various gauges.

"Well, I guess we have one now," I said.

After the exterior doors were secured, the plane rolled down the ramp and waddled into the water, the rear and center sections settling into the ocean while the nose stuck up in the air as if the plane were trying to gasp its last breath before drowning. The pilot revved the engines, and we picked up speed. Water splashed against the windows and oozed through the seals. I pointed this out to my mother, who was similarly alarmed. Despite my fifty or so flights on various planes and jets, I clutched the armrests tightly, thinking this critter possessed none of the light, bird-like qualities of most aircraft. Instead of skimming down a runway, the heavy -bellied Goose appeared quite unwilling and unable to lift off. The noise of the engines was deafening until, after a belabored attempt, the plane heaved itself out of the water. My mother's face, which was surely as white as mine, regained some color.

The flight was short and the descent equally abbreviated because of the low cruising altitude. The plane hit the water hard, and with a great deal of huffing, puffing, and hawing from side to side, the Goose's wheels found purchase on the ramp and up we went, though the plane seemed disinclined to, well, mount the incline. Once the engine was switched off, Mother and I stood on unsteady feet and departed the dripping aircraft, which I half expected to shake itself like a wet dog.

After Mother reconnected with her portfolio, we set off into town, which was charming, with numerous intersecting alleyways designed so pirates such as Bluebeard, in days of yore, could elude anyone chasing them. Flowers were everywhere as were colorful flags and beautifully tended shops and outdoor restaurants. My mother's eyes were bright with shopping fever, though we had business to attend to first. After a few minutes, we arrived at A. H. Riise's elegant store, where we were escorted to the manager's office. Although I didn't catch his name, the man was well dressed in a spotless white suit. He was delighted to meet my mother.

After coffee arrived for the two of them, the manager opened a cabinet and removed a rectangular box.

"I believe these are for you," he told me.

I opened it and was thrilled to see two Nikkor lenses and filters. I touched the black metal on one of the lenses with reverence and thanked my mother and the manager.

"Olivia has a passion for photography," she explained to the man, sounding proud of me for once.

"Maybe one day you'll be exhibiting with us," the manager said, smiling.

Mother cleared her throat, as if dismissing this possibility.

"Now, dear, why don't you leave us so we can discuss my work?"

I came to my feet, smiled, and exited the office, glad to be free. After walking outside, I sat on a nearby bench and removed the broken 50mm lens, mounted the respective filters on the two lenses, inserted the telephoto onto the body, and added a roll of color film. Looking through the viewfinder, I was amazed at the enlargement as well as the sharpness. I composed a shot of fuchsia hibiscus growing in a jade green flower box and made other images of the buildings while wandering through the maze of streets.

Thirty exposures later, I returned to Riise's. Unsure whether to disturb my mother, I strolled around the store and stopped at the perfume counter, where I sampled Youth-Dew. Its dark, peppery scent conjured an immediate vision of Sofiya. Even with the excitement of the flight and the new photography equipment, she hadn't been far from my thoughts all morning. Now, as I had experienced yesterday while swimming, a yearning ache flooded over me. My desire to be with her was as mystifying as my obsession with the blond boy.

"There you are!"

I turned to see my mother, who was smiling.

"Trying some perfume?" She reached for the bottle and sprayed the inside of her wrist. "That's nice, although it might be a little old for you."

I had been wearing Jean Naté over the last year, a light and airy cologne. "Says 'youth' on the bottle."

Mother was in such high spirits that she beckoned the salesgirl to wrap up the cologne, and then explained that the manager, after conferring with the owner, had offered a solo exhibit of her St. Croix series in their gallery next August. After paying at the counter, we roamed around the store, which gleamed in the lights reflecting on the glass cases, but she scarcely looked at the jewelry and clothes, which usually captivated her attention, and instead poured out her ideas for drawings and paintings.

I was delighted for her success but even more excited to hear Mother planned to return the following summer.

"Does that mean we're coming again? For the show?" I asked.

"Yes, of course."

"And I'm included?"

My mother looked at me like I was behaving oddly. "If you would like to be here, that's fine with me. I'd love your company and certainly could use your help."

In the onrush of euphoric relief, I almost missed the positive comment about loving my company, a remark I briefly relished before succumbing to the exhilarating news about seeing Sofiya again.

"We'll have to ship the work here—at least the larger pieces," she added.

Though miles away, I nodded enthusiastically.

—

After lunch and laden with our purchases, we returned on the 5:10 p.m. flight, which was as terrifying as the previous one. My mother didn't help my confidence when she said the seaplane had a habit of conking out hundreds of feet from the ramp, causing passengers to swim ashore or hang onto the pontoons until rescue arrived. It took no imagination to picture this as we wobbled about in the water for a few minutes before making the slow, noisy climb onto the cement apron of the tiny airport.

At the Pink Fancy, Travis greeted us, and my mother related her news about the exhibit.

"That's great," he said, grinning. "As soon as you have the dates, let me know and I'll reserve Fantasy for you and Olivia."

Mother looked uncertain. "Why, I was actually planning to book a hotel on St. Thomas. Since the gallery is there…"

"Oh," Travis said, taken aback.

Startled, Travis and I stared at my mother.

"No, we have to stay here!" I cried.

Travis frowned. "Evelyn, I'm not so sure your husband would think flying into St. Thomas is such a good idea. Pan Am just began flights in January, and there have been issues with the extremely short runway."

"Hmm." Her eyes glistened with mischief. "Well, I guess I'm outvoted." She had been kidding Travis, to see how he would react.

When he realized this, he laughed, placed his arm around my shoulders, and gave me a squeeze. "She had us going there for a minute, didn't she?"

I agreed and then noticed Sofiya leaving her apartment. Quickly, I walked over to meet her by the pool.

"I see you survived the Goose," she said. "Travis mentioned you were in St. Thomas."

"Yes, and I didn't even have to swim home."

She chuckled at my comment and then asked about the gallery visit.

"It went really well. They're giving my mother a show next summer. So we're returning to St. Croix in August. Isn't that great?"

Sofiya's face brightened. "That's excellent news, Olivia!"

We joined Travis and my mother. Sofiya offered her congratulations, which my mother accepted graciously. I removed my camera from the TWA bag, fixed the 50mm lens in place, and snapped two pictures of my mother and Travis as well as two of Sofiya, though she protested.

"Now, if everyone agrees, we should go to dinner and celebrate Evelyn's announcement," Travis proposed.

All of us thought this was a brilliant idea, and an hour later, we set off to the Stone Balloon, my mother and Travis walking ahead. I asked Sofiya what she had done during the day.

"You mean without your fine company?" she teased. "Actually, not much. Some reading, a walk in town, and checking the employment ads in the paper."

"Anything of interest?"

"One or two advertisements. I don't know what I'll do if I can't find a job. At this rate, I might have to try another island."

"You can't leave St. Croix!"

Sofiya gave me a reassuring smile. "Everything will work out. Don't worry."

I hoped so. Being on the island without Sofiya was a depressing prospect, which led to a more imminent concern: my return to America and the loss of this special friend. I shoved this thought out of my mind.

As we approached the turn from Strand Street, I noticed a blond head in the distance. At first, the boy was walking toward us, but then he turned abruptly and hurried away. Why had he changed directions? Had he seen me? I slowed to look at the disappearing figure and fought an overpowering urge to dash after him, throw my arms around his shoulders, and confirm that he was flesh and blood. And not my brother or an apparition.

Sofiya stopped walking and seemed to sense my tension, perhaps even my wish to bolt, because she placed her hand on my elbow, as if to prevent me from running. "What's wrong, Olivia? You look like you've seen a ghost."

He was gone. Despite the warm night, I shivered. "Sort of like a ghost." I sighed, wanting to share what was upsetting me, to confide in someone, especially her, but this was not the time to do it. "It's a long story."

"We seem to have a lot of those, don't we? Long stories."

I glanced at Sofiya, who was regarding me with concern. "Yes. Enough to fill a book. I'll tell you later."

Travis led the way into the restaurant, and we were escorted to a courtyard table, which, yet again, required leveling. Sofiya sat across from me. As the candlelight illuminated her face, I reflected that she was a very handsome woman, one who possessed an air of nobility, perhaps because she held her head erect, yet without rigidity or effort. I listened carefully when she spoke, noticing the sibilant sounds that colored her otherwise perfect English. I found the modulation of her voice hypnotic.

When Mother started talking about the gallery, my focus returned to the boy on the street and the lines from *Lord of the Flies*—those uttered by Simon to the effect that the "beast" was in all of us. I wasn't sure about the beast's existence, but I wondered if Simon—or his spirit—was somehow within me, impatient with his imprisonment and trying to break free into renewed life, perhaps wishing to punish me.

Unconsciously, I inhaled a sharp breath. Sofiya gave me an inquiring look but didn't interrupt my mother. I shook my head a fraction and mustered a smile.

We ordered drinks, salads, and steaks. In what seemed like seconds, a beer and three daiquiris were placed before us, and everyone became engaged, speaking to each other and asking questions. Perhaps because of Travis's presence, my mother behaved in an amiable fashion with Sofiya. However, when Mother gazed at him, her expression shaded into flirtatiousness, a subtle, yet unmistakably sensual look. Travis wasn't missing her signals. While he attended to Sofiya and me, his green eyes glittered whenever he beheld my mother.

I decided to relax my moralistic attitude. Mother had been depleted by the events of the last eight years, turning fifty and dealing with a difficult marriage. Although the idea of her having sex with Travis made me squeamish, I'd just have to deal with the situation.

While I was mulling this over, the salads arrived. Mother took up her fork and began eating, as we all did. A few minutes later, she faced Sofiya and, with no prelude, asked about her experiences during the war.

"Evelyn, I don't think you should—" Travis began.

"It's okay, Travis," Sofiya replied, though she seemed unsettled by my mother's directness. After an awkward pause, she said, "Well, as you may know, Evelyn, I was living in Czechoslovakia when the *Wehrmacht* occupied it. They used the excuse that the Germans in the Sudetenland were in peril, which they weren't."

Mother nodded curtly.

"We began a partial mobilization to fight them, but there was little support from our government or from England and France. In September 1938, the Munich Agreement was signed without the presence of our leaders. The Sudetenland was annexed and the country fell shortly after."

Mother pierced a pitted olive in her salad. I thought she was finished with her questions, but then she said, "I remember something about that, of course. Then what happened?"

Sofiya took a sip of her rum daiquiri and reluctantly continued. "By 1942, the Nazis killed or imprisoned many of the men who resisted them."

As if dissatisfied with Sofiya's speedy condensation, Mother cut a piece of tomato and waved it in a circle to encourage a fuller recounting. "And what about you and your family?"

Sofiya stared at the red and green salad in front of her but didn't eat anything. How could I sidetrack Mother's intrusive questions, which were taking on the unpleasant quality of an interrogation?

"Er, Mother—"

"Don't interrupt, Olivia," my mother snapped.

Sofiya looked at me, which I interpreted as acknowledgment for my support. "My family's home was in the country, near a village, Ležáky. Perhaps you know of it?" Sofiya's tone changed, as if her question contained a test, one she knew my mother wouldn't pass.

No one had heard about it. Travis and I exchanged worried looks, but then he busied himself with his beer.

Mother stared at Sofiya. "And?"

"The town is southeast of Prague," Sofiya explained. "It became famous when Himmler's deputy, Reinhard Heydrich, was assassinated. Hitler thought the people of Lidice and Ležáky were to blame—they weren't. Both villages were destroyed. Most of the people were murdered."

She stopped when the waitress arrived with our dinners. Sofiya pushed her mostly untouched salad to the side, and once the woman left, said, "But this isn't a cheerful subject, Evelyn. On your special evening we should have fun, don't you think?"

Before Mother could raise the subject of the war again, Travis lifted his glass, toasted my mother, and swiftly changed the topic to a lunch he and Sofiya had discussed, a picnic on the beach. While he talked, Sofiya was silent, staring into the courtyard, perhaps recalling the horrors evoked by my mother's insensitive questions, and Mother frowned slightly, as if frustrated in her pursuit of Sofiya's history. I was perplexed as to why she was acting so aggressively about an issue that probably didn't interest her. To assert the pecking order? If Sofiya reacted with pain or sadness, my mother, always cool and in control, was the winner—in her own opinion, at least. I'd seen this mile of road before when Mother felt threatened and regained leverage by making me cry or become upset. Now, the threat was Sofiya, a woman with presence and strength, a woman Mother wanted to demote, especially in front of Travis and myself.

—

After we finished dinner, Mother and Travis switched to scotch. Sofiya and I drank water.

"I think I shall have a brownie," Sofiya announced.

"Me, too," I agreed.

My mother patted her flat stomach. "Not me. I can't afford to gain one more pound on this trip."

I knew this comment was directed toward Sofiya, who didn't possess a svelte figure, and in case anyone might miss the criticism, Mother tossed a glance in her direction.

Then, she turned her attention to me. "And, Olivia, you should watch what you eat as well, though you are a growing girl."

In other words, I was already overweight, and if I kept eating desserts, I would look like Sofiya.

"Don't worry, Mother. I exercise all the time, unlike you, so I don't have to be that concerned with my diet. Besides, those daiquiris were a little fattening, weren't they?"

This checkmated my mother. Sofiya barely suppressed a giggle.

Sofiya and I ate our desserts slowly and with great satisfaction. A second round of scotch was imbibed by the twosome before Travis signaled for the waiter. Everyone divvied up the bill and we left, Travis and my mother in front. She was weaving slightly.

At the Pink Fancy, Mother announced her intentions. "I hope you won't think us rude, Sofiya, but Travis and I have made plans for the rest of the evening. Olivia, can you entertain yourself? Or maybe Sofiya is free?"

Clearly, consultation with me hadn't crossed her mind.

Sofiya and I traded looks. I was primed to comment on my mother's offensiveness, but Sofiya spoke first.

"I'd be happy to spend time with Olivia. If she would like some company."

"Thank you, Sofiya," I said. "Oh, and Mother? I'll be fine. Don't worry about me." I couldn't contain my sarcasm.

I was treated to a wan smile, and Travis and my mother departed.

"God, she can be horrible!" Turning to Sofiya, I apologized, "I'm so sorry for her behavior tonight. I don't know why she mentioned the war. Once she's rolling, you can't stop her. It's like throwing a feather at a bulldozer. And I'm sorry she put you on the spot...having to be with me when you're probably tired."

"It's all right. Besides, I enjoy being with you."

I sighed, still upset. "Well, the least I can do is bring something to drink. I'll be over in a minute."

Sofiya nodded and entered her apartment while I crossed the gallery and unlocked our door. Light rum or dark? I opted for the dark.

—

I felt a happy flush of anticipation as I climbed Sofiya's steps. When she opened the door, I was already smiling. "I haven't had this before, but Mother likes it." I handed her the bottle of rum.

"Thank you, Olivia."

Sofiya had lit white candles on the kitchen table and on the low table between the two beds. The room looked festive.

I turned toward her. "I love candles!"

"No surprise. You are a romantic, after all. Anyone who loves the water as you do also loves the flame." She chuckled. "Doesn't that sound profound?"

I laughed. "Yes, it does, but I have no idea what it means."

"Neither do I." She pointed to the armchairs and, after placing ice cubes in our glasses, poured several ounces of rum on top. Sofiya set the bottle on the adjacent table and joined me.

I clinked my glass against hers. "I'm so relieved my mother isn't here. She makes me crazy."

"I can see that. This is a trying time for both of you."

"It has been for a very long while. Ever since I can remember." I took a sip of the rum, enjoying its smoothness. "Things are worse lately, though. Maybe because my mother is beginning menopause and I'm a teenager." I smiled. "Nothing more difficult than a teenage girl, I guess."

"I don't think you're at all typical."

"You may be right, but being different doesn't make it easier."

"No, it probably doesn't," she agreed. "And by the way, don't drink this rum too fast. It's potent."

"Okay." We sat in companionable silence for a few minutes. "I don't know why Mother interrogated you tonight."

Sofiya swirled the liquor in her glass, considering. "It's fine. She wanted to have a better idea of who I am. She couldn't know that her questions would—"

"Cause you pain?" I snorted. "I'm not sure her curiosity was innocent." Sofiya didn't comment, so after a pause, I added, "I would like to hear more of your story, if you're willing to tell me. You don't have to, Sofiya. I'm not my mother."

She smiled. "No, you're not, thank goodness."

We laughed but her expression changed, growing more solemn. "All right, Olivia, but mine isn't a happy tale, as you realize from what I've already said about my parents and my brother. I hesitate to relate the rest for many reasons, but chiefly because no one your age needs to hear about the atrocities of wartime life. I probably shouldn't have told you all the things I did already."

"Sofiya, I want to know about what happened. I can't imagine how it felt to lose a brother, a father, your home... and to be left wondering what became of your mother." I took a breath and, in a quieter tone, said, "What you experienced matters to me."

She nodded in acknowledgment of my concern, but then the intensity in her blue eyes dimmed, as if the energy needed to continue had drained away. However, after drinking some rum, she began speaking, her voice composed but without its usual inflection.

"After I lost my family, I escaped into the forest, hiding with some of my countrymen who were fighting the Nazis. I cared very little about my life. Risk meant nothing, and revenge was in my heart. I continued to deliver communications and to take photographs, both hazardous. The only reason to exist was for Dano, who was also involved in the Resistance. We met before my brother was killed, but we didn't fall in love until months later. After the Germans had gone, we planned to marry." Sofiya ran a finger around the rim of her glass. "As I told you, he was a handsome young man, with golden brown eyes that sparkled like amber—rather similar to yours, in fact." She smiled sadly. "Dano was kind and sweet. Brave, as young men often are during times of war. He took even more chances than I did, which really frightened me."

"Did you live with him? After your house was burned?"

"Not at first. A girlfriend took me in until she left with her family. By this time, Dano and I were serious about each other, and his parents invited me to stay with them. It was difficult to share such close quarters because we had no privacy—you can imagine two young people in love, trying to find moments alone. We were always sneaking around his tiny house or meeting in the nearby woods. His parents didn't believe we should be together unchaperoned. They watched us all the time."

"I bet you didn't like that. I wouldn't."

"It was frustrating, but his parents were very moral, church-going folks."

"Are you?" I asked. "Church-going?"

She shook her head forcefully. "Absolutely not. After what I've seen and experienced, no one could believe in God."

I nodded in agreement.

"In early 1942, Dano's group heard about a special operation to kill Obergruppenführer Reinhard Heydrich. I shared part of that story at the restaurant."

"Yes, I remember."

"Well, Heydrich was a police general. His nickname was the 'Butcher of Prague,' and we all hated him. Heydrich was also a favorite of Hitler's and was one of the henchmen assigned to oversee the 'Final Solution.' Do you know about that?"

"A little but not much. I've heard about the concentration camps and the extermination of Jews. Auschwitz, Dachau, and Bergen-Belsen."

"There were many camps besides those. About seventy in several countries. So many Jews died." She paused, then added, "And so did thousands and thousands of others."

The direction of the conversation was making me increasingly anxious, but I also wished to understand Sofiya's life. "Go on," I whispered.

"Anyway, Dano and several of his friends signed on to this secret operation to assassinate Heydrich, though Dano, who was supposed to help with the coordination efforts, actually took no part and was nowhere near where it happened. On May 27, 1942, two men attacked Heydrich's open convertible. The killing was ultimately successful—Heydrich died from his wounds—and everyone cheered the news."

"But then you said Hitler destroyed your town."

"Yes, he did. He ordered a massive retaliation, arresting thirteen thousand people and executing five thousand, maybe more, though some of the women and children were shipped to a concentration camp in northern Germany. Both villages were burned."

Here she stopped and rested her head on her hand.

I drank more rum, waiting. Finally, I asked, "What happened with Dano?"

Sofiya closed her eyes, then slowly opened them again. "He was on a list the Nazis discovered. They caught him on the outskirts of town, with his father and mother. They were all shot."

I stared at her in alarm. "Were you there? Did you see this?"

"Thankfully, I didn't. But I witnessed the murder of many people. The Germans were indiscriminate. Killing chickens, dogs, cows, pigs, and people. Blood everywhere. Fires destroyed houses, farms, and fields."

"I can't imagine what it was like." As I said this, one enormous question loomed. Had Sofiya been captured? My hand gripped the arm of the chair; the other tightened around my glass.

"You don't want to imagine it. I wish I couldn't," she said emphatically. After she spoke, the nearest candle flickered. Sofiya pointed to the candle. "You see, Olivia? The ghosts of my family and other tortured souls have followed me to this small island. I am haunted and will be forever."

"But you weren't to blame for their deaths."

She scanned the room several times before settling on me again. Instantly, her expression changed. Her eyes flashed, and the lines on her forehead creased. "No, I was not to blame. Not for their deaths," she said, her voice taut. "But I'm alive and they aren't. I sit here, drawing breath, eating steak at the Stone Balloon, enjoying your fine company. And they lie in the ground, most in unmarked graves, sharing the earth with their poor animals. For this, I blame myself. For this, I am ashamed."

The room suddenly went ice cold. I couldn't suppress a shiver of dread. Watching the misery transform her face, I knew the rest of Sofiya's story would be equally horrendous. Stunned, I made no reply, though for an instant, I thought of Simon, who prowled through my dreams, thoughts, and imagination. I had experienced a single loss; she had experienced so many.

Sofiya blew out a sharp breath, drank the last of her rum, and poured a few ounces in her glass. When she asked if I wanted any, I declined.

She fell back against her chair. "I'm sorry, Olivia. I should probably end there."

I was unsure whether to encourage Sofiya to continue or to agree that she had told me enough. Sofiya was definitely upset by the violent memories. She stared at me and then her attention slid away, as if she was straining to remain present, to sustain a connection. I waited. At last, I said, "I'd like to hear more, but I'll understand if you don't want to go on."

Sofiya gazed at the candles on the table. I scarcely breathed, anxious about interrupting this silent interlude a second time. The candles guttered again, and it seemed as if the room itself was moving slightly. The scene reminded me of being in the eye of a hurricane, an experience I'd had a few years before in New Jersey. Temporarily calm, yet with a storm raging and swirling all around, soon to return.

In a measured tone, she said, "I will tell you some of the rest, but perhaps not everything. Is that acceptable?"

"Yes, of course."

Sofiya stroked her cheek, as if soothing herself before re-entering the turbulence in her mind. "Let's see. Dano and his family are gone," she whispered. "Afterward, I ran into the forest, praying the Nazis hadn't seen me and that they didn't know I was a member of Dano's household and active in the Resistance. I heard hundreds of gunshots in the village. Some close, some far, some single shots, some from machine guns. I knew the Nazis were shooting anyone who was trying to escape the village, not just the adult men and older boys. I kept running until I could no longer hear gunfire and then hid in a cluster of bushes by a stream. The water was drinkable, but I had no food except for some berries. Luckily it was summer, so the weather was warm and I didn't need shelter."

She swallowed some rum, then continued. "I lay on the ground and cried and cried. I was sure I'd be caught and killed. I had no idea where to go or who could help me except some of the partisans, if I could find them, if they were alive. I stayed there for several days, but finally I was too hungry. After darkness fell, I followed the stream, knowing it led to an abandoned warehouse. My friends in the Resistance would conceal messages in the stone wall that ran behind the building, where I had also been instructed to leave rolls of film. Very late, about midnight, I arrived. The place looked deserted, so I hurried to the wall, where I found a pencil and a piece of paper in a can. I wrote a note saying I was alive and asking where I should go. Just as I finished, two beams of light struck me. I hid the tin, hoping the Germans hadn't seen it, but they had. Soldiers poured out of the warehouse, and I was arrested."

"You must have been terrified!"

"I was."

"Did they hurt you?"

Sofiya nodded. "I tried fighting them at first, but one hit me with his gun and knocked me to the ground. When I came to, my head was bleeding, and I was in the back of a truck. At a large farm outside the town, they threw me off the tailgate and dragged me to a wire pen, one used to hold animals. Several dozen women were already imprisoned there with some children and babies. Everyone was afraid, some were wailing, and some huddled in the dirt with their arms around their heads, as if this protected them. Just before sunrise, a soldier threw several loaves of stale bread at us, and another brought four buckets of water. Otherwise, the Germans did nothing except watch us and smoke cigarettes, their rifles slung on their shoulders. Escape was impossible."

I tried to imagine the terror and loneliness she felt, yet Simon's devastating loss didn't compare with Sofiya's. "Did you know any of the women? Were they friends or neighbors? Someone you could talk to?"

"Two women came from farms near Dano's. I spoke with them, but they were so frightened they didn't say much. No one knew what would happen, but everyone expected the worst. The rumors that were passed around were horrifying." Sofiya closed her eyes for a few seconds, remembering. When she opened them, she seemed adrift within the story. "After a while, we were told to form a line. We thought the Nazis planned to shoot us, but instead we were forced to board trucks. They said we were being moved to another area, a nicer one, with better facilities." Sofiya laughed harshly. "We rode for a day, then walked for days more until we reached a train station, where we were forced to sit on the concrete platform along with others who had been rounded up."

"Did they give you something to eat?" I asked.

"Not much. Only a little bread. At least there was a bathroom in the station, with running water, but there were so many people that there was a long line to get in. And at night, the sentries kept shining flashlights at us."

I pictured the bursts of light illuminating the terrified faces. "Why did they do that?"

"Because it amused them." Sofiya shrugged. "They had to stay awake so they figured we would, too."

The cruelty and inhumanity were incomprehensible. Wrestling with how to respond, I remained silent until at last I asked how long Sofiya had been at the station.

She studied me, perhaps worried about continuing. "Probably about two weeks. Sometimes it rained, and we were soaked. On other days the sun was hot, and without any shade, we roasted. Two babies were killed because they were crying, and one old woman was beaten to death because she begged a soldier for food. After that, everyone was quiet."

"Oh my god!" I exclaimed. "How many people were there?"

"Hundreds. More kept coming each day as people were brought in from the nearby farms and the forest." Sofiya sighed. "Finally, late one night, a train arrived with twenty boxcars designed to carry livestock. Half of these were crammed full of women and children. The moaning and sobbing, the smell coming from those train cars—so awful!"

I leaned forward, scared to hear her answer. "Did they put you on the train?"

She pressed her lips together and nodded. "Yes. We were divided into groups, and then each group was driven at gunpoint into an empty car. We were crowded in so tightly it was impossible for everyone to lie down at the same time.

There were two slops buckets in the center of the car, and the soldiers tossed some vegetables at us, causing a frenzy when everyone tried to grab the food. I was lucky to find a spot by the door, against the wall, so I was a little more comfortable than those in the center and at the back. While we waited at the station, the door partly open, I saw three women outside who had tried to run earlier. The Nazis shoved the women against a wall and shot them. The soldiers left their bodies there, on the ground." Sofiya lowered her head. "And then they closed the train door."

Suddenly, she slapped her palms together, and I jumped. "The sound was so loud, so final. The children began scream-ing, the women weeping. We could hardly see each other be-cause the car was almost dark, except for the light between the slats—zebra stripes of white on all those frightened faces, stripes that flickered as the train began to move."

I placed my fingers over my eyes, but the hideous images didn't fade. I dropped my hands and let them slide into my lap. After staring at her for a moment, I reached for the bottle of rum and added to my empty glass and Sofiya's. "How long were you on the train?"

"I don't know. We stopped whenever a troop carrier or a high-ranking officer's train required priority. Then, they shunted us off to a side track, but we weren't allowed out-side. Soon, the car became a nightmare of sickness and unbe-lievable squalor."

"Where did they take you?"

"Only two transit camps existed in Czechoslovakia, but they were not our destination. Instead, we were being trans-ported to Germany, to a camp designed to hold female pris-oners and children."

"What was it called?"

Sofiya took a large drink of rum and whispered, "Ravensbrück."

She stood and walked to one of the windows overlook-ing the pool. The exterior spotlights lit the side of her face, changing the cast of her tanned skin to white.

I feared what Sofiya would say next, and yet I knew. Sorrow—a deep, dragging, almost unbearable grief—overwhelmed me. "I haven't heard of Ravensbrück before," I whispered.

Sofiya turned and looked past me, as if I wasn't present. "It was a camp opened in 1939 by Heinrich Himmler and operated until the liberation in 1945. Over a hundred thousand people were imprisoned. Many were Polish women, but there were a large number of Jews in addition to Russians, French, Czechs, and a mix of other nationalities. Also gypsies, Jehovah's Witnesses, lesbians, prostitutes—anyone the Nazis deemed undesirable. Most died in this camp. From starvation, disease, and horrific working conditions. Some simply gave up. Over two thousand were gassed. Terrible medical experiments were performed on others. But, Olivia, I really can't describe this nightmarish place, only give cold historical facts."

"Facts I didn't know." My voice thickened with feeling. I paused, trying to compose myself. "When you arrived...what happened? Where did you go?"

Sofiya rubbed her neck. "We were herded into the camp's barracks. Three-tiered cubicles fit for animals. Any valuables were taken from us, though I had nothing except my identification papers and the clothes I'd been wearing for weeks. Everyone looked dazed, like they were half blind. Some huddled in the corners, maybe thinking they'd be safer farther away from the door. We were given some disgusting soup—it was mostly water—but at least it was hot. However, the smell in the room was so awful that a few threw up whatever they ate."

Sofiya looked at the ceiling, gently shaking her head from side to side. Then, she brought her eyes to mine. Unblinking, as if in a trance, she said, "At first, I was assigned to build V-2 rockets. We were required to stand in the assembly areas for twelve hours a day, often longer. Even though I was young, it soon became unbearably painful. My back ached from leaning over. I couldn't straighten until I lay down later, at night. One afternoon, I was so weak that I must have passed out. All I recall is being kicked awake by two of the female guards—they were almost more vicious than the men. One of the women who was next to me on the line helped me to my feet. We tried to be kind to each other, but we were so hungry and tired that we hardly talked after we returned to the barracks—and, of course, no conversation was allowed while we worked. That's the way it went. Every day was the same. Putting the same parts in the same places, over and over. I thought I would lose my mind."

I wanted Sofiya to come closer so I could see the expression on her face. Her story seemed like a recitation, yet here and there, flickers of emotion broke through. Suddenly, from outside, I heard laughter and people splashing in the pool. I wanted to scream at them to be quiet, but Sofiya merely glanced through the window, made no comment, and then faced me again.

I had been holding my breath and now let it out slowly. "How did you survive?"

She considered before replying. "I had it better than some—those who did hard labor outside. Others had easier jobs. Darning socks—piles of them. They were allowed to sit." Sofiya sighed. "And then, after a few months, something unexpected happened. One of the administrators learned that I spoke English, some French and German, and a little Italian and Russian. He made me his assistant."

"That must have been a relief."

"A relief?" Sofiya frowned and I realized how silly my remark had been. "I guess you could say that. At least I was fed better—not well, mind you—and was moved to cleaner quarters. They also gave me two sets of clothes, probably from someone who had died. A pair of blue trousers, a brown skirt, a black shirt and a white one, underwear, and socks—mine had worn through at the heels." She smiled. "Now, I own more socks than I could wear in a lifetime."

I almost laughed due to nervousness but stopped myself. I didn't want to be insensitive like my mother had been at dinner, nor did I wish to pry like she had. Even so, I was curious to learn everything about Sofiya's life.

"What kind of work did you do? Was it in an office?"

Sofiya leaned against the wall. "Sort of. I had a desk, though sometimes I was sent to the entrance. To register arrivals—their names, ages, nationalities, races, religions, and the reason for their imprisonment. Other than that, I helped record deaths. And births—there were more of those than you'd think. Some women arrived pregnant, but others were used by the Nazis."

Understanding the implication, I nodded. "Why did the Nazis bother to keep count?"

"For some reason, they loved statistics."

"You'd think they wouldn't want anyone to know what they were doing." I considered this for a moment. "Maybe they were proud of what they did."

"Probably." Sofiya finished her rum and returned to her chair. "I'm not sure you should hear more, Olivia. Although I can't get all this out of my mind, it's selfish to burden you with these nightmares." She raised her fingers to her lips and covered her mouth.

I placed my glass, which I had been clutching, on the table to my right. "I don't think you're being selfish. It may not help to talk about what happened. Only you know that, but I care about you and will keep imagining what you went through. Is it better to tell me the truth or leave me wondering?"

She gave me a searching look, lowered her hand, and sighed. "Okay," she said. "Well, I worked long hours. Toting up figures, keeping ledgers. I wasn't privy to all of the camp's information, but what I saw was shocking. Many nights I couldn't sleep, thinking of the women and children who had died that day. And always, I was hungry. Sometimes, when the administrator left the room, I was able to steal food from his trash can. A roll, a bite of apple. The best was a piece of sausage. I can't tell you how good that tasted!" Her eyes lit up, remembering. "You won't believe it now, but when I was captured, I was a slender girl, and over the months in the camp, I lost a lot more weight. Hard to picture that now, isn't it?" Her laughter was short and bitter, followed by a period of silence.

Sofiya's outbreaks of dark humor contrasted with her somber demeanor, leaving me unsure how to respond and anxious about saying the wrong thing. Shifting in my chair, I leaned forward to encourage her.

"This work went on for some time," she explained. "Then, one day, the camp commander, Hauptsturmführer Suhren, appeared with an officer, who was visiting to gain expertise in running prisons. This man, an Obersturmführer, was ugly and coarse. Thick protruding lips and forehead and pocked skin. I later learned that his cousin held a senior rank in the Gestapo and had arranged for him to receive officer training. Anyway, he entered the room where I was sitting at my desk—I was the youngest woman there, which is probably why he noticed me. At first, the man began talking, then he touched my face." She paused, shuddering at the recollection. "You must understand, Olivia, that we kept our eyes off the Germans for fear one of them would become interested. Being chosen might sometimes improve one's situation temporarily, but when the man tired of the woman, she was tossed back into the squalid barracks. The other women would treat her with contempt, and the female guards would often be physically abusive."

I had an idea where the story was leading. I reached for the bottle of rum and poured a small amount in my glass. Sofiya watched as I took a sip, her mouth set in a firm line. When I asked her to continue, she quietly resumed.

"The Obersturmführer ordered me to step outside. I didn't want to go with him, but I feared what he might do if he became annoyed. So, I followed the man into the square, keeping my head down. There, he stopped and began questioning me about my name and about my family. When I mentioned that my grandmother was English—I lied and told him she was an aristocrat, a lady—he was impressed, as many Germans are with titles and noble ancestry. I made up details—that her family had a large estate in Kent and our lineage could be traced to the thirteenth century. I don't know why I did this except, in an odd way, it felt good to talk about her and to imagine living in a beautiful, safe country. After hearing my story, he seemed satisfied that I wasn't a mere Czech peasant and complimented me on my German, which, after the time in the camp, I now spoke well. Then, he looked at me closely. 'You have very beautiful eyes, Fräulein,' he said. 'I think you should come with me. Maybe we'll have some schnitzel, a little champagne—and get to know each other better. Would you like that?'"

"I hope you didn't have dinner with him."

"I had no choice. He could signal to a sentry, and I would be immediately shot. What could I do? I was hungry, scared, alone."

I shook my head. "He sounds horrible. Why would he be interested in a prisoner? Couldn't an officer pick any German woman he wanted?"

"In many cases, yes, but this man was very unattractive. To be honest, I don't know why he chose me."

"So you went with him?" I heard the disappointment in my voice and instantly regretted it. Sofiya's eyes flickered, almost imperceptibly.

"Yes," she said softly. "He ordered a female guard to take me to the showers and give me a new dress. 'Something red or pink,' he told her. 'And some shoes, with heels.' When I was dressed, I felt like a prostitute. I'd never worn clothes like that in my life. After being made presentable, I was brought to the officer's table, where I was fed huge amounts of pork schnitzel, bratwurst, spätzle—all kinds of rich food that I craved. We drank champagne."

"What did you talk about? I mean, that must have been so weird. Having a conversation with a Nazi. Someone who could snap his fingers and kill you. Someone who might have murdered your family."

"I know this sounds strange, very strange, but for a little while I almost felt alive, human. You must understand that I was starving. Food was all we thought about most of the time. And no one had shown me the slightest kindness except for a few of the other prisoners. This man did, even if he didn't understand how to speak with a woman. His conversation was awkward; sometimes he was shy, mostly he bragged about himself. 'My family is very wealthy,' he said. 'We have a large apartment in Berlin, which I will inherit one day.' It was like he was trying to impress me. 'Very soon I'll be in charge of my own camp.' When he told me this, it was as if he'd forgotten my identity, forgotten I was a woman who would very likely die in a camp like the one he was so eager to run. But then he revealed that his childhood had been lonely and unhappy. His father was strict and quick to punish him. I could see his pain, his suffering, which made him less repulsive."

"Did he say anything about his duties? How he felt about Hitler?"

"No, except to mention his ambitions."

"Did you ask?"

"No." Sofiya let out a long breath. "You have to understand, Olivia, that night was bizarre. Just as he was two men—one insecure and unhappy, a lost, hurt boy, and the other an arrogant and depraved Nazi—I was two people also. It was like a fairy story, like for a few hours I was Cinderella at a ball and not a starving prisoner in a camp. I was even treated with courtesy because the other officers didn't recognize me due to my clothes and clean hair. I had more food than I could eat. Champagne was bubbling in my glass. But as desperate as I was to believe this dream would last, I knew it would evaporate within hours, plunging me back into the nightmare."

What would I have done in her position? Refused to dine with my enemy or used him to help myself survive, even for a short time? "Was he nice to you? Did he ask you questions and listen?"

"He was pleasant in a way but didn't ask questions. He didn't want to be reminded of who I was. Neither did I," she replied. "After dinner, someone put on a record, and we began dancing—a waltz, of all things. Suddenly, I had to rush out of the room because I felt sick. Too much heavy food after such a poor diet. When I returned, I hoped my illness would deter the man. It didn't." As she said this, Sofiya looked away. A few seconds later, I saw that her eyes had filled with tears.

"What was his name?" I asked gently.

She wiped the dampness from her cheeks, turned, and stared at me. At first, she shook her head, as if refusing to answer, but then she stopped and held herself very still. The refrigerator whirred.

"Viktor Florián."

My head jerked upright. "What?" I thought I'd misheard, but one look at Sofiya's face told me I hadn't. "Your husband?"

She nodded.

I was speechless. It was impossible to believe that the assured, attractive woman, who laughed easily and smiled often, had been forced to marry her enemy, a Nazi.

"You may find, Olivia, that knowing these things about my past may interfere with your good opinion of me."

"Why would it?" I asked, puzzled. "You didn't have a

choice, did you?"

Sofiya rose, took a tissue from the box by the bedside table, blotted her eyes, and sat in her chair. "I've witnessed this many times. A person I like, after telling them my story, looks at me differently, as if I've been transformed into a repellent creature or a Nazi sympathizer. People retreat from horror and from those who have experienced it," she said, almost whispering. "So, you see, Olivia, because of all of this, I'm not only displaced from my country and my family, I'm also displaced from the woman I was before I met Viktor Florián."

"I won't feel differently about you," I said firmly.

"It happens. It's a common phenomenon that a good person associated with an evil one takes on the coloring of the bad person. Or a good person, who innocently encounters some terrible occurrence, becomes absorbed into that darkness, is tainted forever by it, and can never be the person she once was."

"I don't believe that." I rose to my feet and kneeled beside Sofiya. "I can't tell you how sorry I am."

More tears rolled down her face. She dabbed at them quickly and forced a weak smile. "There is nothing to be said, really. What can anyone say? It has been many years since Ravensbrück, yet the memories of that place are still absolutely fresh."

I wanted to embrace her but was unsure I should. "What happened after that night?"

Sofiya shook her head. "Olivia, I am ashamed to tell you."

"Please, it's okay."

"Well, I became pregnant. When Viktor found out, he insisted that we keep the baby. He said this could be the only chance for him to have a child. I assumed this was because he might not survive the war, but he also held a low opinion of his appeal to women. The man was deeply conflicted—egotistical about his career abilities, his superior German heritage, and yet unsure of his social skills. I think he was very attracted to me and, in his way, loved me. Viktor decided we should marry, though I never loved him, which he knew. Marrying him was wrong. Immoral and cowardly, but without Viktor's protection, I would have died at the camp. And, even if he was a demon when wearing his uniform, there was a less brutal, personal side that made life with him almost tolerable."

"You didn't have a choice," I repeated.

Sofiya reached out, took my hand, and squeezed it. I wanted her to agree with my statement, but she didn't agree or disagree. A few seconds later, she removed her fingers from mine, though the contact was reassuring for both of us, or so it seemed.

I asked about the baby.

"Fortunately, I miscarried. I hadn't wanted a child and absolutely didn't want his. Viktor had moved us to Poland by this time, but I was dreadfully underweight and extremely depressed. It wasn't surprising that I couldn't carry the baby to term. I was barely alive myself. After the miscarriage, I swore never to have children and haven't. It's just as well."

"I think you would have made an excellent mother, if you had wanted children. You're compassionate, loving, kind—you have every quality a mother should have."

"Thank you, Olivia."

I felt awkward kneeling on the floor and returned to my chair. "How did he take you out of the camp and bring you to Poland?"

"Viktor paid someone to fake identification papers, which said that I was born German in the Sudetenland. He found me some clothes, and we left Ravensbrück one night late. I was sure I would be discovered, but since he was an Obersturmführer, none of the sentries questioned him."

"So you went with him?"

Sofiya placed her fingers over her eyes and didn't answer. There was an extended silence until she lowered her hand. "I didn't know what else to do," she said. "Viktor was already very powerful and had been promoted. To be second in command of a Polish camp, which turned out to be as bad as Ravensbrück. Day by day, I had to watch those poor people being brought in. By truck, by train, on foot. It was excruciating not being able to help. I begged Viktor to be more lenient with the prisoners, but he ignored me. Then, after the miscarriage, he realized how the camp was affecting my spirits and decided I should live with his family in Berlin. He never told them about my history in a camp, but Viktor bragged about my grandmother in England, which was odd since the Germans were at war with Britain."

I thought her story was finished and straightened in my chair, but Sofiya leaned toward me, anger blazing in her eyes.

"I hated his parents. They were cold, unpleasant people." She blew out a puff of disgust. "They refused to let me out of their apartment. Said my husband would be upset if I was hurt on the street. The truth was that Viktor feared I would run away, though where would I go without money or family? I was in another prison, though a somewhat better one." She sighed. "Every night, I had nightmares about being in Ravensbrück, and later, when the bombs began falling on Berlin, I thought I would go mad."

I searched for what to say, yet every question seemed shallow. At last, I asked if Viktor visited her in Berlin.

"Not often, thank goodness. His duties kept him occupied except for occasional days off," Sofiya said. "Viktor was a perfect fit for the Nazis. As with so many of them before the war, he had resented the success of others, especially Jews, so when Hitler spewed hatred, Viktor bought into the mania. When we first arrived at the camp, he lied about his responsibilities, saying he was only a high-level accountant. Much later, in Berlin, out of sick pride, he admitted to his role in the extermination of huge numbers of innocent people. I was horrified, though I was already certain about what he'd been doing. Then, and ever since, I've questioned how a man could be such a monster and yet also have a caring side. I believe many women wondered the same thing about their fathers, husbands, and sons."

"It must have been so difficult to live with him, suspecting what he did and later being sure."

"It was. But remember, Viktor and I did not have a normal marriage. He had his needs, and I needed to stay in an emotionally distant place. Though we never spoke about this compromise, it existed from the beginning. And, as I said, we seldom saw each other."

"What was it like living in Berlin? I remember seeing photos of the city after the war."

Sofiya turned her glass slowly, swirling the rum. When she answered, her voice was once again flat. "Before the war, Berlin was a beautiful place, very avant-garde, though I never visited then. But because it was the key to Hitler's defeat, the city was a primary target and suffered hundreds of bombing raids. Berlin was turned into rubble, with a large part of the population killed or homeless. I was extremely fortunate. The Florián home was hit several times, but I was living in the underground basement. On one of the strikes, Viktor's parents died upstairs."

"Were you upset?"

"No. The Floriáns held the same prejudices as Viktor and were much like him. Although they didn't know my past, I was treated with resentment because I was another person to feed. And they suspected I wasn't German, which made me second class in their opinion. So, I didn't grieve for them, though I was scared about being alone in the city."

Sofiya had become very quiet, as if she were visiting a charred, dead place and saw no sign of life or humanity. She sat without moving for some time before taking up her story again.

"When Viktor heard about his parents, he returned to Berlin and was reassigned to protect the Reichstag from the Allied invasion. On April 30, 1945, the building was attacked by the Soviets. Viktor escaped and hid in his family's apartments with me, but the Americans found him and put him in jail."

I was astonished by this revelation. "How did you feel about his capture? You must have been conflicted—"

"Because he saved my life? I guess I was in a way, but he also destroyed my life. My family and my loved ones. He and the Nazis. What they did was the epitome of depravity."

"After he was caught, was he put on trial?"

A shadow fell over Sofiya's face. "Before Viktor was sentenced to death, he hung himself in prison. It was the right thing for him to do."

She swallowed the last of her rum and set down the glass on the table. The small room grew still, though Sofiya's words echoed in my ears.

"I am really sorry. That sounds so stupid and meaningless, but I don't know how to tell you—"

"I see how you feel, Olivia." Sofiya regarded me for a moment, then her expression softened, and she gave me a look that glowed with warmth. "That's what is important."

Another silence stretched between us. We finished our drinks, and Sofiya slowly rose to her feet.

"I hope you won't have bad dreams tonight." She smiled. "Thank you for listening and for being so caring. Now, my dear Olivia, it's quite late, and we have a lovely day planned for tomorrow. Our beach picnic."

We exchanged glances that shimmered with affection, both of us reluctant to dissolve the closeness. I stood and walked to the table. Sofiya handed me the pint of golden rum, now over half empty, and we continued to the door.

"Good night, Sofiya." I leaned over and gently kissed her cheek.

—

After descending the steps and the path, I stopped under the gallery's awning. The pool was so pretty and magical, glittering with sparkles created by the overhead spotlights, a surreal contrast to the place I had entered with Sofiya. Although the war in Europe seemed like ancient history to me, for Sofiya, it was still raging in her mind and clutching at her large, generous heart. All through her recounting, I had felt a crushing helplessness, yet at the same time, a powerful intimacy; now I felt adrift, severed by the space of a hundred feet and the wall behind which she stood, probably attending to mundane tasks like blowing out candles and washing glasses. There was no way to fully fathom what she had lived through, though I doubted she expected me—or anyone else—to understand.

I pulled the apartment key from my pocket, pondering how Sofiya's nightmarish past relegated mine to a place of lesser significance. In comparison, how could I be so self-involved with Simon and his loss as well as with my mother and our struggles?

And then I remembered Mother. Was she inside or with Travis? I crept into the dark room and switched on the light. The apartment was empty. I checked my watch: nearly midnight. After replacing the rum bottle in the cupboard, I changed into my pajamas and sat on the porch, listening to the wild dogs and cats yowl, bark, and snarl, and, in between, when battles weren't being fought on the street, to the palm trees swishing, a pleasant sound like waves falling on the beach. Exhausted, I decided to go to bed.

Sometime very late, my mother arrived, stumbling in the dark, but she settled quickly and was soon asleep. I was relieved she had returned, though during the hours she was gone, she and Travis had plenty of time to do whatever they had been doing.

—

Simon was being murdered by Nazi soldiers. The setting was a dark forest, everything colorless except for red blood spurting from my brother's bullet-riddled body. Surrounding him were hulking forms wearing helmets and holding huge black rifles.

I lurched awake, hot and frightened, and tossed off the sheets. I silently swore at myself for conjuring up the nightmare, though I had to admit it was a creative unification of Sofiya's story and my brother's, one of many variations on his death I'd fabricated during the last eight years. How Sofiya ever slept, after her war experiences, I couldn't imagine.

Day 7

In the morning, the sun streamed into the bedroom and banished the lingering remnants of Nazi Germany. It was after eight, but my mother was still asleep. I threw on a polo shirt and shorts, grabbed a slice of bread, my book, and the key. Outside, the pool area was quiet, but Travis's office door was ajar and the shutters were half folded. I waited, unsure what to say to him since I could no longer pretend that he and my mother were mere friends. Standing by the railing near our apartment, I ate the bread and wished I'd thought to pour some orange juice. Eventually, Travis opened the door, officially ready for business. When he saw me, he smiled.

"Good morning, Olivia. Hey, I have something to show you." Travis beckoned me to follow him.

We walked past the stone wall into the garden, which was teeming with yellow, red, and pink hibiscus. In the center, a medium-sized tree grew.

"This is a guinep tree." Travis picked a green, semi-shiny fruit that resembled a small lime. "If you peel off the skin, the meat inside is edible." He showed me the apricot-colored flesh and popped the fruit in his mouth. "Use your teeth to scrape the fruit, then throw the pit away." He handed me one.

The guinep was tart, with a thin layer of slippery meat, but it was fun to eat.

"Like most things in life, a lot of work for not much reward," he said, laughing. "Help yourself."

"Thanks, Travis. And by the way, it was thoughtful of you to give me the tee shirt. I wore it at Pelican Cove."

He smiled. "Bring it along today with your snorkeling gear. Maybe you'd like to try some spearfishing?"

"Really?"

He nodded. "Perhaps we can get a grouper for lunch. Or a hogfish—they're both quite tasty."

Travis returned to his office, and I ate two more guineps and wandered around the garden, investigating the various flowering plants and watching a brown gecko dart up a tree trunk. At the stone wall, I stopped to pick a beautiful magenta hibiscus. I skirted the pool, hurried up the path, and placed it on Sofiya's top step. A little embarrassed, I bid a hasty retreat, but as I neared the office, the phone rang.

Travis said my father's name, then popped his head out the door. "Oh, Olivia, there you are. It's your dad."

A call I'd been dreading. As I accepted the receiver, I noted Travis wore a noncommittal expression. I tried to sound enthusiastic. "Hi, Dad."

"Hello! I arrived home last night and wanted to check on you and your mother first thing this morning. How are things in paradise?"

"Fine." I peeked at Travis, who was seated at his desk, wearing his eyeglasses, and occupied with paperwork. He could hear every word I said. "I've done some snorkeling on a nearby reef, and we're planning a beach picnic today. Might have a chance to do some spearfishing."

"That's great, but be careful. You know the drill. Where there are smaller fish, there are bigger fish."

"I know."

"Who's taking you?"

"The owner of the Pink Fancy, Travis—you just spoke with him. He's been very nice. He loaned me a pair of flippers and has shown us some of the restaurants. The hotel is only a few blocks from the main part of Christiansted." I told him about the Stone Balloon and the Comanche, explaining how much he would like them, and about our visit to St. Thomas and Mother's art exhibit next year.

"Wonderful! I bet she's pleased. Another St. Croix sojourn, then?"

"Yes. Will you come next summer?" I checked to see if Travis reacted to this question, but he was facing away from me.

"Well, we'll see how things stand at that point, okay?"

Although this was a typical response, I sensed an odd undertone. Usually, Dad would laugh and say he needed to consult his schedule. He didn't laugh now. Plus this slight variation implied that other issues might prevent him from accompanying us. Probably I was just misreading his words because I was nervous. To change the subject, I inquired about his most recent flight and when he was leaving for Europe next. We chatted for a while until I remembered the camera.

"Dad, Mother bought me a new lens in St. Thomas. A really great one hundred thirty-five millimeter telephoto."

"Glad she did. I asked her to get one at a duty-free shop. Thought you'd have some fun with it now that you've mastered the fifty millimeter lens." Dad chuckled. "But we never master any lens, do we?"

It was disheartening to learn my father had suggested the purchase rather than it being my mother's idea. I had assumed buying the lens was her peace offering, an admission of wrongful behavior.

"And, like you always say, we only master one shot at a time," I said, repeating a favorite remark of his.

He chuckled. "I can't wait to see your photos. And, speaking of your mother, is she around?"

I explained she was still in bed.

"Okay, well, that's too bad. Will you ask Sleeping Beauty to give me a call when she awakens? I'll be here until noon."

After saying goodbye, I handed the phone to Travis and

exited the office, but then turned back. "You know this puts me in a very uncomfortable spot, don't you?"

Travis removed his eyeglasses and laid them on the desk. "I do. And I'm sorry, Olivia."

His simple apology was straightforward, as was Travis himself. Although I was unhappy about avoiding the truth with my father, I didn't want an argument with Travis. Besides, what could I say? Stop fooling around with my mother?

"What's happening between the two of you may be none of my business, but I don't like lying to Dad, either directly or indirectly. I know my parents aren't getting along well. Even so, like I said, I'm not comfortable. So, if you could at least not be too obvious while I'm around, that would be helpful."

"I understand. And, again, I'm sorry."

After thanking him, I walked under the awning, sat on a chaise, and stared at the pale blue water, half blinded by the play of sunlight on the pool's rippling surface. Suddenly, there was movement to my left. Sofiya's door opened and she appeared in her bathrobe, holding a small bag of trash. As she lowered it to the top step, she spotted the hibiscus and reached down to pick it up. Then, she saw me. With her eyes fastened on mine, Sofiya lifted the flower and pressed it against her heart. She smiled, lingered for a few seconds, and returned inside.

I was pleased that I could give her a small token of reassurance after last night. I remained on the chaise, sorting through parts of her story again as well as the situation with my parents.

About forty-five minutes later, Mother plodded out of our unit, perfectly, though casually attired. Befitting our picnic plans, she wore a straw hat and sunglasses, blue shorts, and a lavender scoop-neck blouse. Underneath her clothes was a purple bathing suit—one strap was visible. She mumbled good morning to me, though her interest lay elsewhere, namely with Travis. Once she spied him, she strolled to his office. The two exchanged greetings, Mother leaning in close, but after Travis said something to her, she backed a few inches away, and then walked over to where I was sitting.

"We're leaving in an hour or so. Travis and I are going to buy a few things, and we'll return for you and Mrs. Florián."

"Sofiya," I corrected.

"Yes, of course."

I nodded, rose to my feet, and followed her into the apartment, where she lifted her pocketbook over her shoulder.

"Anything in particular you'd like?" she asked.

"Nothing special," I replied. "And I assume Travis told you Dad called?"

"I heard."

"Aren't you going to phone him?"

"Later. When I have time."

She left to join Travis.

—

After locking the front door, I headed into the bedroom, stripped off my clothes, and examined my sunburn. My back was peeling slightly, as were my shoulders. The difference between unprotected skin and skin covered by my bathing suit was dark red versus pale white. I took a shower, applied some cream, and dressed in my black tank suit, shorts, white tee, and a long-sleeve blouse. I fastened my hair with a tortoiseshell barrette and placed my snorkeling and beach gear in the flight bag. From my camera, I removed the roll of Tri-X and hid the film in the closet, in a pocket of my yellow linen jacket, and then sat on the porch to read my book.

In my present mood, returning to the novel proved unwise because I soon came upon a disturbing passage where Simon is alone, in an almost hallucinatory state, and stares at a sow's head, which the boys had thrust on a stake after sadistically slaughtering the animal. The grinning head is covered with flies, hence the title. In Simon's delusional imagination, the pig begins speaking, saying that "the beast" couldn't be killed because the beast was within him. Simon has a seizure, starts to bleed through the nose, and loses consciousness. I was certain what would follow and equally certain that I was in no condition to read more.

I closed the paperback and wrote in my secret journal about what happened to Sofiya's village, to Dano, and about the train ride and Sofiya's first months in Ravensbrück. Afterward, I wedged the journal behind the dresser in the bedroom and lay on the porch bed, contemplating how we were both incarcerated in emotional prisons, though hers was much darker and more difficult to escape than mine. Would Sofiya ever be able to free herself from these terrible memories? Did she even possess the strength to try? What motivated her to trudge onward? The hard fact was that she had little reason to continue, at least as far as I could tell. I had lost only one person, yet his absence had extinguished the sunlight in my life and, on several occasions, led me to consider diving into the black river. If I felt this way, how did Sofiya survive? There were still traces of that young, high-spirited, romantic girl who loved to laugh; of a compassionate and open-hearted woman who deserved to be loved and treasured. But who truly loved her and whom did she love?

I heard my mother enter the apartment. She called and asked if I was ready. I appeared in the doorway with my bag and flippers, and we walked to the office where Travis waited, looking neat in khaki shorts, an olive green tee under an unbuttoned, long-sleeved white shirt, and brown leather sandals. A web belt circled his waist, from which hung a skin-diver's knife. Wondering about Sofiya, I watched her door, concerned she might cancel, but she emerged carrying a large straw bag and wearing sunglasses, tan shorts, and her beach jacket. Her hair was hidden under the pink kerchief, as it had been the first time I'd seen her, which now seemed like weeks ago. Although I couldn't see her eyes through the dark glasses, I sensed she was observing me and not my mother or Travis. I reached for her bag.

"Let me carry that for you," I said, slipping the bag's handles over my arm.

Travis's car was a Nash Rambler station wagon, two-toned aqua and white, freshly washed for our adventure.

"A 1957," he told me. "Second set of whitewalls. The first four disappeared one night, leaving the car flat on the street. Don't know how they managed to do that."

"At least the thief has a matched set of tires," I replied.

He laughed and threw up his hands. "You're right!"

We stowed our things in the rear, with his flippers, speargun, knapsack, and a large cooler, into which Sofiya added a bottle of white wine. My mother had already placed a bottle inside, along with three Coca-Colas and a few perishables bought while shopping with Travis. She took the front passenger seat, while Sofiya and I sat in the back. I gave Sofiya a smile, which she returned, and we both rolled down our windows because it was stifling hot inside the car. Travis drove us out of town and into the countryside, chatting happily with my mother, while Sofiya and I were mostly silent. We passed an enormous red-orange flame tree, brilliant in the morning sun. My mother insisted that Travis pull over so I could take a photograph for her, which I did.

Eventually, Travis exited onto a narrow, sandy lane and continued for several hundred feet to a cleared area overlooking the ocean. He parked the car, and we decided who was best able to carry what items. I slung the strap of my TWA case over my shoulder, placed my flippers under my arm, and grabbed the heavy cooler's right handle. Travis took the left one after slipping on his knapsack and gathering the speargun and snorkeling gear in his other hand. Sofiya toted her straw bag and two cotton tablecloths, while Mother managed her carryall and a grocery bag. Off we trooped down the steep hill, Travis and I sliding several times in the sand

and disturbing our tandem performance, causing him to emit sharp barks of laughter and the ice in the cooler to rumble as it shifted inside. We walked quite a distance, my mother huffing and puffing and asking to stop several times to catch her breath.

"Smoking will do that to you," I muttered, mostly to myself.

"That's enough, Olivia," she retorted.

By the time Travis selected a location, we were all perspiring heavily. He found four long driftwood branches, and we shoved them upright into the ground, forming a square. Travis removed laundry line from his knapsack and coiled it around each corner of a white tablecloth, tying the ends to the poles in order to create an awning. Mother spread the other tablecloth below while Travis and I dug a pit downwind for the coals, which were also in his knapsack, along with a spatula and tongs, silverware, paper plates, and napkins. Next to our makeshift grill, Sofiya placed potatoes, onions, and mangoes, all wrapped in tin foil. After setting out a selection of cheeses, Mother played bartender, dispensing a beer to Travis, opening Sofiya's bottle of white wine, and pouring plastic glasses full for Sofiya and herself. She handed me a Coke.

"No wonder the cooler was so heavy," I said. "There's an entire liquor store inside."

Sofiya chuckled at this. To my mother, she said, "I hope you like the wine, Evelyn. It's a Riesling from Alsace-Lorraine."

"Thank you, Sofiya."

Sofiya smiled, then clicked her glass against my Coke. "To a lovely day, Olivia!"

I sat beside her and watched Travis toss balls of newspaper, driftwood kindling, and coals into the pit. He flicked his brass lighter on the paper edges. The flames rose quickly, fanned by a light sea breeze.

"Now, who's up for a swim?" he asked, taking a large gulp of beer.

Sofiya and I were ready; my mother announced she preferred to sketch some nearby sea grape bushes laden with purple and green fruit.

"Okay, maybe after lunch," Travis told her. "Evelyn, in a few minutes, when the coals turn gray, will you place the potatoes in the bottom, close to the briquettes? The onions can be added later, the mangoes when we cook the fish."

Sofiya removed her scarf, and we trimmed down to our bathing suits, as did Travis, except he retained his green tee shirt as I kept on my white one. We entered the ocean, Travis with speargun in hand. He swam about thirty feet ahead, while Sofiya and I stayed near shore. I wanted to join him but also wished to be with her.

"Are you okay, Olivia?" she asked, sitting in shallow water.

"Are you?"

Sofiya sighed. "Yes, but I think it was unwise to confide so much last night."

I shook my head. "I needed to hear it." I sat beside her and wedged my feet into the flippers. "Have you told your story to many people?"

"Only a few. The military personnel in Berlin knew—I was hired as a translator by the U.S. Berlin Brigade after Viktor's death. Years later, in 1950, I reunited with my grandmother in England and related everything to her. She was almost eighty-one."

I stared at Sofiya, surprised. "Did you stay with her?"

"I did but only for ten days because of work. As much as I was overjoyed to see my grandmother, the trip to England was extremely upsetting. Her health was failing, and she was living in a shabby care home after being forced to sell her house and the family farm shortly after the war."

"Even so, I'm very glad you found her. Did you return to England later?"

"My grandmother lived several more years, but sadly, her mental capability began deserting her soon after my visit. When I came again, she didn't know who I was. At her funeral, I learned she had left me her pearl necklace and earrings plus some money—not much." She watched Travis for a moment, then continued. "After my job with the army was phased out, I was employed as an office manager for an export company in Berlin. This spring they were bought by another firm, and my position was terminated. So, I decided to take a vacation."

"Vacation" seemed an odd word for what surely was not a holiday. "And come to St. Croix?"

"Well, at first I traveled to South America, then to some of the islands, but I chose to stay here."

Was St. Croix the end of the line? With mounting anxiety, I began to realize the extent of Sofiya's predicament. "What will happen if you don't find work?"

She touched my arm. "Don't worry, everything will be fine. I've managed for this long. Something will turn up. Now, shall we swim?" She stood and waded into the surf.

After glancing at my mother, who was preoccupied with a drawing, I followed behind Sofiya. A few minutes later, Travis lifted a speared fish into the air.

"Hurray!" he shouted.

We applauded his success.

He swam toward us. "A nice snapper."

Coming ashore, Travis showed Mother the fish. She admired his prowess, and then he placed the snapper on a large rock and began filleting the fish with his knife. My mother wrapped the two sections in foil and laid the packets in the shade of the awning while Travis used the tongs to turn the potatoes and insert the onions. After a swallow of beer, he returned to the water.

"Okay, Olivia, let's see how you do with a speargun."

I cast a glance at Sofiya, hesitant to leave her, but she smiled and waved her hand to go. I donned my mask and snorkel, as Travis did his, and followed in his wake. There weren't many fish swimming nearby, but when we reached the broken coral reef where he had speared the snapper, there were many more. Travis removed his snorkel and explained how to use the speargun, warning that it was a dangerous weapon and could kill somebody.

"Namely me, since I'm the only big target near you," he said, laughing.

I was intimidated by the gun but followed his precise instructions about holding it pointing down and away from us. We replaced our snorkels and cruised along, with Travis gesturing at various fish and indicating with a "thumbs down" if they weren't edible or big enough. Finally, he halted and pointed to a brown, big-mouthed grouper hunkering by the coral and signaled "thumbs up." I removed my snorkel and, as smoothly as I could, descended to the reef, where the large grouper eyed me with suspicion. I tried to anticipate a sudden move, but he remained almost stationary, perhaps imagining that he blended into the rocks and was invisible. I aimed the speargun and squeezed the trigger. To my absolute surprise, the spear hit the fish. Travis clapped me on the back and swooped in to retrieve the second part of our lunch.

Everyone fussed about my brilliant shot. Sofiya teased, calling me a markswoman, and even my mother seemed impressed. After Travis fitted the mangoes near the potatoes and onions, he prepared the grouper, and then cut some green branches, doused them in the ocean, and fashioned a criss-cross grill over the coals. He laid the foil-wrapped packets of fish on top, and the bar was reopened. The three of them lazed under the awning while I composed a few photographs of the group, their glasses raised. When I finished, I set the camera in the flight bag, in the shade.

"I'm going to look for shells," I announced.

Sofiya placed her wine glass on the sand and offered to accompany me. She slipped on her beach jacket, and we started walking along the wrack line where many small treasures had entangled with the seaweed and twisted grasses. I began picking up keyhole limpets, about an inch in size, each with a hole in the top, with stripes extending from the hole. Some were mostly white, others had alternating rust and ivory rays.

"They look like little hats," I told Sofiya.

"Or miniature volcanoes," she replied, laughing.

"Maybe I'll make a wind chime using a piece of driftwood, like this piece here." I saw a smooth branch about a foot long and grabbed it. "I'll tie a string to the ends as a hanger, then dangle strings from the branch and space a series of limpets on each string."

"Give the shells to me, Olivia. I'll put them in my pocket."

I did so and we kept strolling until Sofiya noticed a large sea urchin, bleached white by the sun except for tiny knobbed rows of pale pinkish lavender. She gently lifted it off the sand.

"What a beauty!" she exclaimed.

Together, we examined its underside as it lay in her hands. The bottom curved gracefully into a hollow interior space. The skeleton was extremely thin, perfectly round.

"This is for your collection," Sofiya said.

"How will I get it home without breaking it?"

"Stuff the inside with cotton, and maybe your mother will buy you a case to carry on the plane."

"One of the small straw suitcases they sell in Cavanagh's would work."

"Yes, good idea."

We found four more urchins, a piece of purple coral, helmet and triton shells, a squiggly corkscrew that we thought was a worm shell, and a reddish-pink sea fan. When we could carry no more, we joined the others. Mother was excited about our discoveries and showed us a large brain coral that she intended to lug home.

Lunch was a feast. The two fish and the grilled mangoes and onions were cooked perfectly; the potatoes had a smoky flavor, enhanced by salt and pepper and butter. After we had eaten, Mother removed her street clothes, revealing a purple, low-cut suit. Travis cast an appreciative eye over her figure.

When they walked toward the ocean, Sofiya began to chuckle.

"What's so funny?" I asked her.

"Oh, ho! Your mother has turned Travis into a love-struck puppy."

We watched as Mother held his hand as she waded into the water, acting like she was entering treacherous seas and might fall. Travis happily obliged her tentativeness, though the sandy bottom was clearly visible and free of rocks. Sofiya and I kept sharing looks, turning away from the cause of our amusement and breaking into peals of laughter. When the twosome tired of their watery games, they returned to finish their drinks.

The afternoon disappeared, as did two bottles of wine and five beers.

—

On the return drive, Travis began singing "Jamaica Farewell" and everyone joined in, mostly on key. Mother was sometimes close to the pitch but tended to dance around it, sometimes nipping over the note, sometimes sinking below it. To be fair, she couldn't sing well when sober. To be fair, I couldn't sing much better.

When we arrived at the Pink Fancy, we divided to our various residences, mellow in spirit but tired from too much sun and partying.

"Are you going to call Dad?" I prompted my mother.

"Oh, no," she said, yawning, "I'm taking a nap."

We changed from our swimsuits, and Mother settled on the living room couch and instantly fell asleep. I retrieved my secret journal, headed for the porch with it and the paperback of Lord of the Flies, and began recording more of Sofiya's saga, citing her life with Viktor, her Berlin experiences, and her visit to England. Replaying the story depressed me, but the day had been a fine antidote.

After an hour of writing, I closed the journal and took up the novel. The plot followed the expected, sickening line. Simon is murdered by the boys, as they turn into savages. William Golding had created a story that demonstrated the thinness of our social veneer and how readily the ferocious and immoral inner beast could break through. As I finished the book, I thought of Sofiya and the Nazis, the camps, the trains, the executions and murders, the sadistic cruelty, and realized Golding had been inspired by the atrocities of World War I and II.

I presumed this would be another evening without dinner, but at least I wasn't hungry. After checking on my mother, who was still asleep, I crept into the bedroom, hid my journal behind the dresser, and returned to the porch. The Goose buzzed in the harbor, then noisily mounted the ramp to its nighttime sleeping spot. To the west, the setting sun gilded the palm trees and rooftops, and the sky created an impersonation of a rainbow, migrating from red to orange to pink to lavender, soon to darken into cobalt blue. Late afternoon floated gracefully into early evening. This time of day was my favorite, which Sofiya would attribute to romanticism. More simply, I loved the light, the colors, and how the wind died and the air stilled.

I switched on the bed-side lamp. The porch enclosure became intimate despite its openness to the darkness. The light threw shadows from the shutter slats upward and extended long black lines from the furniture legs across the floor. Even with these eerie effects, my corner was enriched with a cheerful yellow glow, reminding me of my narrow room at home, one of the smallest in a big house.

I opened my travel diary and began to describe the shells on the beach, the fish we speared, and the food we ate at the picnic. These details were perfunctory, but I wanted to keep up to date with my writing in case Mother snooped, which I was sure she was habitually doing.

I had written only a paragraph when I heard a dog fight below and a male voice shouting at the animals. I stood and leaned over the railing, craning my neck to the right. On the street, a pack of mongrels were running down the road, away from town. A lone figure was heading in my direction, his springy gait similar to Simon's way of walking, as if he were about to break into a sprint. The person wore black, but of greater significance, his hair was blond. I couldn't see his face—in the dusky light, it was a pale disk without features—but it was definitely the boy.

Probably because I was illuminated by the nearby lamp, he noticed me and slowed his fast pace to a stop. Spellbound, we stared at each other for a minute. Imagining Simon as a fifteen-year old, taller but still slender, he might resemble the young man on the street. My heart quickened with happiness and hope. I raised my hand in greeting and was about to call out to him, when the boy suddenly dashed away. Was he embarrassed because I had seen him peering at me, or was he in a hurry, returning from a seaplane flight and late for dinner? Or—more chilling—perhaps he couldn't maintain his ghostly image for very long, which was why he always disappeared.

Desperate to find him, I rushed past my sleeping mother, grabbed the apartment key, and ran outside and down the steps, wishing I was wearing my sneakers instead of loose sandals. Across the street, the old black woman was sitting in her chair, her hair backlit from the light shining through the windows. A man, perhaps her son, sat beside her, watching as I turned right on Prince Street. By the time I reached the intersection at Strand, the blond-haired boy was already sprinting into the darkness.

"Wait!" I shouted, but he didn't turn around.

I followed him to Queen Cross Street, down which he had traveled in the taxi. At the corner, I stopped, bent over, hands on my knees, while I tried to catch my breath. There were people roaming about, several of whom looked at me askance, but when I peered down the road, the boy was gone.

"Damn it!"

Reversing course, I walked toward the Pink Fancy, feeling despondent, confused, and anxious. At the gate, I ascended the steps and then checked Sofiya's apartment. No light was showing. Her reassurance that I wasn't crazy would have been very welcome, though what could she say about a boy who might not exist?

—

In my absence, Mother had roused herself from her slumbers and was now sitting upright, smoking a cigarette. I locked the door behind me, tossed my key on the counter, and flailed at the smoky haze.

"Where have you been?" she demanded. "Or perhaps I should ask why you ran out of here?"

"It was nothing."

"Nothing? I saw you go down the street. What were you doing?"

"I don't feel like explaining."

"That's not an acceptable answer!"

I rummaged around the cupboard, removed a bag of potato chips, and ripped it open. "Let's forget about it, Mother."

She snorted her displeasure. "Olivia, I don't understand why you won't talk to me like a normal child."

"Maybe because I'm not a child. And I'm not normal, whatever that is." I ate a chip, crunching loudly to disguise my anger and to avoid making a barbed response. But I couldn't help myself. "And while we're at it, Mother, do you consider yourself a normal parent? Do you know how to have a normal conversation with me?" I shook my head in disgust. "I don't think so."

She bit back a reply, which would no doubt have been acidic. "All right. I give up. Run around the streets at night and see if I care. You're old enough to know better but also old enough to make your own decisions."

I poured a glass of water and took a big swallow. "Then we understand each other." I walked out of the room.

Day 8

Mother wasn't much nicer the next day. When I woke, she was drinking black coffee and working on an acrylic painting of palm trees twisting in the wind. No "good morning" greeting, smile, eye contact; no acknowledgment of my existence. I looked at her hopefully, prepared to be pleasant, but the frost was thick in the warm room. After she pointedly lit a cigarette and blew smoke in my direction, I fixed a bowl of cereal, poured some juice, and fled to the porch to eat, surprised to see that the sky in my mother's painting matched the one in front of me. The clouds were piling themselves higher and higher, resembling white wedding cakes in which each tier was smaller. The east wind gusted with growing force and tangled with the uppermost sections of the thunderheads, blowing their neat, curvy tops apart and spewing them westward. The sky was turning dark gray with sections of bilious green; in the distance, shafts of yellow sunlight burst through the clouds and blasted the white wave crests below, which churned and boiled with the coming storm. I finished my breakfast, changed into shorts and a blouse, and then returned outside to watch nature throw a tizzy.

A few minutes later, I heard Travis in the living room. "Evelyn, we need to put this tarp on the porch bed. We're about to have some bad weather."

The two of them stepped onto the balcony. Travis greeted me and reiterated what he told my mother. "We might have some lightning, too," he said, as we tucked the tarp over the bed, end table, and lamp. "So stay out of the pool and in the apartment."

I agreed to do so and gathered up the breakfast dishes and my belongings, bringing them into the living area and the bedroom respectively. After he left, I carried my camera outside and joined my mother by the railing. A procession of fierce clouds skimmed across the horizon.

"I think I have this in memory, but would you take a few shots for me?" she asked.

This passed for ice-breaking.

"Okay." I increased the Nikon's shutter speed to stop-action the movement of the trees, raised the camera to my eyes, and snapped several pictures. Afterward, we stood watching until the rain plunged from the sky, slashing white diagonal lines against the green foliage and sounding like steel nails pinging on the nearby tin roofs. The street was instantly flooded; then the wind veered and thrust the rain straight at us. I covered the camera with my blouse, and Mother and I bolted for the living room, laughing despite our earlier tribulations. Our departure was greeted with a booming clap of thunder.

I used a towel to dry the camera while she returned to her painting. It seemed like the storm would hover over St. Croix for a while, so I retreated to the bedroom and began a new book, an Agatha Christie mystery, *Murder on the Orient Express*. It was a disturbing irony to read about murder for pleasure when the murders experienced by Sofiya were still haunting my thoughts.

About eleven, the rain and wind exhausted themselves. Water drained swiftly along the street gutters, and steaming mist rose from all surfaces. Palm leaves littered the roofs, front porches, parked cars, and the road. When Rosita brought clean towels for our apartment, I removed the tarp and used the old towels to dry the porch furniture. I returned the tarp to Travis, who was mopping the gallery floorboards, and helped him by wiping the chaises, setting one upright because it had blown over.

"We needed the rain," he said, twisting the mop head into a bucket. "Fills the cisterns."

"Good. Maybe now I can take a shower."

Travis stared at me for a second, realized I was kidding, and laughed.

I tossed the towels into a basket of dirty linens and checked Sofiya's apartment. No lights were on, which didn't necessarily mean anything since the sun was now shining brightly.

"Have you seen Sofiya this morning?" I asked Travis.

"Yeah, earlier. She had a job interview."

I nodded and then grabbed the net skimmer. "Should I clean the pool?"

"That would be great, Olivia."

It took about twenty minutes with a net to remove all the leaves and flowers floating on the surface and those drifting below. In the apartment, I changed into my bathing suit and then returned to swim.

—

After lunch with my mother, I offered to do our laundry, having been apprised by our maid that one of the commercial washers was available. Rosita instructed me how to use the machine and pointed to the clothesline tucked behind the lemon tree to the right of our apartment. I gathered our clothes and fit everything into one load. While waiting, I brought my book poolside and corralled a raft so I could read and float about.

A half hour later, Travis removed his sandals and sat on the gallery deck, dangling his feet in the water.

"I'd join you except we have some new guests arriving soon," he said.

It occurred to me that a week and a day had passed since we came to the island. It seemed much longer than eight days. "That's good. To have more people." I closed my book, tossed it on one of the nearby chaises, and sat astride the raft.

Travis sighed. "Yes, it's good for the old bank account, but between you and me, I like fewer guests about. So I can spend more time with ones I like, such as you and your mother."

I smiled at him. "And Sofiya."

"Of course. I love having her at the Pink Fancy."

I paddled closer to Travis. He kicked the water playfully. Even his feet were handsome—high instep, slender toes, evenly trimmed nails.

"I just hope Sofiya can stick it out until she finds a position," he continued. "Don't know what her financial situation is, but I'm a little worried about her. I'm giving Sofiya a discount, like I do with most of my long-term renters." Travis chuckled, then whispered, "Except for the guys from Texas and Oklahoma who are here to work at the oil refinery. The company is subsidizing them, so I figure they can help subsidize someone like Sofiya. That's our secret, right?" He winked.

"Okay. But what happens if she runs out of money?"

Travis rubbed his chin. "I'll spot her for a few weeks unless I get a ton of reservations, which is unlikely at this time of year—the two apartments next to yours are empty now and might be for some time. Sofiya won't need to leave anytime soon."

"I'm glad to hear it."

Travis regarded me with a friendly expression. "You've taken quite a shine to Sofiya, haven't you?"

I tucked my legs up on the raft, which required some balancing. "Yeah. I find her fascinating and...well, very sympathetic."

"Like the mother you haven't had?"

This surprised me. "In some ways, maybe." I wrapped my arms around my knees. "In other ways, Sofiya is like the friend or sister I don't have." I hesitated before adding, "Our relationship is hard to describe. It's very different."

"I kind of think it's different for her, too," he said. "Sofiya hasn't had an easy life, as I'm sure she's mentioned. In fact, my guess is she's told you a lot more than she's told me."

I wanted Travis to return to his comment regarding my mother and her parenting, but I didn't wish to place him in an awkward position. And this new topic, about Sofiya, was equally interesting. "Why do you think she confides in me?"

Travis shrugged and his green eyes narrowed as he reflected on a response. "There's something special about you. Like you know things. Sofiya is the same way."

"You think we're alike?"

"I do. That might not make much sense due to the big difference in age and experience."

"Actually, Travis, it does. She understands me better than my mother."

"You might be right," he agreed. "I may be speaking out of turn, but Evelyn seems bewildered by you." Travis placed his hands on the deck behind him and leaned back, thinking. "No, that's only part of it. She's frustrated, almost angry. Like the two of you are in an entrenched fight."

"Do you know why?"

Travis shook his head. "I'd just be making things up if I said anything else. Whatever Evelyn is feeling, it can't make living with her easy."

I wanted him to speculate further, but he seemed reluctant. "I'm curious, Travis. Why do you like her? Other than that she's beautiful."

"For some men, beauty would be enough. But Evelyn is also fun to be with. I love making her laugh, love to share a good time with her. That's what our relationship is about. Not very complicated." Travis lifted his legs out of the water and rested his feet on the deck. "I guess we get on because Evelyn and I are new to each other. We can ditch our past stuff. In my case, coming to St. Croix has allowed me a fresh start. For your mother, perhaps that's also true."

"What's going to happen when we leave?"

Travis threw up his hands. "There're quite a few days before that happens. My philosophy is to let things flow. You might have trouble understanding that."

"Why, because I'm young?"

"No, it has nothing to do with age. Evelyn and I are naturally built to live in the present, though circumstances have kept her mired in the past until now. You and Sofiya tend to look backward, into your history, your memories. I don't know if Sofiya can change her perspective and move on, but that's not true for you."

I took this in, aware that Travis's words contained some significant truths. Obviously, he was referring to Simon's death, which Mother must have told him about. The fact that she'd had this exchange with Travis made me revise my estimation of her and of him, who, up until now, had seemed like a lighthearted spirit, a nice guy, but not a profound thinker or confidant.

"I'll consider what you said."

"Good." Travis came to his feet.

"By the way, she hasn't called my dad, has she? This morning?"

"She didn't." Travis gazed across the pool, as if uncomfortable. "It's not really my place to remind her."

"No, it isn't," I agreed. "Not mine, either, though I did."

"Your father will be concerned, won't he?"

"Yes. Mother usually stays in touch with him, even when Dad is overseas. We don't talk long—too expensive—but he likes to know we're both okay."

Travis nodded. "Well, I better get some work done." He grasped his sandals and began to walk toward the office. Then, he faced me again. "You know, it was funny. A little earlier, just before the storm, this guy came up the steps from the street. I thought of you. Maybe because his hair was the same color as yours, though his was much shorter."

I stared at him and inhaled sharply. "What did he look like?"

"About my height. Your age or thereabouts."

"And his face?"

"Sorry. He was only here for a minute," Travis said. "He was dressed in black. I remember that because it was odd in this heat. Anyone you know?"

"No," I replied, trying to sound offhand. "He didn't ask for me, did he?"

"Nope. Only said he was looking around. Before I could offer him a tour, the guy hurried off. We get people checking out the hotel sometimes. Not unusual."

As I watched Travis enter his office, my head began spinning with thoughts about the boy. I was too excited to stay in the pool any longer, so I hurried to the steps and climbed out. In a daze, I rubbed my arms with a towel. The boy was surely the same one I'd seen last night below the hotel. Had he returned to find me? Maybe I wasn't delusional after all. It was sorely tempting to do something other than stand around dripping water on the cement, but it had been hours since the young man left. He could be anywhere. I lay on the chaise, closed my eyes, and tried to forget about him.

A short while later, a young couple arrived with suitcases, flushed from the heat and out of breath from climbing the steps. Travis hastened to greet them, and after they completed some paperwork, he unlocked the door to Fertility. Aha! Newlyweds. I chuckled to myself and felt like an old-timer at the Pink Fancy.

—

The laundry was ready to hang, so I borrowed clothespins from Rosita and set to work. As I clipped shorts, blouses, and skirts to the line, I remembered Sofiya's remark about Mother being old yet young, versus me being young yet old. In many ways, her comment dovetailed with what Travis had said, except he stated the differences in terms of living in the past versus in the present. He had also implied that Sofiya and I possessed deeper personalities, whereas he and my mother were more interested in pleasure and enjoyment. Though she was a very dedicated artist, this was probably an accurate assessment, yet I had to admit that I didn't really understand my mother. And, certainly, she did not know or understand me, either.

After I finished the laundry, I rounded the lemon tree and saw Sofiya walking toward her apartment. She was wearing a pearl gray linen suit and carrying a pocketbook and a black leather case. I called to her and she turned, shading her eyes against the sun. Then, she beckoned to me.

I tossed the clothes basket inside the apartment and hurried to her side. "How did the interview go?"

"Who knows? Another beach resort in search of a manager. The salary is acceptable, and I would have a nice three-room unit near the beach, kitchen included."

"That sounds good."

"We'll see. Now, let me change clothes, and I'll return."

I sat at the round table beneath her apartment, glad that Sofiya might be offered a job but also worried this might necessitate a move before I left St. Croix. I scolded myself for this selfish reaction, and by the time Sofiya reappeared, I was once again enthusiastic about her opportunity.

She took the chair across from me, the late afternoon sun warming her tanned face and glinting highlights in her black and silver hair. She had forgotten her sunglasses, so I could observe her eyes, which I compared to Travis's. His sparkled, as if they possessed the power to steal sunlight or candlelight. Sofiya's blue eyes smoldered, lit by an enigmatic fire, more hot coals than flame. It was as if her emotions were constantly stoked in an inner furnace, illuminating her eyes from within.

I broke from this reverie and listened attentively as she discussed the job in detail. When she finished, Sofiya tapped the table with both hands. "Okay, that's enough talk about business. What have you been doing today?"

I laughed, told her about my exciting laundry chores, and relayed Travis's observations about his relationship with my mother. "So, what do people do when they're having an affair, and one of them leaves the other? And that one is married?"

"It depends on how serious they are. Travis might be having fun, with no real intentions. Or Evelyn might consider him a fling."

"Has Travis done this before? Become involved with one of his guests?"

"Possibly. When I first arrived, he seemed to be dating a woman who was staying at the hotel."

"Do you think he makes a habit of this?"

She shrugged. "He's a very attractive guy."

I nodded.

Sofiya crossed her legs and resettled in her chair. "Olivia, while the situation with Travis may be of real concern, your mother's willingness to be with him may have additional significance."

"Why?"

"I don't mean to worry you, but could your parents' marriage be heading toward a divorce? Sometimes couples decide on a brief trial separation. Perhaps Evelyn agreed to this before coming to St. Croix. If so, she might already feel disconnected from your father."

I considered this angle. "I have no idea if my parents have an arrangement." I explained the layout of the house and that I couldn't hear conversations or arguments unless they occurred in the living room or kitchen.

"How would you feel about a divorce?"

"Things have been tense for years, but if they broke up, I'd get stuck living with my mother because Dad is frequently away. And Dad might decide to move closer to the airport. He's always complaining about the commute. So our time together could be even less than it is now."

"I see. Well, maybe the best way to view the situation is to realize it would be short term. You'll be heading off to college in two years, right? I imagine that seems like ages, but it isn't."

"I suppose not." The mention of time reminded me about my departure from St. Croix. I folded my arms on the table and lay my chin on top.

"Two years will go by quickly." Sofiya observed me and added in a more somber tone, "But twenty days will go by even faster."

I looked at her, surprised that she knew, once again, exactly what I was thinking and feeling. "Yes, it will."

—

When my mother came out of the apartment, Sofiya and I watched her stroll over to the office. She said a few words to Travis, who disappeared inside again. Then, he gave Mother the telephone and left so she could speak in private. Sofiya and I exchanged looks.

"I guess she remembered to phone Dad."

"It seems so," Sofiya agreed.

We waited until Mother emerged, her face drawn.

"Is everything all right?" I stood, intending to go to her.

She held up her hand. "Yes, of course. Just chatting with your father. He's tired of eating out every night." She walked toward Travis, spoke to him, and turned to me. "We're going for a hamburger. About seven."

I didn't know if the "we" included Travis, Sofiya, and me, or only Travis. "Who's going?" I felt foolish having to ask.

"Don't be daft, Olivia."

I supposed this was a "yes" to me, but a tacit "no" for Sofiya, the one with whom I wished to dine.

After she left, Sofiya said, "Go with your mother—or with them. I'm fine. I have chicken to cook tonight."

I laughed. "How do you always know what I'm thinking? No one else does."

"To me, dear Olivia, you're transparent." She chuckled. "Now, I must get busy in the kitchen." She rose and pushed her chair under the table. "I'm not sure if you're free tomorrow, but I was hoping we might go to Buck Island. What do you think?"

I gave her a big grin. "I'd love it!"

Sofiya smiled at my enthusiasm. "I'll make reservations for the afternoon trip. Would your mother like to come?"

"I don't know. She's not much of a swimmer, as you saw at our picnic."

"Ask her. The boat leaves at one thirty, after lunch. I'll borrow gear from Travis, and Evelyn can, too."

I returned to the apartment, excited about visiting the Buck Island Reef National Monument, which I'd read about—acres of magnificent coral reefs, home to several hundred species of fish. Mother was sitting on the sofa, smoking, and studying a painting.

"Would you like to go to Buck Island tomorrow afternoon? With Sofiya?"

She took a long drag from her cigarette and exhaled slowly. "I have a lot of work to do." Mother lifted the painting and contemplated it. "But I suppose we can." She puffed on her cigarette, squinting her eyes at the canvas.

Pleased at her unusual display of agreeableness, I smiled at my mother, who surprised me by smiling back. I rushed to Sofiya's apartment and asked her to make three reservations for Buck Island.

—

Before dressing for dinner, I unpinned our laundry and folded everything in hers and hers piles. Mother thanked me, and together we hung clothes in the closet and stored items in the chest of drawers. I then opened my suitcase, wondering what outfit to wear for the evening, and noticed the Youth-Dew box. I unwrapped it and smelled the cologne. Heady with its scent and the emotions it evoked, I opted to save the perfume for home, feeling that I shouldn't dilute its poignancy while Sofiya was still present.

At seven, we met Travis and walked to the waterfront bar near King's Alley, the same one I had visited several days ago. Steel band music was playing interspersed with some American popular songs. The place was hopping with activity— people dancing, standing by the bar drinking, and seated at seaside tables opposite the dance floor. We were shown to such a table and ordered daiquiris and hamburger platters. The sky had become moody, as if another storm was conjuring itself. As our cocktails arrived, a fierce downpour began, yet there was little wind and no rain blowing on us. Water dripped off the awning, and then, as quickly as the weather had started, it stopped, and the clouds retreated. The crowd greeted the return of the sunset with a roar of enthusiasm and regained the dance floor.

Travis asked Mother to dance, a slow number. To my knowledge, this was their first dance, but they were well matched and comfortable. Mother was an excellent dancer—in contrast to me, who was not—and she fitted into Travis's embrace smoothly, gazing into his eyes with adoration. I watched, sipping my drink, and wished I was dining with Sofiya.

While I enjoyed the music, it was awkward sitting by myself, so I turned to face the harbor. Halfway through the song, someone tapped me on the shoulder. Startled, I swiveled in my chair and encountered the man from the last time I'd been here. He was in his thirties, dark-skinned, and dressed in a sapphire-blue knit shirt. He smiled and asked me to dance. Unsure what to do, I hesitated. Mother wasn't paying attention and couldn't be counted on for guidance. I accepted, sorry that the song wasn't set to a faster beat so we would dance separately. When we reached the floor, the man pulled me much closer than I would have expected a stranger to do. Except for attending my eighth-grade graduation dance and a freshman sock hop, with five outings with different boys, my most frequent partner had been my father, who was so tall and strong that following him required little skill. While this man's sense of rhythm was excellent, I stepped on his toes several times and felt mortified with embarrassment.

Mother finally noticed us. Her expression froze, and she nudged Travis, who whispered something to my mother. When the song ended, I thanked the man and returned to the table, where Travis and my mother had already taken seats.

"What do you think you were doing, Olivia?" my mother hissed.

"Dancing."

She rolled her eyes at me. "You don't want to give them any encouragement."

I sighed. "I didn't give *them* ideas. All I did was dance with one guy."

"Well, don't do it again!"

Travis frowned and pulled Mother aside. "Evelyn, it's okay. Jimmy is a nice fellow. He's a guard at the museum."

Mother stared at Travis. "I don't care if he's governor of the island, I won't have it!"

He raised his eyebrows, glanced at me, and focused on my mother again. "It's their island, Evelyn."

Before more could be said, the waitress came with our dinner. As she placed the plates in front of us, I realized that my discomfort hadn't been about dancing with a Crucian. It was about dancing with anyone, whether I knew them or not. However, my mother's prejudiced reaction stiffened my attitude so that I half wished Jimmy would ask again. He had been observing us, and although he couldn't hear the conversation, it was obvious my mother was upset. I gave him a small smile, nodded my head, and started to eat my French fries.

After our meal, Travis danced with me, though I was self-conscious. Despite my nervousness, I felt the power in his arms, smelled the lime cologne on his neck, and was pleased to be with such a handsome man. He twirled me around, exhibiting fine moves, and I managed to follow, with only one misstep.

"You did the right thing," Travis whispered. "Dancing with Jimmy. Just don't tell Evelyn I said so, okay?"

"I won't. Thanks, Travis."

"But be a little careful. There are a few men here that are trouble."

"Who?"

"Those two white guys behind me. They're drug dealers."

I took a quick peek and saw the two he meant. They were thin, with uncombed hair, ruddy features, and wore loud clothes and ropes of gold necklaces.

I couldn't help laughing. "Mother would have a cow if I danced with one of them!"

"Yeah, she would," Travis said, grinning. "So don't get any smart ideas."

Day 9

In preparation for our Buck Island visit, Sofiya selected gear from Travis's stash. Then, he attempted to outfit Mother. Sofiya and I sat together at the round table by the pool and observed this scene as he offered her one pair of flippers after another.

"Too big," she told him.

He gave her a child's flipper. She grimaced. "Ouch! Too tight."

Travis tried a black set. Mother waved them away. "Too masculine."

This fussing was reminiscent of her shoe-shopping expeditions, which I had always avoided when possible. Travis then began playing a Parisian salesman.

"Oh, *Madame*. Zee best. *Magnifique*!" An orange pair.

"Loose in the heel," my mother insisted.

"*Sacre bleu*!" He tapped his forehead in mock anguish. After rooting around in the basket, tossing flippers over his shoulder, he proffered a pink flipper. "Ah, *parfait*." He rolled the "r" to comic effect.

As she placed them on her feet, I was already giggling at his antics, which caused him to roll his eyes. Realizing she was being laughed at, Mother threw darts of annoyance in my direction. Sofiya turned away, her shoulders shaking with laughter.

"Oo-la-la!" he exclaimed, as Mother flashed flippers in the air.

"Okay, these will do, Travis."

The pink pair. Chosen, no doubt, for color rather than fit. Travis handed her a mask and helped her adjust the strap. While everyone looked bizarre in the gear, myself included, my mother in a mask and snorkel was hilarious. Because of our ill-disguised mirth, she refused to do a wet-run in the pool.

———

The Buck Island ferry left from the Comanche dock with us onboard. We sat abreast of each other on a wooden bench, with Sofiya in the middle. She engaged Mother in dialogue, asking about her artwork and where she had exhibited and studied. These were my mother's favorite topics, so the two of them chatted while the boat skirted the harbor. I was content to enjoy the warm sun and to experience a sense of solidarity with Sofiya even when her attention was elsewhere.

The island was about a mile long and a third as wide. The captain moored the boat close to the beach on the western side, explaining that the National Monument was on the opposite shore. The idea was to give the inexperienced snorkelers a chance to practice in shallow water, in the lee of the island, where the seas were calmer. I jumped off the boat's deck, eager to explore, but Sofiya waited for my mother to sort herself out. The two climbed down the ladder facing outward, flippers flipping, and splashed in, Mother in a rather ungainly fashion. I steered clear of them, too fascinated by the sights below, but when one of the black mates began assisting my mother with her mask and snorkel, Sofiya joined me, her face lit with amusement.

"I bet she wished that Travis had instructed her," she whispered, treading water.

"You're right. I don't think she's happy having that guy's help. A little prejudice is rearing its ugly head." I recounted my mother's bigoted reaction last night when the Crucian museum guard had asked me to dance.

"Oh, dear. You really know how to upset her, don't you?" Sofiya replied, laughing. "Now, I suppose it's our job to swim around and prove we won't drown when we're in the park."

We did as Sofiya suggested. She was obviously comfortable with the equipment, having had an opportunity to practice at Pelican Cove, but I also suspected Sofiya was naturally more athletic than my mother, who, while coordinated, was terrible at sports with the exception of lawn croquet, a game in which she delighted smashing her opponent's ball into the weeds.

Side by side, Sofiya and I swam away from the ferry, peering at the fish below, and then she pointed to an orange-gold conch, with pearly pink folds, resting on the bottom. I nodded, ripped the snorkel out of my mouth, and dove down for it, immediately glad I was wearing flippers since the clear water had disguised the distance. I surfaced and took a huge gulp of air, waving the shell at Sofiya.

"A perfect queen conch!" she cried, examining the shell that I held in my hand. "You'll have to leave it in alcohol or bleach so the animal dies. Otherwise you will have a very smelly friend in your suitcase."

We returned to my mother, who had more or less mastered the snorkel, with a few coughs and sputters. About ten minutes later, the mates called everyone to the ladders. The swimmers climbed onto the deck, and the ferry proceeded to the windward side of the island, where several catamarans and small boats were already moored near the park's underwater entrance. We dropped anchor, and one of the mates jumped overboard while two others uncoiled a series of black inner tubes connected by ropes and tossed them in the water. We were told that eight of us would compose the first group. Confident snorkelers could leave the line if they wished.

The captain began reciting his speech. "Buck Island Reef National Monument is run by the U.S. National Park Service and encompasses about eight hundred and fifty acres. Please don't dive down to the reef," he warned. "The coral is razor sharp. In particular, watch out for the yellow-green coral. If you bump into it, it hurts. Like a jellyfish sting. And don't be alarmed, but we have some local visitors, one large fish we call 'Barry Barracuda.' He swims around but won't bother you if you don't bother him."

We were chosen in the first group with a family of three, one of whom was a girl about nine years old, and a young couple, who couldn't keep their hands off each other. Fertility apartment candidates, for sure. I slipped on my white tee shirt and stepped over the side. Once everyone was splashing around in the water—the girl and my mother making the most commotion—the mate assigned positions: Sofiya was first, I was second, Mother third, the family next, and the lovebirds brought up the rear. Our guide pulled the lead rope, though each person was expected to self-propel, one arm draped over his or her inner tube.

Compared to the western side of the island, the National Monument was crammed with dense clusters of elkhorn and brain coral; masses of undulating sea grasses and fans; and fish of all sizes, shapes, and colors. It was a brilliant panorama that elicited much excited gesturing by the swimmers. Here, everything was bigger than at Pelican Cove because this was an extensive barrier reef that ran the length of the island, whereas Pelican Cove was a fringing reef that grew close to the beach, in much shallower water. I tried to identify the fish and knew many, but eventually I became so dazzled by the processions passing below and around me that I succumbed to a state of wonder.

The guide queued us behind another group, and after swimming a short distance, he told us to look down—as if we weren't already doing so. On the sand, about twelve feet below us, was a plaque that said, "Underwater trail starts here." We followed along, reading signs explaining the types of coral. Another plaque warned, "Don't poke around. Holes in coral may contain moray eels."

After a short time, I grew impatient with the slow progress

and disconnected from the conga line. I tapped my mother on the shoulder.

She lifted her head out of the water, her eyes large. "It's amazing! I wish you could take underwater photographs for me."

"I wish I could, too. You'll have to take pictures in your mind," I told her. "I'm going off for a bit. Be back soon."

I passed Sofiya, indicated that I was departing the tube train, and set out to the right of the underwater trail yet remained close to its path. The honeymooners had a similar idea to separate from the group, or rather they had other ideas. Under the surface, their hands were on each other, then within each other's suits. Instead of staying for some sex education, which was apparently about to get quite explicit, I sped away.

I marveled at the variety of fish. The tinier school fish angled in all directions, and for a while, I amused myself by swimming into their midst and flicking my hand, which they avoided with unified precision. The neon colors of other fish were breathtaking: vivid sapphires, yellows, and oranges, with black-and-white zebra fish providing a sober look. I was so enraptured that I hadn't noticed I'd drifted to the far side of the reef. Here, the water was deeper and unprotected from the open ocean, with bigger fish, which were exciting to see. Exciting until I saw four barracudas about twenty feet away, each at least a yard long and one even longer. Barry had some pals, silver fighting machines with way too many sharp teeth. I decided meeting them up close was not wise and retreated, keeping them in sight until the foursome disappeared. Shaken by this reminder of the dangers nearby, I returned to the tour, thinking that if any of the barracudas decided snorkelers would make a fine snack, the inner tubes would be all that remained.

The wind picked up and the heights of waves increased, causing seawater to top some snorkels. Along the line, people started coughing, my mother especially. I instructed her to remove the snorkel and let it dangle, which was easier than constantly clearing liquid from the tube. Sofiya had already figured this out, but like Mother, she was tiring. The guide asked everyone to reverse direction and swim to the ferry. Though I was sorry to end my time in this underwater garden of delights, the barracuda sighting had filled me with apprehension. I shared what had happened with Sofiya as we waited in the water to board the boat.

"I'm glad you didn't tell me about them when we were back there," Sofiya said, laughing nervously.

After climbing the ladder and sitting on the bench, I mentioned the episode to my mother.

"You got that close? My god, Olivia! You shouldn't be so independent." She sighed with exasperation. "One of these days you're going to land in real trouble."

—

The return trip to Christiansted was pleasant, although the back of my neck and legs were deepening into sunburn, and where the short sleeves of the tee shirt ended, my arms were smoldering hot. Mother was worse because she hadn't worn any protection and had no tan. Before the tour, Sofiya, who was already dark, had slipped on a tee shirt and seemed to be in good shape. All of us were drowsy and warm, despite the breeze.

When we reached the dock, I suggested dinner at Club Comanche, but Mother and Sofiya announced they were too tired. Instead, we bought some sandwiches, potato chips, and two six-packs of beer. After mounting the hotel steps, we headed into our apartments to change into dry clothes. I left the conch on the porch, thinking it looked smaller and less colorful out of its watery element, though it was a beautiful shell. I'd need to buy some rubbing alcohol to kill the animal—Mother wouldn't be thrilled if I used her rum.

The three of us gathered at the poolside table with the beer and food. Travis was busy with guests, but once they were settled, he came over and grabbed a can. We were already imbibing, thirsty from the sun and salt water. Beer wasn't my favorite alcoholic beverage, but I drank the first one quickly.

"Whoa...it's not soda, Olivia," Sofiya said.

The sandwiches were polished off along with two rounds of beer. We sat nibbling potato chips and watching the sun silhouette the lemon tree and the roof across the street. Travis seemed unusually subdued. His face was flushed, as if he'd already had a few drinks, though usually this made him funnier and more talkative. Mother tried to rouse him from his strange mood, but after his third beer, he rose and announced he was fetching a bottle of scotch. "From Upper Joy," he said joylessly.

When he left, we discussed the curious change in Travis. No one knew the cause, and all agreed it was atypical. The consensus was that something had occurred while we were at Buck Island.

Travis returned with a nearly full bottle and a partially filled ice bucket. He took glasses from the bar behind him and poured a hefty amount of scotch for himself, a lesser amount for Mother, and none for Sofiya, who insisted beer was fine.

"And Olivia isn't having any," my mother told him, lighting a cigarette.

He frowned, as if to protest her restriction, but she explained that I didn't like scotch, which was true. Travis agreed it was an acquired taste, and from the size of his first swallow, it appeared he was doing his best to acquire more of a taste for the liquor.

Sofiya tried to create a happier atmosphere. "So, Travis, you should know that your friend Olivia was playing with Barry Barracuda this afternoon."

"And his best pals Bart, Barbara, and Barney," I added, smiling.

"You didn't tell me there were four of them!"

Mother exhaled a white cloud that stung my eyes.

"You didn't ask."

"It appears that Olivia is on a first-name basis with the silver devils." Sofiya gave me a teasing look.

This elicited some laughter from everyone except Travis, who only smiled weakly, his thoughts elsewhere. My mother, noticing this, drew her chair near to him, but Sofiya spoke first.

"Travis, what's wrong? You're not yourself tonight."

He looked up and tried harder to smile, but the smile faded before it lit his eyes. "I'm sorry. Just a little off." He took a large gulp of his drink and wagged his head side to side, as if it was too heavy to hold upright.

Mother placed her hand on his. "What happened today?"

"Nothing special." He reached for her cigarette that balanced on the lip of the ashtray. After he took a puff, he murmured, "You know the drill. No old history."

Sofiya studied him for a moment. "Travis, please tell us. We're concerned."

He inhaled again and blew out the smoke. In a choked voice, he replied, "I can't."

I sat back in my chair, surprised, and noticed Sofiya cock an eyebrow, apparently as puzzled as I was. It didn't seem appropriate for me to question him. If anyone could help, it would be Mother, though I didn't usually cast her in a Florence Nightingale role. Sofiya and I remained silent while my mother encircled his neck and pulled his head against hers.

This show of intimacy was stunning. My mother rarely demonstrated such tenderness to my father and certainly not to me. To Simon, yes.

Sofiya finished her beer and gazed at me again, a question on her face: what to do? Break up the party or have another beer and be quiet? I lifted my shoulders in a half shrug. Sofiya nodded in response, opened two more beers, and nudged one in front of me, all the while casting worried glances at Travis.

Mother whispered in his ear, words I couldn't make out, and smoothed Travis's hair.

Travis returned the cigarette to the ashtray, then pinched the bridge of his nose and sighed. "It's her birthday."

No one spoke.

My mother caressed his cheek. "Whose birthday?"

Travis swallowed more scotch and turned toward my mother. "My daughter's birthday. Maddie would have been eighteen years old today."

"Oh, Travis. How old was she when..." Sofiya couldn't finish the sentence because Travis looked so troubled.

Slowly, he mustered his composure, though his face remained clouded. "Eight when she died."

"Only a small child," Sofiya replied gently.

"Yes. Almost the same age as Simon," Travis said.

Mother stiffened. After shooting me a sharp look, as if I had been the one to mention Simon's name, she took a puff on the cigarette, angled a stream of smoke to the side of her mouth, and stubbed the butt into the ashtray. Finally, she leaned over and kissed Travis on the temple and suggested they return to his apartment.

But he wasn't finished with his story.

"Might as well explain everything now that I've gone this far." He fortified himself by replenishing the liquor in his glass, though he spilled a few drops.

"If it's too difficult, you don't have to tell us, Travis," Sofiya said.

"It's okay," he replied. "It was ten years ago, in September 1956. We'd been invited to a cocktail party but couldn't find a sitter. The host said Maddie could come. I drove us to the house, which was several miles away, on a big hill. The winter before, Maddie and I had gone tobogganing there." He paused, his expression almost happy as he recalled the memory. "Maddie was a cheerful little girl, extremely pretty like her mother, Diana." He exhaled an uneasy breath.

"Before we left for the party, Diana and I argued. She thought I was having a relationship with a woman at work. I wasn't but she didn't believe me." He sipped his drink. "Diana was almost perfect except for one fault. Jealousy. You have to understand, I never was unfaithful. I loved my wife. But some people are like that," he mused, half to himself.

I was staring at my mother when Travis said the word "unfaithful," but she was facing him and didn't react.

"So, when we arrived, both of us were still upset. Diana headed for the bar right away, which wasn't a good sign. We both liked to drink—don't get me wrong—but Diana began putting away one gin and tonic after another. When I tried to slow her down, she grew angry and accused me of flirting with the hostess. This was ridiculous—I'd only spoken to the woman for a few minutes." Travis leaned an elbow on the table, folded his fingers into a fist, and supported his chin. "I went into the den and sat with some of the guys who were watching a football game. I figured that was the safest place to be while Diana was on a jealousy tirade. Maddie joined us, sitting next to me. A while later, Diana walked in and whispered that she was sorry. I gave her a kiss, said I was sorry, too, and thought we'd patched things up. Diana asked Maddie to come into the living room, saying she wanted her company."

Sofiya and I knew where the story was headed. We drank our beers and were silent.

"I was wrong that Diana was over our quarrel. In hindsight, I think she was jealous but also depressed. After Maddie was born, and during a few other periods in our marriage, she had psychological breakdowns. I rarely knew exactly what was bothering Diana because she didn't like to talk about her feelings." Travis swallowed more of his drink. "After Maddie left the den, she didn't return. I decided to join the main party, which was quite large—forty or more people. I couldn't find my wife or Maddie anywhere and became worried because Diana had a set of car keys. As I was leaving the house to check outside, the hostess ran in, crying, and told me they had hit the big tree at the bottom of the hill."

He shut his eyes tightly. "I rushed out of the house and down the driveway. The car was on its side. Diana was trapped behind the steering wheel, dead. Maddie had been thrown through the side window and was lying against the oak tree. Her little body was all twisted—neck, arms, and legs broken. I lifted her up, hoping she was alive." Travis opened his eyes and raised his hands. "But she was dead. Like my wife."

"Oh, Travis," Sofiya said. "How terrible!"

"I'm so sorry." My mother embraced him.

He nodded. In a voice thick, he repeated, "It's her birthday. Maddie's." He threaded his fingers through his bronze-colored hair.

We were quiet, unsure what to do.

Mother straightened slightly. "This is too hard on you. Maybe you should stop."

I wasn't sure he wanted to stop. He looked grief-stricken but made no move to leave, only glanced at us, one by one.

"Travis, let's continue this in your apartment." She glared at the bottle of scotch, as if accusing it of making Travis drunk and emotional.

He didn't answer.

"Come on." Her mouth tucked up at the left. I could see she was done.

Rising, Mother took his arm and forced him to his feet. He lurched slightly, losing his balance, which she corrected. Together, they left the table and started up the path.

Travis looked back at us and tried a smile. "'Night, guys."

Mother turned him around and steered Travis toward his apartment. After they disappeared into the darkness, Sofiya and I regarded each other.

"What a tragedy!" I said.

"Yes, it is."

I thought about the scene Travis had described. "It sounds like the accident wasn't Travis's fault."

"No, I suppose not," Sofiya replied tentatively. "I guess his friend mixed up the story he told me or else I misunderstood it. He said Travis had broken some bones in the car accident. I assumed Travis and his wife were in the car together. The only unclear part was who was behind the wheel."

"Do you think Travis was truthful just now?"

"I have no idea. I doubt Travis knows his friend talked to me about the accident." She considered and added, "Maybe Travis changed the story because he didn't want Evelyn to think badly of him—or us, if he caused the deaths of his wife and daughter."

"I've heard that people sometimes deny reality. Or they reshape it until it's more comfortable to handle." As I said this, I wondered if my memories of Simon had been altered. I never could recall the final ending by the river, though I ran hard against that point in dreams and visions.

Sofiya nodded. "Yes, sometimes. Especially when traumatic events occur. That's very astute."

"I really hope Travis was being honest."

"I do, too," Sofiya agreed, staring at the path, deep in thought. "I imagine hearing the story was difficult for you. And for your mother. Losing a child, someone close." At last, she asked, "How old was your brother—"

"Simon," I replied. "He was seven years old. I was eight. Like Travis's daughter, Maddie."

"Was this when you hurt your foot?"

I was astonished that she connected the two, but Sofiya possessed an eerie perceptiveness. "Yes, it happened in the early spring, on a dock, at night."

"What were you and Simon doing out so late?"

I finished my beer and tried to think of a way to avoid the subject. Yet, I also wanted to tell Sofiya everything. "I suggested fishing for winter flounder—they were beginning their spring run. Dad was in Rome so we decided to go ourselves. As I already mentioned, our bedrooms were on a separate wing from my parents. It was easy for us to sneak outside without being heard or seen. We got our gear in the garage and walked through the forest. Even though the moon was nearly full, I was really scared because the trees were very dark. Simon was fearless. It never occurred to him there was any danger. He didn't think ahead—just plunged into things."

"Different from you," Sofiya inserted.

I nodded.

"So the two of you walked through the forest and then what?"

"I walked. Simon ran ahead. When I arrived at the cliff above the river, he was already sliding down the hill. I finally caught up to him, and we decided not to carry the toolbox onto the dock." I explained how he loaded his pockets with sinkers and how I planned to tie a can of cat food to attract the flounders. "Before I could remind him to be careful, Simon dashed up the steps." Up until now, the retelling had been fairly painless, but at this juncture, my chest began to feel tight. It took effort to breathe.

Sofiya's voice was gentle. "Your brother ran onto the dock and you followed?"

I fought a surge of panic. "I tried to stop him. I really did! But he was in such a hurry!" I pressed my eyes shut, the violent images flying through my mind with surreal speed. "There were no railings, and some of the boards were rotten. As I went after my brother, my foot broke through. A huge nail punctured my foot. I couldn't move."

"And Simon?"

My eyes flew open. I looked at her, misery swallowing my words. All I could manage was to shake my head.

"Did he come to help you?"

I gasped for air. "Don't know."

Sofiya came to the obvious conclusion.

"He fell off the dock."

I shook my head again and began to cry. "I can't remember any more. One second he was there, and then he wasn't."

"Oh, my dear," Sofiya murmured. She moved closer and laid a hand on my shoulder.

I smelled her spicy perfume and wanted to disappear into her embrace. Yet, I didn't reach for her. Didn't believe I deserved what I wanted most. "I keep thinking I see him. Simon."

"I understand. For people who've lost a loved one, this happens because we're so desperate for the person to be alive. To believe they aren't gone."

"I'm so confused! Do you imagine people from your past? Your parents or Dano?"

Sofiya smiled sadly. "Of course. But I also see others like Viktor, the Nazi soldiers and guards, people dying in the camps. Sometimes they're so real that I think I'm in Ravensbrück again or in Berlin, with bombs falling. I'm sure Travis has pictured the car, the tree, his daughter, and his wife many times. Your mother, too, with Simon, though it's worse for you, Olivia, because you were there and have real mental pictures."

"His body was never found," I said, shutting my eyes again and picturing the dock jutting into the black, fast-moving river. Simon's blond head bounced back and forth as he ran. Then, Simon transformed into the boy standing on the street below the hotel, his face featureless.

I opened my eyes to dispel the terrifying visions, but as I looked at Sofiya, she was covered with images of the dock, the blood on my foot, Simon's face and the boy's, as if these were slides projected on a curtain between us.

"It's okay, Olivia," she whispered.

"No, it isn't! I try to forget him and can't."

"Time may help, but I don't sound convincing, do I? Me with all of my nightmares."

I tried to quiet my disordered thoughts, but I felt as if one foot was pierced by the nail and the other foot was here, under the round table. Both worlds were vivid, or rather, both seemed equally tremulous and illusory. I clenched my teeth and tried to stop crying.

"Sofiya, I feel lost. And my brother is lost, too. I can't find him."

Sofiya nestled her chin in her hand, appraising me, her expression serious, yet kind. "Olivia, there's nothing anyone can do right now. As much as I'd like to make Simon appear, alive and well, I can't. And neither can you." She paused, then added, "You have no idea how much I wish I could help you."

Listening to Sofiya made me calmer. The boy was imaginary, a product of my grief, and the young man who came to the Pink Fancy was only a coincidental visitor. "I guess a body that can't be buried will always feel alive."

"I understand that completely."

I thought of Sofiya's mother and all the others whose graves she couldn't visit. Indeed, she did understand what I meant.

We sat together, letting the quiet settle over us. I didn't want to end the moment, to leave Sofiya, but it was late. "I suppose we should say goodnight," I said, wiping my damp eyes.

"Are you sure?"

"Yes," I replied, though I wasn't. I gazed at the path rising toward Travis's apartment. "I doubt Mother will be home tonight."

"Maybe not. Are you okay by yourself?"

"Yeah. I'll lock the doors."

We stood and hugged, both wishing to express the depth of caring we felt for each other.

Day 10

Mother stayed with Travis until early morning. I didn't sleep well, thinking every creak in the apartment marked her arrival. W he'd been upset and needed company, he didn't need my mother all night, nor was it likely they had been discussing the accident for long. I knew I was being unfair blaming her for their affair, but Travis had no marital and family commitments and my mother did. I tried to talk myself out of my anger, tossing this way and the other way, but my irritation was fully steeped by the time she finally entered the bedroom. I turned and glared at her.

"I know! I know!" She threw up her hands. "I don't want to hear about it, Olivia."

I rolled over and faced the wall. "I won't lie for you."

"I won't ask."

This conversation was more abbreviated than I expected, especially after the diatribes I'd practiced. Even though it was six o'clock, Mother made me get out of bed and apply cream on her sunburn. She then crawled under the sheets and was out like the proverbial light. Since my brain was stuck on a squirrel track, going round with all the things I wished I'd said to her, after another hour, I gave up trying to sleep, went into the bathroom, changed into my swimsuit with street clothes on top, and packed my bag with the Nikon and the exposed film, including the roll containing the photos of Travis and my mother kissing.

I waited on the porch until eight, then left the hotel. Heading toward the harbor, I still felt rough with hostility, yet as

I approached King Street, my mood softened, and I became entranced with the arcades, the curved shadows echoing their arches, and the subtle pastel colors. Few tourists were out before the shops opened, so I began taking photographs. After finishing two rolls of Kodacolor film, I wandered to the café and ordered bacon, eggs, toast, and gooseberry jam.

As I ate, I considered the impetus for my previous searches for the boy. I wanted my brother to be alive, and therefore my imagination had produced a synthetic version of him. This awareness and the substantial meal made me feel somewhat better. Renewed, I set out to shoot more pictures, and then, when the photo shop was open, I dropped my film for development, asking for two sets of prints—one batch for my mother, who would handle them with paint-stained fingers. At my request, the owner promised to develop the black-and-white film himself.

On the way to the hotel, I stopped at a pharmacy to buy rubbing alcohol to kill the conch, though the thought of drowning the poor thing was loathsome. I also purchased a bag of cotton balls to stuff the sea urchins for their perilous journey north.

When I opened the apartment door, Mother was drinking coffee and feathering an area of green vegetation in an oil pastel. She said nothing. I said nothing. After walking past her to the porch, I unscrewed the cap on the bottle of alcohol, tipped the conch, and hesitated. Finally, I decided the animal was probably half dead, and I was being kind to end its torment. I filled the shell's interior and listened to the liquid gurgling as the alcohol filtered through pockets of air within the shell.

This task done, I stripped to my bathing suit, walked outside to the gallery, placed a record on the stereo, and read my book while floating on a raft. At noon, I returned to Fantasy and was surprised to find my mother in a better temper. After we ate sandwiches, she showed me two studies and a finished drawing.

Observing my mother's creative energy encouraged me to construct my wind chime. I asked Rosita for some white string, which she gave me along with a pair of large scissors. At the porch table, I assembled everything and began by tying a section of string to the two ends of the driftwood branch, creating a hanger, then affixing four strings to the branch, each a different length to avoid symmetry. I threaded the vertical strands through the holes in the limpet shells, adding knots on the undersides to keep the shells in place. When I was finished, I brought the wind chime into the living room to show to my mother.

"I like it," she said. "Very pretty. Why don't you hang it from the molding above the door?" She handed me a thumbtack. "I might incorporate the wind chime into a drawing."

—

That night Mother and I dined at Café de Paris. Sofiya had begged off, saying she was tired, and Travis didn't accompany us because he didn't feel well—due to a physical or emotional hangover? I wanted to ask my mother about their relationship, to express concern that Travis might be prone to having brief affairs, as his wife had once believed. I also wished to discuss the car accident, but our peaceful coexistence was fragile and bringing up thorny issues would ruin the evening. Instead, we spoke about our planned car trip to the rain forest, which, surprisingly, Mother had arranged with Sofiya, and skated through the meal without a skirmish.

After dinner, we retired to the apartment. I brought the Agatha Christie paperback onto the porch, turned on the lamp, sat by the railing, and determined not to think about the boy or about Simon.

I was successful until a pebble struck the shutters. I closed the book and stood. Another stone hit below the balcony. I leaned over the railing to check the street and noticed movement in the darkness. Whether it was the blond-haired boy, a large dog, or a ghost, I wasn't certain. A shiver ran up my neck. Dogs and ghosts don't throw stones.

I turned off the light and looked again, but saw nothing.

Day 11

The rainforest was located in the northwestern part of the island. We sat in Sofiya's small Ford—me in the passenger seat and my mother sprawled in the back, her sketchbook in her lap and a box of oil pastels and pencils beside her. After driving to a station, where Mother paid for gas, we continued on into the rainforest. The road was full of potholes and ruts, jiggling us often, which amused Sofiya, who was in a jolly mood. She kept saying "Whooaa, look out!" as she avoided one tire-gobbling abyss after another. Overhead, the vast trees grew together in a thatched canopy of leaves that almost choked the sky.

My guidebook featured six illustrated pages about local vegetation, so I was able to identify the huge mahoganies, towering seventy-five feet high, their trunks ridged and scaly; the turpentine trees, with their red, flaking bark, locally called "tourist trees" because their trunks resembled peeling sunburned skin; and the breadfruit, banana, sweet lime, and mango trees. My favorite was the kapok tree, which grew to heights of eighty feet and girths of eight feet. It seemed like an enormous hand had pulled and twisted their sinewy trunks from above, stretching them like warm caramel taffy. Throughout the rainforest, snaky vines hung low, occasionally scraping the car's roof. Sofiya stopped several times so Mother could sketch and I could photograph, though whenever I stepped outside, it took a few seconds for the viewfinder and lens to clear because of the humidity.

While I was investigating the gnarled roots of a kapok tree, Sofiya called to me.

"Olivia, best get in the car!"

I turned, half expecting a tiger to come bounding through the jungle-like greenery. The instant my door was closed, rain burst through the trees as if a switch had been thrown. I rolled up the window—like Sofiya and my mother had already done with theirs—and we sat in hot silence, the damp and heat rising within the car, causing the glass to mist with condensation; outside, the windows were sheeted with rain, smearing the view into green and tawny blurs.

"I think we're cooking." Sofiya pinched her sleeveless blouse and flapped the fabric several times. "Wow! I feel like I'm in a pot of goulash."

Mother and I laughed.

When the downpour stopped, we lowered the windows, which only allowed an equal exchange of humidity and steam, yet the air temperature, at least, was slightly cooler. Because the road was awash with water, we decided to wait before continuing our drive.

Sofiya faced my mother. "Evelyn, how was Travis the other night? That must have been difficult for him—telling us about the accident."

"He was pretty upset. All the scotch didn't help."

"No, I suppose it didn't," Sofiya agreed. "He's usually so cheerful. It was a dramatic change to see him sad."

"Yes, it was," Mother said. "I was surprised."

"A real contrast to our beach picnic. Travis looked so gallant then, with his belt, knife, and olive tee shirt. Like a navy commando emerging from the ocean waving his speared fish."

Mother's expression became dreamy, picturing Travis. No doubt we all looked the same.

"I wonder why he wears a shirt when he swims. He has such a good tan that he doesn't need it." As soon as I said this, I recognized I'd made a connection no one else would follow, but a flicker of suspicion had ignited.

"Oh, that's simple," Mother said, her attention drifting from the conversation to her drawing. She picked up a pencil to darken a shadow. "He's embarrassed by the scars on his chest."

"Scars? What type of scars?" I shared a glance with Sofiya.

"From a construction site accident." Mother erased a smudge. "Travis used to be an architect. He was on a ladder, inspecting a building, and fell off. He broke several ribs and badly scuffed the skin."

"I didn't know about that," Sofiya said, "although Travis told me he was an architect in the States. He said he was tired of the profession and wanted to try something new here." She rubbed her cheek thoughtfully. "Travis has certainly had a tragic life."

"That's why he doesn't like talking about his past. He was grieving from the deaths of his wife and daughter, and then he fell and was laid up for some time and lost his job."

Another peek at Sofiya confirmed she was also distrustful of this tale regarding Travis's work-related accident. Probably, as I did, she wondered if the scars were due to the car crash. My mother didn't know about the story Travis's friend had related to Sofiya, and obviously Travis wasn't aware that his friend had shared it, so perhaps he felt safe falsifying what happened. Engrossed in her work, Mother didn't catch the looks passing between Sofiya and me.

Once most of the surface water had drained on the road, Sofiya started the engine and drove carefully through the rainforest, the car lurching as she swerved to avoid holes. I kept thinking about Travis and the information provided unwittingly by my mother, who seemed to accept that he had suffered through two separate events. However, if Travis had been in the car with his wife and daughter when they left the party, he was most likely the driver. If so, had he been intoxicated and at fault? Had Travis been fired from his job because of a fall, as he had told my mother, or was he fired because of a problem with alcohol or culpability in the deaths of his wife and daughter? If his version was a fabrication, what about his description of his wife's jealousy and his declaration about being a faithful husband? There was no way to resolve my questions short of demanding answers from him, which I wasn't going to do. Perhaps Travis was exactly the wonderful man he appeared to be, with the innocent history he described.

That evening, Travis, Mother, and I returned to Club Comanche. We ordered conch soup and lobster curry with rice pilaf; I drank iced tea while they shared a bottle of wine. Because of Sofiya's absence, I felt an urge to talk about her, which I did for some time, though Travis and my mother were attending to each other more than to me. I continued until Mother frowned to indicate I'd been overdoing my topic. I stopped and remained silent through the rest of dinner, turning my attention to Travis, admiring his happy grin and handsome features, and laughing at his stories.

—

Mother spent the night with him again. I went to bed with my book, wondering how I could be attracted to Travis—though who wouldn't be?—and still prefer to be with Sofiya. While it was true that he was dazzling, with a charismatic personality, my feelings about Sofiya were deeper and more complex, even unsettling. Too distracted to read, I laid down the paperback and pictured her large grayish-blue eyes and the special light that filled them when she looked at me. Did my eyes shine as brightly when I regarded her?

Earlier, when I learned she wouldn't join us for dinner, my mood had plummeted, despite the fact that we'd been together for hours in the car, though in my mother's company, and planned to visit Pelican Cove the following day. I'd never experienced this fascination with anyone else. Not with girlfriends, and no boy had ever caught my attention like this.

I turned off the light and stared at the ceiling. The air conditioner rumbled in the window. The room was cool but my body felt hot, as if heat was bursting through my skin. What the hell was wrong with me?

Day 12

Mother suggested we sit on the porch and have breakfast: pan-fried toast with an egg in the center, coffee, and orange juice. The morning was hot and still, with only an occasional easterly breeze. I was in a chipper mood, dressed, and anticipating an afternoon at Pelican Cove with Sofiya.

I washed our dishes and returned to the table. From her case, Mother shook out a cigarette and flicked her lighter at it, then sat straight in her chair and dropped her chin, a formal posture communicating that an unpleasant judgment was about to be rendered.

"Olivia, there is something I wish to discuss with you."

Instantly, I became alert. Feeling happy was dangerous; so was Mother whenever she slipped into omnipotent mode.

"What?"

She exhaled a cloud of smoke and waved her hand ineffectually through it, as if attempting to divert the toxic fumes.

"Well, first let me say how lovely Sofiya is. A very remarkable woman."

More warnings were shooting off. "Yes, she is." I crossed my arms, preparing for the attack.

"As much as I find her company pleasant, however, I'm worried that she isn't a proper companion for you. An occasional get-together wouldn't be a problem, of course. Or being with Sofiya when I'm with you, as we were yesterday. But I'm concerned you're becoming—and it pains me to say this—too interested in the woman." She pursed her lips in disgust. "Perhaps even a little infatuated. And, though I hope and pray I'm incorrect, she seems to regard you with an intensity that is not entirely appropriate. Particularly by an older woman."

"What?" I stared at her in horror. "You can't mean what you're saying."

"I do mean it. I think the two of you are spending too much time alone together." Mother sipped her coffee in an offhand manner, as if her demand would be met without argument. "So, please, no social engagements with Sofiya unless we've discussed them first."

"How dare you!" I said, enunciating each word. "Absolutely not! In case it's escaped your attention, Sofiya is the first real friend I've had. The only person who understands me—and that includes you."

"I understand you perfectly well. Better than you realize."

"No, you don't. You have no idea how I feel or what I think or what my life is like." Anger was rising inside me, congealing into a heady emotion.

"That's not true."

"Yes it is. And let me tell you, Mother, my life is hell because of you!"

She frowned, surprised by my sudden vehemence. "I can see from your behavior that Sofiya has influenced you against me, which is precisely what I thought."

"You ruined our relationship without any help from Sofiya!" I shouted. "All she's done is listen, be kind, and care about me. Which you have never done. Not ever."

"You're completely wrong." Mother inhaled on her cigarette and let out a white stream of smoke. "And you know it."

I jumped to my feet, no longer able to contain myself. "Liar! You've never loved me. Not like you did my brother. Don't deny it."

"That's off the subject." With studied care, she tapped the ash off of her cigarette, which seemed to interest her more than our quarrel.

"No, it isn't. It *is* the subject. Ever since Simon died, you've treated me worse than you did while he was alive. But from the first day he was born, you preferred him to me."

"Oh, dear, that's just sibling rivalry you're talking about. Every older child feels that way. What's sad is you persist in these feelings after—"

"You can't even say Simon's name, can you?" I cried, gripping the top of my chair.

"Olivia, you're becoming quite undone. Perhaps you should go into the bedroom and rest for a while, calm down a little."

"And cede the high ground to you? No! Tell me why you hate me so much."

Mother looked away and shook her head side to side, as if aggrieved. "I don't hate you. That's nonsense. Perhaps Sofiya has told you that for some purpose of her own—"

"Purpose of her own? What the hell could that be? Sofiya has no agenda—not like you do. You're jealous of her. That's the issue with Sofiya. And you should be, Mother, because she's a lot finer person than you are. Her life has been a nightmare, and yet she is a warm human being."

She took two more puffs, then stubbed out her cigarette with considerable force. Her face flushed, and her eyes hardened as she scowled at me. "This sort of insubordination is not acceptable. Sofiya has filled your head with ridiculous and dangerous notions."

"She has not!" I retorted. "But if giving me the courage to stand up for myself is her doing, well, thank you, Sofiya!"

"You are acting very badly. I wish your father could hear you."

"Oh, yeah? I wish he could hear you cooing over Travis. Or see you in bed with him. My god! Who's acting badly?" I thrust a finger at her. "You are. Dad will be thrilled to know what you've been doing, and after our conversation this morning, I'll tell him every single detail. I might even call him myself."

"You'll do no such thing, young lady!" Her eyes were now ablaze with anger. "We'll deal with everything when we return home."

"Then lay off Sofiya and leave me alone."

I thought I'd won this round, but a strangely serene expression passed over her face, which sent a chill down my back.

"I see you leave me no choice," she said in a stern voice.

I looked at her with trepidation and waited.

"First, you will not call Steven. As I said, we will talk in private—the two of us—and not with you."

"And as usual, our family is none of my business because I don't count."

"There is a proper order to do things. That order will be followed. Now, second, about Sofiya. You will see a lot less of her."

"No. We have plans to go to the beach this afternoon, and I'm going." I pushed the chair hard against the table.

Mother heaved a large sigh, which implied she was fatigued with the exchange, but in fact, it was obvious she was furious with my defiance. "You simply don't understand what's happening, do you?"

I glared at her and didn't answer.

"I suppose I have to spell it out, then." She fingered a partially withdrawn cigarette but pushed the pack away. "Well, I grant you Sofiya is an attractive woman, in her own way, though she certainly should lose some weight—"

I hooted at this. "She's fine the way she is! Not everyone needs to weigh ninety pounds." I shook my head violently. "You are so superficial. And, besides, did it ever occur to you that Sofiya is suffering emotional effects after being starved in a concentration camp?"

"I didn't know that." Mother fell silent.

"Well, now you do."

Her mouth turned down, as if she regretted saying more, yet this pseudo-reluctance was an old ploy, usually preceding the deliverance of another blow. "I'm sorry, Olivia, about what I must say."

I shrugged, waiting for Mother to unleash a new travesty. "No, you aren't."

Her face darkened, a malevolent look I'd never witnessed before. "All right, you leave me no option except to be brutally honest. What if Sofiya is one of *those* women?"

I sank back against the porch railing as if struck. "What are you talking about?"

Mother withdrew a cigarette and lit it at her leisure, inhaling slowly, her mouth curling with satisfaction. After she propped her elbow on the table, she pointed the cigarette at me. "Oh, surely you're not that naïve, are you? Come on!"

Suddenly, I felt dizzy, then sick. My thoughts from the previous night flashed through my mind, but I refused to lose my composure. "Sofiya is not that way."

"Maybe she isn't," my mother replied. "Maybe Sofiya isn't the problem at all."

I took a few steps toward the bedroom door before realizing there was an ominous insinuation embedded in her words. I spun around to face her.

Mother studied her well-shaped nails, which to me, at the moment, resembled claws. "I might have this all wrong," she said. "I certainly hope I am mistaken because it is hard to fathom how any daughter of mine could be, well, one of those types."

"Are you accusing me of something? What is it now? Huh? Loving Sofiya?" I was incensed but also felt a vague sense of shame in case I *was* one of those "types." I reminded myself this was one of Mother's tactics, mud-throwing in the hope something would stick.

"Caring for her as a friend, for someone who is so lonely and sad, that's one thing...but—"

"Lonely and sad? You are really pathetic. Who's shacking up because her ego needs fluffing? I am not listening to anything else, Mother. And as for Sofiya, I will care for her however I wish. Do you hear me?"

"Olivia—"

Enraged, I added, "And let me tell you one last thing. Caring for her is a lot easier than caring for you!"

I turned on my heel and left the porch, slamming the door. In the bedroom, I stood still for a moment and tried not to burst into tears. Uncertain where I would go, I hurriedly slipped on my sneakers and reached for my TWA bag and camera. As I did this, I noticed my hands were shaking badly, and my breathing was fast and erratic. I stuffed several tissues in my pocket, grabbed my wallet and key, and tore out of the apartment.

Rosita was sweeping near the pool, but when she saw my face, she lowered her head and said nothing. I rushed across the gallery, relieved Travis wasn't in the office and that Sofiya wasn't about—I couldn't see her until I was calmer. I took the steps fast and hurried to King Street. Tears were now flowing freely. I swiped at them, hating that my mother still possessed the ability to exploit my weaknesses. This time she had excelled, landing a direct hit where I was most sensitive: my feelings for Sofiya, and Sofiya's feelings for me. Whatever they were.

I walked along the shopping arcades. A few stores were opening, their lights illuminating their wares: crystals, jewels, clothes, watches, porcelain; all had seemed so beautiful and exotic before, but now, because of my despondent mood, everything appeared flashy and too bright. At the harbor, I collapsed on my favorite bench and stared at the sailboats rocking at their moorings, the wood masts swaying back and forth. I considered calling my father and asking him to fly me home, but I couldn't bear the thought of leaving Sofiya. Then, for a moment, I fantasized about living on St. Croix, attending high school here, and working part-time to pay my expenses. This was a ridiculous notion, but I felt happier contemplating that possibility rather than imagining what life would be like in New Jersey, with Mother goading me at every opportunity, my parents arguing and maybe divorcing, and Sofiya being so far away. Yes, we were scheduled to return next summer, but twelve months was a long time, and a great deal could happen to prevent the trip, especially with the family turmoil looming ahead.

I couldn't cry any more, not in public. Using a tissue, I dried my eyes and considered the label with which my mother had attempted to brand Sofiya and then me. Although I understood she was implying that one or both of us were homosexual, I knew little about the subject. At school, there were two boys and a girl who were taunted about being "queer," but I had assumed these were instances of teenage cruelty. The only homosexual I knew was Charles, the owner of the beauty parlor—a man I liked, whom Mother professed to adore when in his company. Yet, at my parents' cocktail parties, any mention of "gay" people was accompanied by derogatory comments or cruel jokes. Clearly, my classmates and my mother and father considered homosexuality disgusting and depraved. But my feelings for Sofiya weren't disgusting or depraved, they were the opposite: fine and good. I had no sexual interest in her, though the thought produced some anxiety. Was I blocking these desires because they were too fearful? One thing was certain. Sofiya was not this way. She couldn't be.

The other, older issue of Simon was like some type of treacherous archaeological dig, with walls that constantly threatened to collapse and suffocate me. I tried to deal with my responsibility for his death on my own, to endure the nightmares and disturbing visions, but I suspected Mother also concealed private torments, like her wish that Simon had lived and I had died and her belief I was responsible for his death. This morning, we had come within a razor's edge of confronting those issues.

The sun became intense, the heat uncomfortable. I had nothing planned except for the beach outing at one o'clock with Sofiya, which would require a foray into Mother's lair to get my bathing suit and snorkeling gear. I didn't feel strong enough to face my mother yet, so I decided to visit the photography shop and check if my prints were ready. I wore my sunglasses to hide my red eyes.

The air-conditioned store was a welcome relief, though the AC did nothing to conceal the chemical smells of developer and fixer. The owner recognized me and pulled out a thick stack of envelopes containing the prints and the paged negative sleeves.

"Did you take these?" he asked.

"Yes, sir."

"Well, you're very talented. I see a lot of tourist pictures, but many of your photographs are quite artistic. Excellent focus, exposure, and composition."

"Thank you. I hope to be a professional one day. Maybe a journalist."

"Hey, go for it," he said, grinning. "You're already good!"

Though I was still upset, his compliments pleased me. I paid for the prints and development and planned to ask my mother for more money. A number of the photos had been taken at her request plus a second set printed, so she should reimburse me. And I would need a few more dollars this afternoon for the prohibited beach outing.

In a shady area under a palm tree, I sat on a low wall and flipped open the first envelope. The owner had been correct. The photos were sharp, with almost perfect exposure, two technical areas I'd been trying to improve. Some of the images I'd taken while roaming around town were really fine—thrilling, in fact. Others, shot to provide reference for my mother, were more workmanlike, as expected. Overall, I was very happy until I came across the two black-and-white pictures of my mother and Travis kissing. Although the prints were grainy and dark, their identities were clear as was the activity. What should I do with the photographs? If Mother knew I had them, she would destroy them and might confiscate my camera. I decided not to mention my trip to the store and to ask Sofiya if I could leave the envelopes with her.

—

Travis was assisting the newlywed couple in Fertility when I passed by. He smiled and waved. I hesitated to knock on Sofiya's door because she would know I'd been crying, and I'd have to explain the tortuous argument that had transpired with my mother, yet there was no way around it. I needed to stash the prints before my mother spied them.

Sofiya answered my knock immediately, and just as immediately registered something unsettling had happened. She took my arm and led me inside. I felt as if I had entered a safe haven, a cool, dark place where my mother couldn't find me.

Sofiya showed me to a chair, poured a glass of ice water, which I drank quickly, and sat opposite, regarding me with concern. "Okay, Olivia. What has Evelyn done?"

"She was on the warpath this morning."

Sofiya gave me a questioning look. "What about?"

I exhaled slowly. "She says I can't come with you to Pelican Cove this afternoon. But I will. I'll explain everything later, when we're at the beach, if that's okay."

Her eyes widened in alarm. "Why won't she allow you to go? I don't want to cause a problem with Evelyn."

"It's complicated. She has no valid objection and may have already changed her mind," I said. "This may sound like I'm putting you on the spot, but if she absolutely refuses, I'll know when I get my gear from the apartment. Please don't worry."

Sofiya hesitated, then nodded her head. "As you wish, Olivia. I trust you to make the correct decision."

I smiled. "Thank you." I withdrew the photo envelopes from my bag. "And would it be okay if I kept these prints here for a few days?"

"Of course, but why do you need to hide your work?"

I leafed through the set of black-and-white photographs until I found the two prints. Sofiya's expression transformed from perplexed to amused.

"Oh, dear!" She covered her mouth to hide a smile. "Evelyn wouldn't be happy you took those."

"Frankly, I don't know why I did, but I don't want Mother to have them. She might get angry and destroy the rest."

"Surely she wouldn't damage your other photographs?"

"Oh, yes, she might. She broke my camera lens."

"That's true," Sofiya agreed, becoming more serious.

"Everything will be fine." I placed the prints into the envelope. "You're probably busy, but is there any chance we could go to the beach earlier?"

"I don't see why not, so long as your mother doesn't go 'on the warpath,' as you said. I'll make some sandwiches for our lunch."

—

I walked around the pool, growing more nervous as I neared our apartment. I reached for the knob with trepidation, as if touching its metal would electrocute me, and opened the door. Inside, Mother was sitting on the sofa, working. She treated me to a guarded look. Her red eyes suggested that she had shed a few tears since my departure.

Without saying a word, I entered the bedroom and removed my camera from my flight bag. Because it contained no film, I figured it was safe to leave it on the dresser. After changing into my swimsuit, I added shorts and a blouse, washed my face, combed my hair, and placed my beach things in the bag. For a few minutes, I sat on the bed, mustering courage, then marched into the living room. "I need some money for Pelican Cove."

She looked surprised. "You're not going, are you?"

"I am. I don't know when I'll be back."

Mother slowly lowered her sketchbook and laid it on the coffee table. I stood before her, trying not to appear anxious. With reluctance, she reached into her purse and handed me fifteen dollars. I thanked her and left.

—

Sofiya stood by the steps, an eyebrow raised to question whether our outing was on. I managed a smile and told her that it was. We descended the hotel's stairs and entered her rental car without saying a word. As she extricated the Ford from a tight parking spot and drove toward Pelican Cove, I felt a wave of luxurious relief wash over me. Without consciously being aware of doing so, I sighed.

"That bad?" Sofiya asked.

"Uh-huh. I guess you could say everything exploded this morning...or nearly everything. Mother always holds back a little for later use, though not much."

"And you? Did you hold anything back?" She glanced at me to see my reaction.

I chewed my lip. "Yes, I did. Because I couldn't think fast enough in the heat of battle, with all of Mother's accusations flying around."

Sofiya drove for a few miles before turning at the entrance to the beach club. "Let's get settled, and we can talk more."

The thatched-roof cabana farthest from the restaurant was vacant. We stowed our bags inside and removed our street clothes. Sofiya had prepared tuna fish sandwiches and handed me one with a soda. After we ate, we applied her lemon and olive oil concoction, pushed the chaises into the sun, and sat down. Sofiya extended her legs and crossed them; I hugged my folded knees and faced the sea.

Sofiya waited for me to speak, employing her usual tact and patience. Finally, she asked, "So, what horrible thing have I done to make Evelyn unhappy?"

I shook my head and laughed. "You've been kind."

"Hey, remind me not to be so nice. That's it?"

"Not entirely. Yes, you've been kind, but the effect of your kindness and attention is the issue. She's jealous because I enjoy your company and dislike hers, as she dislikes mine. We've had trouble for years, ever since my brother died... even before."

"The two of you are not compatible, I agree. That may change with time. What else?"

I sensed Sofiya was anticipating a more dire problem, though I doubted she expected what I was about to say. I lowered my legs and considered dashing into the water, anything to avoid relating Mother's accusation.

"My goodness!" Sofiya removed her sunglasses. "Tell me."

I rubbed my neck, then looked into her eyes and saw that she was apprehensive, which suggested she was as invested in our relationship as I was. Instead of giving me confidence to continue, her concern caused me to hesitate. How could I convey Mother's indictment of her without offending Sofiya? Or without explaining how I felt about her? Or without asking how she felt about me?

"My mother thinks we're together too much. That's why she didn't want me to come here with you."

"Hmm. I see."

"As I said, she's jealous and resentful because I'm becoming more independent. She's trying to control what I do and, at the same time, bind me to her. In order to do that, she needs to push you away or make me turn away from you."

"Even though you believe she dislikes you."

"Yeah. It doesn't make sense. Perhaps it's as simple as this—a child has a toy she no longer wants, but a second child takes that toy. The first child is furious and tries to get the toy back, even fighting for it. And when the toy is in the child's possession again, she doesn't play with it."

"Are you feeling pulled between us?" Sofiya asked.

"No, not at all. I don't wish to be Mother's possession or to be viewed as an inferior attachment to her. You treat me like a person. I feel valued by you."

Sofiya smiled. "I'm relieved to hear it. I don't want to participate in a destructive tugging match with Evelyn."

"From my point of view, you're not, Sofiya," I replied. "Now, could we swim for a while?"

"Okay, but then I want to finish the conversation because there's more, isn't there?"

I nodded.

We entered the tepid water. She swam away from the reef while I slipped on the mask and snorkel and headed alongside it. The fish were magnificent—a circus of dazzling colors and blitzing activity—but my heart was too heavy to enjoy the show. When Sofiya waded ashore and returned to the chaise, I waited a few minutes before joining her. We toweled dry, and Sofiya asked for my wallet, which she slipped in the pocket of her beach jacket along with the car keys.

"I don't want to leave anything valuable here," she said, "because we're going for a walk."

We headed away from the cabana, strolling around the curve of the beach. This section was deserted, with no swimmers or beachgoers in sight. Small waves scrolled onto the white sand; palm fronds swayed overhead, split with gold sunlight when the breeze blew; a few birds called to each other. We walked along the sand but didn't reach for any shells, nor did we speak. It seemed as though the two of us had entered a new zone, allied yet uneasy.

At last, I stopped, as did Sofiya. We looked at each other. The intensity seemed to rise between us, the space collapsing as if it didn't exist. I felt dizzy, my thoughts jumbled one on top of another, while she appeared calm, perhaps a more studied pose than a real one.

"I have to ask you something, Sofiya, and I don't know how to do it," I whispered. "And maybe I need to tell you something also, and I don't know how to do that, either."

"Go ahead. I'm listening."

I ran my fingers through my hair. Fear constricted my throat. "I don't think this is true at all, but Mother implied that you might be...different. Different, as in—"

Sofiya tucked in her chin. "Not liking men?" She gave me a relieved smile. "Is that all? You had me convinced your mother thought I was a Nazi murderer or something."

"No, nothing like that."

"Well, Olivia, she is correct that I hated my husband. However, I loved Dano, my fiancé, but between the two extremes, one wonderful man and the other so terrible as to shadow my life to this day, I've never found anyone to love since. Both memories are too painful, I suppose. No one can measure up to Dano because I've turned him into an idolized god, and I fear anyone might transform into Viktor. Now that I'm growing old, it's less likely I'll meet someone. I guess that I've pretty much lost hope." She smiled again. "So, you find me alone and grieving for the woman I once was, the woman who died in a concentration camp."

"I wish your life had been full of happiness and love. Is it really too late?" I asked.

She looked at me for a long time. "Probably. My life is what it is, and I must continue living it."

The resignation in her voice was alarming. It sounded so fatalistic and defeated. How could she maintain her sense of humor, her empathy, when she felt this way?

Sensing her response had upset me, she added, "You should know, dear Olivia, that meeting you has been such a heavenly gift. But you understand that, don't you?"

"I do, yes," I replied. "I feel the same."

"I know. How you feel shows on your face, in your eyes," Sofiya said quietly.

The simplicity of her words touched me. I felt known; I felt I knew her.

We were silent until Sofiya spoke.

"I believe your mother was feeling rather desperate this morning. As you described so clearly, it might be a toy situation. If she can remove me from the equation, she can have the toy, which is you. Some people become upset when they're threatened—or they imagine a threat—and will use any means to keep the upper hand." Sofiya regarded me intently. "And as for being different? Sadly, Evelyn, like so many others, is confined within a narrow perspective. People love each other in a variety of ways. Who they choose to love may not always be the person society deems the correct choice. But, ultimately, we must be true to ourselves and be open to whatever happens, to a person who inspires a passionate reaction, a person with whom we feel a powerful understanding. Race, sex, background, religion—those don't matter. Love is an emotion that must be free and light, without boundaries." Here, Sofiya chuckled. "I sound like a philosopher."

I thought about what she said and realized Sofiya had not absolutely put to rest my initial question—was she different? But after listening to her lengthy commentary, I decided it didn't matter. She hadn't been offended, which was a huge relief, nor had she been defensive, which told me she was comfortable with who she was.

"A philosopher like Plato? Didn't he write about love in *The Symposium*?"

"You've read it?"

"Last year. In English class, as an extra-credit project."

"Then you know Plato discussed the subject at length. Such as about the four different types of love—*eros*, *philia*, *storge*, and *agape*. Plato believed that physical or sexual love, *eros*, isn't the highest form of love. In fact, he wrote that *eros* was a manic, fiery, irrational desire, a type of madness. *Agape* is more significant—a brotherly love, what one feels for a child or a friend, or what is felt between any two people when a pure, non-physical—"

"A platonic love..."

"Yes, when a platonic love exists. This love is selfless. It's about great affection, charity, empathy, and a shared appreciation of beauty."

"And this is what we are experiencing?"

"That's what is between us. Because we share affinities. Do you agree?"

"I suppose so," I replied, thinking about *eros* and my undeniable excitement whenever I saw Sofiya. I wanted to ask if *agape* could produce that reaction, but she continued.

"Now, earlier, you said there was something you needed to tell me, but you didn't know how to do it."

I'd hoped this remark had been forgotten. Suddenly, I was anxious again. "It's nothing."

"Oh, yeah? Doesn't seem like nothing, Olivia. It's okay. Please tell me."

"Well, mostly we just covered it in the Plato discussion—the feelings that exist in our relationship, that have existed from the beginning. In fact, it almost seems like we were fated to meet here on St. Croix."

"Perhaps we were."

"The problem is I can't forget Mother's insinuation. That more is happening between us. She thinks...that I'm infatuated with you."

Sofiya frowned. "Oh, dear. That word carries such a negative connotation. Like our friendship is one-sided and superficial, and your side is not very mature."

"I know. I felt insulted, which was the purpose of her comment."

"So we agree Evelyn was being destructive as well as inaccurate?"

"Probably."

"But you still sound troubled."

"A little. I can't explain how I feel about you, Sofiya. It's like nothing I've ever experienced before. I want to be with you, to laugh and cry and go swimming, to walk on the beach as we are now. Even the simplest activity means more when you're with me."

"Which is exactly what I said earlier."

I nodded. "Is that why I feel so happy when we're together?"

Sofiya sighed. "I think so, yes. Finding someone who understands and cares is exciting. You are not alone in these feelings."

"I'm not?"

"No," she replied. "You've made a big difference to my mood and outlook since I've known you. I won't say otherwise, even to please your mother."

"Really?"

"Really."

There was a lengthy pause. I became aware of how much I wanted to touch Sofiya's cheek. From the warmth of her expression, I sensed she was experiencing strong emotions, too. Words hovered between us, unspoken.

She gave me an affectionate smile. "Now, if it would help, I'll speak to Evelyn. Reassure her that nothing *different* is going on. Of course, something different is happening, just not in the way she's implied."

"Maybe that would be a good idea."

Sofiya nodded. "So we're okay? Have you told me everything?"

"Yeah."

She placed her hand on my shoulder. "We will continue as we have."

With this, we turned and walked toward the cabana, pocketing a few shells as we went.

—

At the Pink Fancy, I watched from across the pool as Sofi-ya knocked on our door and disappeared inside to face the lioness. I would have given anything to overhear what was being said and very much hoped my mother would be polite, respectful, and reasonable. About twenty interminable minutes passed, and Sofiya emerged, smiling, and joined me at the round table.

"I think I've cleared up Evelyn's misconceptions. She's invited me to have dinner with you tonight at The Buccaneer. Quite a grand hotel, with a great view and restaurant, or so I've heard."

I was astonished. "My mother is difficult to predict."

"You're right, but sometimes a direct approach works. At least it works when age is not a factor."

"And you're not her daughter."

Sofiya chuckled at this. "Actually, Olivia, I think Evelyn was quite upset about what she said this morning."

"She'll never admit that to me."

"No, she probably won't, unfortunately. She doesn't seem to be the apologetic sort, which makes it hard for you," Sofiya said. "Evelyn didn't tell me much, but I asked about her side of your argument so she felt someone was listening, though I didn't broach certain issues, and I didn't imply solidarity with her. Perhaps the conversation helped."

"Is that all you can tell me?"

"For now, yes. Just know that Evelyn regrets her comments and will try to be more understanding," she replied. "I'll see you later, and we'll have a lovely evening."

When I cautiously opened the door, Mother was sitting in the chair, waiting. No cigarette was burning—a positive sign—and she seemed more relaxed. She explained that Sofi-ya had been forthright in her appraisal of our friendship.

"We'll let the matter drop, if that's acceptable to you, Olivia."

And how! I was amazed by the sorcery Sofiya had conjured and fervently wished I could borrow her magic wand to wave over Mother whenever I needed it.

She mentioned the night's outing at the restaurant and said, "Why don't you wear that pretty new dress we bought at Cavanagh's?"

I agreed and headed for the shower, the cool water relieving my sunburn and my anxiety. After I brushed and dried my hair and gathered it with a gold clip, I donned the sleeveless, cotton dress printed with turquoise, green, and white flowers. With my deep tan, I looked about as good as I ever had. White sandals completed the outfit. Mother wore her emerald green dress, high heels, a gold necklace and earrings, and radiated glamour.

"Travis will be impressed," I said. "He is coming, isn't he?"

"Yes, of course."

When we walked outside, Travis saw us and whistled. "Wow! You both look sensational." He examined Mother and me from head to foot, made us turn, and laughed. "I'm a lucky fellow to escort such beautiful ladies."

He was dressed in navy slacks, a blue linen jacket, starched white shirt, and a silk tie that almost matched my mother's green dress. Mother made him do a twirl, too, which he did grinning happily, his arms raised like a prima ballerina. Sofiya came down the path, elegant in an aqua suit, white silk blouse, and a pearl necklace and earrings, which were probably her grandmother's. Her hair was swept up and fastened with a broad black barrette.

I realized I was staring at her as if Travis and my mother didn't exist. *Agape* or *eros*?

We piled into Travis's car. He drove east around Christiansted, then north, up the hill. The Buccaneer was composed of tiered arcades painted seashell pink topped by a white roof. Numerous outbuildings were scattered on the grounds, as was an old sugar mill, which Travis said had been part of a mid-1700s factory. In the spacious lobby, I was instantly drawn to a square oak table, a kind of enormous specimen box topped by glass. Inside, lying on a layer of white sand, were dozens of shells, sea urchins, brain and elkhorn corals, sea fans, and stuffed fish. If Christmas would be celebrated this year, if my father would be around to help me, I decided to have a smaller version built for my mother's Christmas present, with the shells and coral we had collected displayed on black velvet.

We sat outside on the patio, surveying the half-circle beach below, which was fringed with several rows of mature palm trees. Near our table, a calypso band was setting up their instruments. Everyone ordered banana daiquiris.

Sofiya sat across from me. She looked stunning in her suit, but I was drawn to the notched lapels of her blouse. They crossed below her neck, draped like two caressing hands, and gave an impression of elegant gentleness reminiscent of Sofiya herself. Even Mother complimented Sofiya on her outfit and pearls, the ultimate accolade from the priestess of fashion. She also asked Sofiya friendly questions, executing a tasteful charm offensive with no detectable undertones of animosity. For the millionth time, I was astounded by Mother's changeable behavior, from morning harridan to evening enchantress.

Travis was his usual compelling self, teasing my mother and flirting, but more discreetly than during our last dinner. The food was excellent—grilled fish and local vegetables. When the band started to play, Travis danced with my mother first, then took Sofiya in his arms. I watched with interest, perhaps a tiny amount of envy. She seemed to be a graceful and confident dancer, neither of which I was, though when it was my turn with Travis, I didn't mangle his well-shod toes. Everyone enjoyed the infectious music and several rounds of drinks.

—

Upon our return to the Pink Fancy, we gathered at the round table and drank the last of our gold rum. Eventually, Travis and my mother left for his apartment, and Sofiya and I retired to hers so I could show her my color photographs. Inside, the overhead light was garish, and we both squinted like moles emerging from underground burrows.

"Ohhh!" Sofiya moaned, shading her eyes with her hand. "Where are my sunglasses?"

I laughed. We sat side by side and opened the envelopes. Sofiya examined each print carefully, preferring the ones that I did. Like the shop owner, she thought the composition and the technical aspects of the photographs were accomplished. We were well into the packet of market pictures when I stopped at one image. Amid the numerous people milling around the fruits and vegetables was the blond boy, his face blurred, as if he had turned away. To avoid having his photograph taken?

Sofiya glanced at me. "What's the matter?"

The boy was real. He had been standing about twenty feet from me. In the crowded picture, his head was small, which was why I'd missed him on first viewing the prints.

I tapped the image. "This guy reminds me of my brother." But was it a stranger or was it Simon?

"Really? The picture isn't very clear." Sofiya scrutinized the photo. "His hair is the same color as yours."

"Yes, like Simon's. I haven't had a close look at him, but I think he's about my age and slightly taller than I am."

"Really? You're how tall?"

"Five foot eight."

"You don't get that from your mother."

I smiled. "No, I take after Dad."

"Have you seen this young man before?"

"Yes, several times. On the street below the Club Comanche, in a taxi, and on Prince Street several nights ago. When I was standing on the porch."

"And that evening when we were walking to the Stone Balloon?"

I nodded, impressed she remembered. "Anyhow, it's strange that I keep seeing this boy. He's always at a distance, and when I run after him, he disappears."

"You've followed him, Olivia?" Sofiya asked, her voice rising with concern.

"Well, yes, but he just seems to evaporate."

Sofiya checked the photograph again and frowned. "Even if he does resemble your brother, please be careful and don't assume he's a well-behaved young man. There are all sorts here. Some are involved with drugs and crime."

I hadn't mentioned Travis's report about the boy who had wandered into the hotel. Before I could tell her that, Sofiya asked if my mother was returning to the apartment later.

"I don't know. She's been sleeping with Travis. Most likely she won't show up until tomorrow morning."

A worried look passed over Sofiya's face. "You'll lock the doors, right?"

"Of course. I'll be fine."

Sofiya nodded and clasped her hands together. "You know what? This is crazy, but I'd love a quick swim before bed. What do you think?"

I liked the idea and said so.

"Good. Go change and I'll meet you outside."

As I crossed through the gallery, my heart overflowed with happiness. I stood for a moment to appreciate how the spotlights illuminated the pool and how the lights set under the deck's overhang, just above the waterline, added to the glowing magic. I thought about my nighttime swimming fears that had erupted after Simon's death in the river and was relieved tonight's experience would be different because Sofiya would be with me.

After removing the key from my pocket, I opened the door. The living area was dimly lit from the exterior porch lamp, which I had left on earlier, and the apartment was warm. For a second, I felt a rush of dread as something clattered, then laughed at myself. It was my wind chime in the open doorway, blowing in a soft breeze, the limpet shells throwing tiny shadows on the floor below.

Walking through the semi-dark bedroom, I entered the bathroom, closed the door, used the facilities, and removed my damp bathing suit from a hook in the shower. As I did so, there was a noise, either in the bedroom or on the porch. Probably a gust of wind banging the chimes against the door frame. I listened again. Floorboards creaked. My mother had returned.

The sounds stopped. I stepped out of the bathroom, but she wasn't there. Scared, I stopped, too, and dropped my suit on the bed. I sensed the presence of another human being, but this couldn't be the case. My overactive imagination, amplified by several drinks, some high-proof rum, and my potent conversation with Sofiya was distorting my perception.

I slipped off my sandals and cautiously edged past the twin beds, pausing a few feet from the open door to the porch. I saw no unusual shadows, heard no footsteps. There was no reason to be spooked because the front door had been locked. But then I remembered the downspout. It ran from the roof to the cistern below, with brackets attached that could serve as a ladder to the balcony. Had the boy climbed it? Or had Simon?

I held my breath and crept to the doorway. No one was sitting at the table. I stepped onto the porch, and as I turned to check the bed, a black-clothed arm suddenly lassoed my neck.

"So here you are," whispered a male voice. He tightened the pressure against my throat, grabbed my waist, and crushed his body against my back. "We meet at last."

I saw a flash of blond hair but couldn't see his face. "Let go!" I cried, trying to pry loose his grip.

He forced us to the edge of the bed and threw me upon it. Instantly, I flipped over, and instantly I was terrified. The teenage boy I beheld was not Simon—looked nothing like my brother. His asymmetrical features were strangely contorted: thin, pliable lips twisted in an uneven sneer and one eyebrow cocked higher.

"What do you want?" I demanded.

"Ask yourself that. First, you photographed me—"

"I did not!"

"Oh, yeah, you did. In the market."

"I just photographed the local people selling things."

"Where's the film?"

"At the photo shop, but I didn't take your picture."

His expression relaxed slightly. Then, his small brown eyes darkened. "Okay, so how come you've been following me? And parading up here every night? Like a cat in heat?"

He took a step closer. I edged backward on the bed, real-izing what he wanted. Before I could scream for help, he was on top of me, covering my mouth with his left hand. With his right, he began pulling up the hem of my dress, his fingers on my thigh. I tried to shove him off, but he was determined. We fought, twisting side to side. With effort, I freed my hand, swung wide, and punched his ear. Stunned, he jerked away.

"Damn you!" He removed his hand from my mouth and pinned my wrists against the bed.

"Stop it!" I shouted.

His eyes were wild. "Come on, girl, you want this!" He leaned down to kiss me.

I bit his lip. He yowled as blood spurted from his mouth. He tried again, but I wrestled us onto the floor. Our faces brushed as we fell, smearing my cheek with his blood. He unzipped his pants, then reached up and tore my dress and seized my breast. Fear shot through me like sizzling lightning.

I tilted my hips violently, throwing him against the balco-ny wall. He cursed and gathered himself to stand, but I was quicker to rise to my knees. With the heel of my hand, I thrust upward, crunching his nose. He cried out and his fingers flew to his face. Blood seeped between them.

"You bitch!"

I staggered to my feet. My breath was coming in sharp rasps.

He was mad with fury. As he drew himself up, I saw the scissors I'd used to assemble the wind chime and grabbed them from the table. Suddenly, he sprang forward and landed a powerful blow on the side of my head. I slammed against the wall, and he closed in, his hands curling around my throat, blood whipping off his face onto mine. Gripping the scissors, I stabbed him in the side as hard as I could. His eyes widened, and he grunted in pain. I twisted the scissors and pulled them out. Slowly, he crumbled to the floor. I stared at his body, prepared to strike again. The boy didn't move.

I looked down at my ripped dress—the scarlet on the turquoise, green, and white flowers—and the bright red on the silver scissors. The porch seemed to gyrate, and I retreated a few feet, staring at the still figure before stumbling into the bedroom and bashing into the dresser. I fell hard on one knee, but clutched a chair for support, rose, and glanced back at the porch.

The boy was gone. In a panic, I edged to the living room doorway and peeked inside, positive he was there, waiting. The room was empty, but through the other porch door, I saw his black figure escaping over the railing. I dropped the scissors and rushed out of the apartment. Took fast strides across the gallery and dove headlong into the pool, landing flat. My brain exploded with the shock of hitting the water. I lay face down, willing myself to drown. Then, I saw Simon. Simon running to the end of the dock. The black river. "You killed me!" Simon shouted. His face merged into the boy's twisted sneer. "You want this!" the boy screamed.

I desired nothing more than to breathe in water. Part of me insisted it was air. Part of me knew better. My body seemed weighted with despair, sinking, the water closing around me so that soon I would be consumed, and everything would end. Then, I heard someone calling out, sounds of splashing. Hands grasped my shoulders, turned me over. Stars and lights were spinning above me.

"Olivia!"

I struggled to free myself. I saw the boy's fierce eyes, his bleeding mouth. "No!" I shrieked.

"Take it easy." A soothing voice. Sofiya's. "I'm here."

I took a deep breath and moaned. Allowed her to pull me close. My head fell against her chest.

"Put your arm around my neck."

I did. Everything was in slow motion as Sofiya half-carried me across the pool, murmuring softly.

By the stairs, she told me to stand. I placed my feet on the bottom and tried to balance, holding onto the railing and Sofiya.

"That's it, good." She continued to support me as we stepped from the pool to the round table. After I slumped into one of the chairs, Sofiya stared at my torn and bloody dress. "My god, what happened?"

I began to shiver. "The boy."

She swiftly wrapped her towel around my body. "The one in the photograph?"

I nodded. "In our apartment. He left…he's gone."

"Are you hurt? Do you need a doctor? The police?"

I shook my head. "Just you." I looked up at her. "Please."

"Shall I get your mother?"

"No." I gestured toward Sofiya's door and tried to stand. My legs were quaking so badly that I needed help to walk up the path and climb the stairs. Once inside her dark room, I leaned on the kitchen table. My teeth began to chatter.

Sofiya rushed to turn off the air conditioner. "Let's get you out of these wet clothes." She removed the towel, unzipped the back of my dress, unfastened my bra, and eased off my damp things, replacing them with a terry robe. Her hands were warm, sure, comforting. Using a towel, she dried my face, neck, and hair. My shivering increased.

"You're in shock, Olivia." Sofiya switched on the dim stove light, opened the refrigerator, poured some orange juice, and gave me the glass.

I drank, all the while focusing on Sofiya, who had become my only connection to the real world. As the chills grew worse, she led me to one of the twin beds and wrapped the spare spread around my body. Quickly, she hurried into the bathroom to remove her bathing suit and returned in a house dress, joining me on the bed. Sofiya placed her arms around me and kept saying everything was okay, but it wasn't. I was so cold! I burrowed my head into the curve of Sofiya's shoulder, and the room seemed to go black. Pictures began sprinting through my mind. Fists, bloody faces, silver scissors coated in red, and beyond those images, Simon, the fast-moving river, my bleeding foot.

"He's dead!" I cried.

"Who is?"

"I don't know...the boy...Simon..."

"You said the boy escaped."

My brother and the boy were fusing and separating, one with blue eyes, the other with brown eyes, their features, their faces flipping back and forth. The dock became the porch, the porch became the dock. My brother was running. The boy dissolved into darkness. "Simon, stop! Wait!" I squeezed my eyes closed. Saw Simon's blond head silhouetted against the night sky, the blond-haired boy above me, felt him pressing into my body, tearing at my dress.

Sofiya rocked us gently, speaking in a low voice, telling me I was safe. I clung to her, desperate for the tumultuous visions to vanish.

"Simon's at the end of the dock. Turning, shouting, 'Come on!'" I groaned. "I can't! My foot. The nail. Help me!"

"Sshh, Olivia. It's all right."

The images froze, as they always did here. Like the film unspooled or snapped. But this time, the film started again. Simon was leaning the fishing pole against a piling. He called my name and rushed toward me. Gladness filled my heart. He was alive! He was coming to help! My breathing grew faster, excited and frightened, as I slid down the chute of memory. And then I saw the bag of cat food ahead on the dock where I'd dropped it. I shouted at him, but a curtain descended. As it lifted, there was the dock, the black river gushing underneath. "Where is he?" I gasped, opening my eyes. Tears poured down my face. "I can't see Simon!"

Sofiya tightened her embrace. Her perfume mixed with the smell of salt from the river and from the blood and the acrid odor of creosote from the dock.

"He's gone! I killed Simon. I killed him!"

"Olivia! You didn't...he fell. It's not your fault."

"No!" I wailed. "I made him come to me. I murdered my brother!"

Shattered by this revelation, I clamped my eyes shut and sobbed. As I did, I instantly flew back into that swirling night. The cold rising from the river. The white-hot pain searing my ankle. My hands thrust hard against the boards of the dock, and my arms quailing from the effort to keep my body upright. Desperate to save Simon, I shoved upward with all my strength and ripped the nail loose. I felt the pain, the flesh tearing, and moaned.

Sofiya stroked my head. In silence, we swayed back and forth. My breath was ragged, as if my lungs had partly collapsed. "Oh, Simon. Oh, Simon...you're gone." Uttering this, I realized this was true. My brother was dead. I would never see him again. The connection that had stretched over eight years had been severed. No longer would I visit the river on spring nights.

As this awareness sank into my being, I began to cry harder, slowly at first, until the sobs wracked my body. I wept and wept until no more tears came. Exhausted, I lay slack against Sofiya's breast, her arms holding me, and opened my eyes. She reached for tissues from a box on the table and handed some to me.

I straightened to use them and whispered, in a voice cracked with emotion, "I couldn't remember the ending...until now. Sofiya, I tried so many times."

"I know. I know," she said. "Tell me."

I bunched the tissues in my fist, blew out a tense breath, and related every detail that I had always recalled and those I now remembered. "After I freed myself, my foot was really bleeding. I'm not sure how I got off the dock, but I did. All I remember is crawling up the cliff, then limping through the woods using a branch as a crutch. Oh my god! I was so cold! And it seemed to take forever to get to the house...to the laundry room...to get help for Simon."

"You poor dear child. You were so brave."

"Mother came and turned on the light. The room was very bright."

"What else?"

I shook my head. "I don't know. I think we drove in the car to the river."

"Sometimes we forget when the pain is too great," Sofiya said. "But, Olivia, you didn't hurt Simon. It was an accident."

"He was my little brother." A spasm passed through me, and Sofiya renewed her embrace. "I was responsible."

"You were a small child yourself. Simon tripped or a board broke. You were helpless to prevent his fall into the river."

I stared at her, dazed. "Mother blames me."

Sofiya thought for a moment. "Maybe she does. A tragic accident, the death of a child. Your mother needed to blame someone. It's too difficult to accept that bad things happen without a reason." She paused before adding, "And perhaps Evelyn couldn't deal with her own guilt."

Sofiya's face was lit by the faint light from the kitchen. I grasped that she was saying something significant. "I don't understand."

"You said your parents' bedroom was in another part of the house, right?"

I nodded. "They bought the place when I was five."

"Which separated your parents from you and Simon, even though you were very young children. They placed their wishes above your welfare."

I had never thought about this before. "My parents didn't know when we left the house at night. Not that time or the many times after Simon died when I went to the river alone, trying to reenact the scene, hoping to recall exactly what happened."

"Or to magically create a different outcome?" Sofiya suggested.

My brain swirled with confusion. Slowly, her words solidified into sense. "Yes, I suppose so. If I walked to the river through the dark forest, which terrified me, it was a kind of penance. And, maybe by doing this, I could make Simon return, alive." As I said this, I knew Sofiya was right. This was what I had unconsciously believed.

We said nothing for a while, then her forehead creased with concern. In a quiet voice, she asked about the boy.

Her question made my head spin. My ears seemed to fill with water, like I was once again submerged in the pool. "I can't talk about him..."

Sofiya held me, patiently waiting. "Tell me, Olivia. Otherwise tonight will become like the night of Simon's death. Only half remembered."

I lowered my head into the safety of her shoulder. Resistance buffeted me like a powerful headwind. I swallowed hard, fighting to speak. "Ever since Simon's death, I've had nightmares and flashes of memories about my brother. When I saw this guy who looked like him—on the first night we were here—I thought the nightmares had become hallucinations. Or that Simon hadn't really died and was now living on St. Croix, haunting me because of what I'd done. I thought I was going crazy."

"You must have been so upset, so tortured." Sofiya smoothed my hair. "I wish I'd known before now. Maybe I could have helped."

"You did, Sofiya." I pulled a few inches away to be sure she believed me. When she nodded, I continued. "Anyway, I kept seeing this guy in town, but he always disappeared. In the market, he must have noticed when I took his photograph, though I was unaware of him. And then, one night, I was sitting by the porch railing, and he passed below. We looked at each other, but it was too dark to see his face. By the time I ran down the steps after him, he was gone. After that, I was so stupid! I left the light on and sat outside, hoping the boy would return. Maybe he did. And maybe he took this as an invitation. Travis also told me that a blond-haired young man came to the hotel but left when Travis spoke with him."

"So it was this boy who attacked you?"

"Yes. On the porch. I went out there because I heard someone. He grabbed me from behind and threw me on the bed."

"Oh, no..."

"We wrestled. He pushed up my dress, tore the top, and unzipped his pants." I began crying again. "I knew what he was going to do." In a rush, words flooded out, as I described what occurred afterward.

"I can't believe this! Did he—"

I shook my head. "He tried, but, no, he didn't succeed. I was strong enough to stop him...and, luckily, I found a pair of scissors on the table."

"Thank goodness! My dear, dear girl."

She was quiet, though I felt tension in her arms. I looked up and saw tears streaming down her cheeks. She was affected by my story but also by something else.

"Sofiya?"

"I am so sorry." She blew out a long-held breath. "I understand."

Although I was deeply shaken, I made the connection. "This happened to you?" I whispered.

"Yes." She wiped tears away, but they kept falling. "I'll tell you sometime..."

"Please, Sofiya."

"I don't know if I should...if I can."

"I need you to explain." My eyes didn't waver from hers. "It was at Ravensbrück, wasn't it?"

She appeared on the verge of refusing, but my expression may have changed her mind.

"Very well. Yes, at Ravensbrück." She loosened one hand and plucked a tissue from the box. After drying her tears, she cleared her throat. "As I told you, Viktor and I had dinner." Sofiya paused; her gaze left mine and wandered restlessly around the dark room, as if she preferred to focus on nothing real or concrete.

"Yes?"

Sofiya inhaled, then let the air slowly release. "And afterward...he raped me."

"What?" My hand flew to my forehead. "He did?" I searched for some words of empathy, to express my support, but her confession had startled me.

Her voice broke. "And raped me the following night and for weeks."

"What a bastard!"

"Yes, he was." She went silent and, once again, turned away. Her mouth trembled, as if struggling to contain a scream of pain or a sob of anguish.

I gave her shoulder a gentle shake. "Please, tell me more?"

"I knew he would hurt me or worse, so I let him do it." This admission was delivered in a whisper. "I didn't fight him."

"You didn't?" I already knew Sofiya had become pregnant, yet I'd naïvely assumed she had agreed to have sex with Viktor and was ashamed of consorting with a Nazi. Instead, he had used his power and attacked her, and she was ashamed of not defending herself.

She closed her eyes. In a flat tone, she said, "I told him no. I pleaded with him. I begged him and I cried. But that's all."

I tried to imagine allowing the boy to rape me without trying to stop him. "That's still rape."

Sofiya opened her eyes. Her response was tentative. "Yes."

"He could have had you killed. You made the wise choice."

"Did I?" A fresh tear fell. "Or did I save myself? Was I willing to give in to my enemy so maybe I could have another fine dinner? And more champagne?" she asked bitterly. "Did I somehow encourage Viktor? So that he kept at me, night after night? And then, when I became pregnant, so he would marry me and take me away from Ravensbrück?"

"You would have died in the camp."

She stared at me. Her anger, shame, and sadness mixed with my own emotions.

"Yes, like all the others. Those women and children who couldn't escape. Who were dying, sick, too old or young or too unattractive to interest a man like Viktor. The ones that never had a chance to sell themselves to save their lives."

I brought my fingers to her face and caressed her cheek, removing the tears that had fallen. "What else could you have done?"

Sofiya let out a tremulous breath and didn't offer a defense. "I loathed that man. I never understood why he chose me. Why he would marry a prisoner, a Czech, who the Nazis considered an inferior race. But Viktor did care, even though he knew I agreed to go with him to escape the camp. That makes what I did later even worse."

"What do you mean? Marrying Viktor?"

She shook her head. "No. I mean in Berlin. In the end."

"You told me the Americans caught him and that he hung himself in prison."

"Yes, but what I didn't tell you was how he was caught." Sofiya searched my face, perhaps hoping to find reassurance that I was with her. I nodded and her eyes softened. "After the Germans surrendered, Viktor was hiding with me in his parents' home. He had purchased fake Swiss passports so we could flee the country. The morning he shared his plan, I convinced him to let me go out, to find food—he was afraid to appear in public because he might be seen and recognized by the Americans, who administered our quarter of Berlin. As soon as I was away from him, I rushed to their command post and reported Viktor's activities in Poland at the concentration camp. Viktor was arrested, charged with crimes against humanity, and held for trial."

I placed my arm around Sofiya's neck and pulled her close. "It was the right thing to do."

"But he saved my life!" she cried. "And I thanked him by destroying his."

I thought of Sofiya living in the basement of a bombed building. "You took a risk reporting your husband, didn't you? If he had escaped and learned of your betrayal—"

"He would have killed me. Yes, I'm sure of that," she replied. "Yet, I felt an obligation to my country, my family, to atone for...well...to atone." Sofiya drifted off and didn't fully explain what she meant.

"How did you survive afterward? You were by yourself."

"I was. Fortunately, the Americans offered me a job."

A prolonged silence spiraled between us, the stillness absorbing the anguish we each had expressed. I relaxed my embrace. "We all feel guilty about something, don't we? You, me, Travis, and my mother."

"We do. And I suppose we need to forget that guilt and move on." As she said this, I heard the discouragement in her voice, though she tried to conceal it with a faint smile. "It will take a long while to get over what occurred tonight and with your brother, but I hope you can."

"I hope you can, too, Sofiya."

"I'll try," she whispered without conviction. After drying the last of her tears, she asked if I was better.

"Yes, I think so." I didn't want to end this moment, to separate from Sofiya, but I let go and moved to the edge of the bed. Instantly, I missed the physical closeness.

She seemed to feel the same way and laid her hand on my shoulder. "Olivia, if you're ready, we should telephone Travis and have him call the police. The boy needs to be found and arrested. All right?"

I turned to look at Sofiya. "I don't want to see anyone, especially my mother."

"I know. But you must. If you want to spend the night here, that's fine. I can explain you're unable to be in the apartment. Is that agreeable?"

"Yes. Just don't leave me alone with her. Please."

"I won't," she promised. After a brief hesitation, she walked to the phone in the kitchen.

—

Travis knocked on Sofiya's door and entered, his expression grave, his arms full of clothes, my flight bag and camera, and sneakers, all of which Sofiya had requested he bring from the apartment. He placed everything on the table, sat on the bed, and embraced me.

"Olivia, are you okay?"

I drew back and studied his concerned face, lit by the light from the kitchen lamp, and nodded.

"Thank goodness! I'm so sorry!"

Sofiya came to stand beside us. "Any signs of the boy?"

"No, the police and I just checked the apartment and outside on the street. Don't worry, they'll find him. This is a small town. Not that many blond-haired young men are roaming around."

"And he's wounded," I added.

"We saw blood on the railing and downspout, but I'll tell Chief Larsen," Travis said. "And speaking of him, he's waiting to talk with you. Are you able to answer some questions?"

I nodded again.

Travis glanced at Sofiya, then at me. "Evelyn is there, too. Sofiya says you're not sure you want to see her, but I hope you will. She's very upset."

"Okay, Travis. I'll come out in a minute."

Feeling unsteady, I stood and slowly unwrapped the bedspread. Travis took my elbow and helped me across the room to the table. After an anxious look at Sofiya, he left. I selected some clothes and walked into the bathroom, whereupon I encountered a reflection in the mirror that was absolutely shocking. Purple and red bruises covered my neck, face, and arms. My eyes were bloodshot from crying. I looked haunted and fearful. Holding onto the sink, I washed, then dressed, all the while staring at myself, afraid that if I glanced away, I might shatter.

When I emerged from the bathroom, Sofiya had replaced her house dress with slacks and a long-sleeve blouse. Her arms were wrapped around her body as if she were cold.

"Can you do this?" she asked.

"I guess so."

Sofiya opened the door. I stepped outside, feeling exposed. Immediately, my mother rushed up the path and hugged me. She had been crying and began to cry again.

"This is my fault, Olivia! If I had been there, nothing would have happened to you. I'll never forgive myself!"

She continued apologizing and holding me. I was so weary that I could barely stand. Sofiya realized this and led us to the table, where the police chief waited with a second policeman. Once we were seated, Mother laced her fingers through mine, and Sofiya took a chair on my other side, laying a reassuring hand on my back. Travis positioned himself behind us.

The police chief, a Crucian, introduced himself as Clifford Larsen. He was soft-spoken and possessed a presence and a powerful physique that inspired confidence. He and the other officer, also an islander, began writing down my account, including a description of the boy, his clothing, and the locations where I'd seen him in Christiansted. When I related the details of the attempted rape and physical struggle, my mother shook her head repeatedly, as if to erase what she was hearing.

At the end of my story, Chief Larsen assured us that my attacker would be captured. He said the hospital and local doctors had been alerted in case the boy sought medical treatment and explained that a team was taking fingerprints and blood samples from the balcony. Then, he instructed the policeman to collect my torn dress. After we finished, he clasped my shoulder and promised to return in the morning.

Once the policemen left, Mother insisted I stay with her for the remainder of the night, but Sofiya prevailed, saying I didn't want to sleep in the apartment.

"I meant we could go to another hotel," Mother offered.

I refused.

"Are you sure?"

"Yes, I am. I want to remain with Sofiya."

She wasn't happy with my decision but reluctantly agreed. "Okay, well, I'll be with Travis if you need me."

After everyone was gone and we returned to Sofiya's apartment, she locked the door, then donned a nightgown and her robe while I changed into the pajamas Travis had brought. She made hot tea and toast, and we sat at the table, talking about Chief Larsen, the attack, and a little more about Simon.

When we had finished eating, I wiped my mouth with a napkin. "I've told you so much tonight. Thank you for being there." I hesitated for a moment. "But I also want to thank you for telling me about your life. How you endured the camp and what happened with your husband—I have no idea how you lived through it, though I understand why you made the choice you did." After I said this, Sofiya stared at the table, her mouth twisting slightly. More emphatically, I added, "Your death wouldn't have helped anyone."

She raised her eyes to mine. Her tanned face had grown pale; its usual animation transformed into an unreadable stoicism. Had she accepted my point or had she discounted my words? A silence ensued, which made me uncomfortable.

Sofiya took a swallow of tea. "Olivia, very few people know I was at Ravensbrück or married to Viktor—or how I came to marry him." She pushed the cup away. "And I've never confided in anyone about the rape. Never. I've always felt ashamed that I lived with him rather than stay in the camp. As for reporting my husband, only the American authorities were aware of what I did." She paused, then continued. "And that I rewarded Viktor's gift with betrayal, essentially killing him. Maybe it's like I said before—if you come close to a monster, you begin to think you are a monster, too, and others will see you that way."

"I don't. You know how I feel."

"I do. That's why I was honest." Sofiya gave me a tender look, came to her feet, collected our plates and cups, and brought them to the sink. She then replaced the spread on the left bed and turned down the covers. "Come on, it's time to sleep."

I realized how exhausted I was. I rose from the table and slipped under the sheets. Sofiya tucked me in and placed a kiss on my forehead. I couldn't remember when my mother had last done this. Certainly not since Simon died.

"If you need anything, wake me, Olivia. I mean it."

I wished her goodnight. She switched off the light and moved one of the easy chairs in between the twin beds and sat facing me. I gazed at her still figure, her hands resting on the armrests, and felt protected for the first time since I could remember.

Day 13

My body ached the next morning, especially the side of my head, where the boy had struck me, and my knuckles, where I had struck him. Sofiya was already awake, dressed, and preparing breakfast.

"Well, you look colorful today," she remarked, pointing to the bruises. "How are you feeling?"

I sat at the table and told her. She placed a bottle of aspirin and glass of water in front of me.

"Thank you." I swallowed two pills. Then, quietly, I added, "And thank you for sitting with me last night."

Sofiya smiled. "You're welcome. It was only a short while. You fell asleep very soon."

"Before I did...I felt sheltered. Safe."

"I'm glad, Olivia."

The warmth of her expression recalled last night's intimacy. I blushed. Seeing this, Sofiya resumed scrambling eggs and buttering toast. After carrying our plates to the table, she poured coffee for us and took a seat.

I wanted to say more, much more, to acknowledge the intense connection we had experienced, but words failed me. I took a sip of coffee, frustrated by my reticence, yet aware that everyone in my family suffered from the inability to express emotion. Or, rather, we understood how to show anger, not love. This was especially true of my parents.

Sofiya laid her hands on the table. "So, a lot is going on in that head of yours, isn't there?"

I nodded, ate a bite of egg, and swallowed some orange juice. "Yes, there is." Mustering a smile, I said, "Well, to be honest, I feel really shaky. And vulnerable—a word that has always frightened me." I placed my fork on the plate and met her gaze. "But you know what? Despite everything, I'm better this morning. Like what occurred last night blew the top off the volcano. Finally remembering the conclusion to Simon's story after all this time is a relief."

"Good."

"One thing is still confusing. Why does my mother blame me for Simon's death? I know it's because I was older than my brother and should have been more careful."

"The same reasons why you tormented yourself for so many years." Sofiya eased back against her chair. "And, yes, your mother probably did believe you were at fault, even if that's inaccurate. However, if you recall what I said last night, it's possible your mother couldn't accept her own role in what happened."

"Why should she? Mother wasn't there." I thought about this for a moment. "Are you saying it was easier to blame me rather than admit she had been...I don't know, negligent?"

"And to blame your father, too. You said he was away then."

"Yes, he was," I said. "Since Simon died, Dad seems to be gone a lot more, and even when he's home, he's kind of not there. Perhaps you're right. She's mad at Dad, too."

"Some people aren't able to understand their own behavior. In her heart, I believe your mother knows she's being unfair to you."

"Unfair? Is that why I'm so angry with her?"

"Yes. And why she vacillates between punishing and caring for you."

I considered her words. "I think you and I have hidden our suffering, though yours was so much greater than mine. You had no one close, and your losses kept growing and growing. For me, after Simon died, I was too afraid to talk with anyone for fear they would think I had lost my mind. My parents refused to speak about the accident or mention my brother's name."

"They wanted to forget, I suppose."

"And to condemn me in silence. They never gave me a chance to admit how responsible I felt for his death. This left me with nowhere to go. The only way I could release some pressure was to write in my journal or to return to the river at night."

"Which didn't really help, did it?"

"No, but doing something, anything, felt better, at least for a little while," I said, recognizing this was the truth. "And, from what you've told me, you haven't shared your feelings much, either."

"Many of us buried the tragedies we accumulated during the war. In that, I am not alone. But some of us remain alone because of our experiences."

I puzzled over her comment. "I hope you don't feel as alone now."

She reached over and touched my hand. "No, I don't."

We finished our breakfast. Sofiya and I washed the dishes, then sat at the table.

"You know, Olivia, this might be an excellent opportunity for you and your mother to discuss everything. Hopefully, without harsh words. Evelyn has endured years of pain, too. Perhaps one of the reasons for the affair with Travis—other than that he's irresistible—is that she needed to be with someone who wasn't part of her history."

"And in a way I also needed that," I said. "I was desperate to get past Simon's death and couldn't. I was stuck, making no headway climbing out of the pit. Kind of like that nail was still in my foot—"

"Nailing you to your brother?"

"Yes. But as I did then, I guess I had to tear myself in order to become free."

The morning sunlight brightened the room but didn't shine directly through the windows. In the soft light, Sofiya's blue eyes radiated quiet satisfaction.

"I couldn't have done this without your help," I said. "In the pool, I might have...well, I don't know what would have happened." My coffee was cold, but I swallowed some, trying to gather courage to make the most honest admission. "What I'm trying to say is...you rescued me."

Sofiya seemed to pass through several emotions until they blended into a serene smile. "Thank you for saying that. I appreciate it. Mostly, I was fortunate to be present."

"Fortunate for me."

"I believe you're stronger than you realize, Olivia. However, if I was able to give you any comfort, that means a lot. I care greatly for you." She studied me for a few moments. "If you were stuck in a pit, I've been in one, too, as you just said. And for many more years. I don't think it's possible to fully extricate myself from my memories, but you've made an enormous difference in my life. All the fine qualities you attribute to me I also attribute to you. You are an empathetic, kind, and intelligent young woman. For both of us, this was the right time to meet each other."

—

After I showered and dressed, Travis and my mother arrived with Chief Larsen. They asked how I was, to which I responded in minimal detail. The policeman reported that the boy had been found and was in the hospital. The scissors had punctured just above his spleen, bruising the organ sufficiently to require observation.

"But the doctor says he'll be okay," Chief Larsen explained. "Do you want to know about this guy?"

I nodded.

He flipped open his notebook. "His name is Erich Haller. Nineteen, from Miami. The police in Florida have listed him as a primary suspect in a series of assaults on a local campus. He arrived on St. Croix four weeks ago—confirmed by the airlines." The chief looked up. "We received a photo of Haller on Monday from the sheriff in Miami. I called him for more information, and he said Haller's parents admitted their son was here but wouldn't reveal where he was staying. According to the sheriff, his parents are wealthy and may have paid for his flight to keep him out of jail. We think Haller was involved in some recent criminal activities in Christiansted—a number of house burglaries and two sexual attacks—one on an older woman he met at a bar." He paused before adding, "You're lucky. Some of his other victims didn't fare so well."

I thought of the woman in the taxi and described her to the chief.

"Could be the person I was just talking about." Chief Larsen then asked if I would be willing to examine several photographs in order to identify my assailant. "Instead of coming to the station and viewing a line-up. It might be easier on you."

I agreed and was presented with head shots of six men. I stopped on the third photo. The young man was better looking than I remembered, but here his features lacked the aggression I'd witnessed. Even so, his face, with its strange misalignment, was disturbing. "That's him, but his hair isn't brown. Did he dye it as a disguise?"

The policeman nodded agreement. "Okay, thank you, Miss Livingston."

Travis checked the photo. "Not that it matters, but that's the guy I confronted near the office. I suppose he was looking for Olivia."

"And surveilling the hotel's layout," the policeman said.

I showed Chief Larsen the picture I'd taken in the market. He commented that Haller probably turned away to avoid any record of his presence on the island. "I guess taking the photo put you on his radar."

"I'm sure he regrets going after Olivia," Travis said. "She proved to be an impressive adversary."

After Larsen left, I told Travis and my mother I'd seen Haller in town and thought he might be Simon.

"What do you mean? Why didn't you tell me?" Mother demanded.

I was about to list the reasons, such as that she was mostly with Travis and froze whenever Simon's name was mentioned, but Travis rested his hand on my arm. Addressing my mother, he said, "Let's talk about this later, don't you think, Evelyn?"

"Yes, this is a time for everyone to be kind to each other," Sofiya said.

———

Once the policemen were finished with the apartment, Travis, my mother, and the maid scoured the place, removing all traces of the attack, but I still refused to return there. I stayed with Sofiya, reading, thinking, and talking. Mother called my father, and after hearing the news, he booked a flight to St. Croix, to arrive the following afternoon. She checked in with us several times, and Sofiya invited her for a spaghetti dinner, which Sofiya and I began to prepare late-afternoon. The aromas of sautéed garlic and onions, browning meat, and bubbling tomato sauce filled the room, adding to the sense of comfort Sofiya provided. Although I was unsure whether I wanted to be in my mother's company, Sofiya believed it was a good idea.

When Mother entered the apartment, she smelled of smoke and clutched her cigarette case like a hand grenade she might toss if the going got rough. Sofiya politely explained she preferred her not to smoke in the apartment. My mother frowned but returned the case to her purse, a concession that felt like a small victory. We took places at the table—Mother across from me, Sofiya at the head, to my right. Acting as the referee? My mother might not cede that authority, however. She had already adopted a superior air—sitting stiffly upright, her head held high. She was dressed in a pink sleeveless dress, a polished cotton material that shone in the candlelight. A three-strand, white bead necklace and matching earrings served as decoration, though she scarcely needed enhancement. Mother looked glamorous, her violet eyes dark and glittering, her makeup flawless, with lipstick the same light shade as her dress. By comparison, in my shorts and blue polo shirt, I felt awkward.

Sofiya opened a bottle of red wine. Because I preferred to drink water, I shook my head, so she poured wine into my mother's glass and hers. She then offered Mother some cheese, which was delicately accepted, as if my mother's pink nail polish was still wet.

"So, how are you doing, Olivia?" my mother asked.

"I'm all right."

Mother took this in, swallowed it with her cheese and cracker. "Glad to hear it, dear. I've been very concerned." She thanked Sofiya for the wine and took a sip. "In fact, darling, don't you think it's time you returned to our place? The police said it was okay, and Travis fixed the downspout so it can't be climbed. He was so upset about everything."

"I know he was," I said. "He told me."

Since I hadn't responded about her request, Mother puckered the side of her mouth, a sign of irritation I didn't miss.

"Olivia, I believe you've imposed on Sofiya's kind hospitality long enough. I'm sure she's busy—on her job search—or…" She fluttered her hand in the air.

"Evelyn, I'm enjoying Olivia's company."

"And I'm enjoying being here," I added. "I'm not ready to come back." A wave of doubt washed over me, and I looked at Sofiya to confirm I was still welcome. She nodded.

Mother softened her tone. "Please…stay with me tonight. Or tomorrow, when Dad arrives."

I shook my head. Sofiya cleared her throat, as if she might

say something, but instead poured my mother more wine. Then, she rose to her feet. "Let me finish making dinner. It's almost done."

After Sofiya walked to the stove, Mother and I faced off. It seemed like whoever spoke first was yielding to the other. I moved my water glass in a tight circle.

"Olivia, you know I miss you."

This unusual admission caught me by surprise. Did she mean it? Or was this a pro-forma statement designed to look good in front of Sofiya? Whatever its aim, I felt my cheeks color and prayed my tan would hide this reaction. Perhaps sensing my distress, Sofiya interrupted the conversation.

"Come over and help yourselves," she said, using two pot-holders to lift the large pot of spaghetti onto a trivet.

We did, and when we returned to the table, Mother spoke about our picnic on the beach, the trip to Buck Island, the warm weather. Anything to avoid difficult subjects. Sofiya chimed in here and there, but mostly she was quiet like I was. Observing my mother, I noticed she had become ill at ease: sending nervous sidelong glances at me and, at other times, smiling too broadly.

When we had finished eating and our plates had been brought to the counter, Sofiya offered sliced mangos with lime for dessert. Mother declined but welcomed a second bottle of wine, even though her first three glasses had already affected her speech. Intending to take out her cigarettes, she reached for her purse and then remembered her promise. She placed the purse on the empty chair.

I felt the pressure rise in the room. The détente had run its course.

"Mother, I think we should talk about it."

She arched her eyebrows. "About what?"

"That night." I realized I wasn't being clear. "The night Simon died."

At the mention of my brother's name, my mother tucked

in her chin. "I doubt there is much to say on the subject."

"The subject is Simon. I know you hate for me to say his name. But I just did and I won't avoid his name any longer."

Sofiya placed her arms on the table, creating a symbolic double fence between the two of us. "Evelyn, I'm sure it's difficult for you to recall the night your son died, but it might help Olivia to hear more about it. From your point of view."

My mother cast a suspicious glance at Sofiya. Then, her eyes seemed to sharpen with annoyance. After a brief hesitation, in a controlled voice, she began. "Very well. I suppose Olivia doesn't recall much because she was only eight years old." Mother swallowed some wine. "Apparently, Olivia had suggested night fishing and Simon agreed—that was my son, a bit impulsive and always willing to try anything. Olivia was usually more careful."

I started to protest the implied criticism, but Sofiya gently touched my hand. As she did, a resentful expression swept across my mother's face. Though it disappeared immediately, I knew my mother was unsettled, perhaps jealous.

"Children don't always use the same judgment as adults," Sofiya said quietly.

My mother sighed. "You're right. However, Olivia was quite mature for her age and always took excellent care of her brother."

"I did, didn't I? Because I wasn't allowed to refuse." I pointed a finger at her. "However, you left us whenever it suited you...when we became inconveniences. When you wanted to play bridge or go out for lunch or dinner. When Dad was traveling or when he was home and you couldn't find a sitter." My voice was growing louder. I didn't care. "You even left us at night by disappearing into your bedroom. Where were you and Dad when Simon was crying after he had a nightmare? You were too far away—because you chose a house designed to keep us separate."

Mother's lips drew together. "I resent that accusation."

"But you can't deny it's true!" I grabbed my water glass so hard I thought it might crack.

"It isn't. And you were rarely left alone with your brother."

"With Simon! Say his name!" I shouted.

"With Simon," Mother muttered.

We glared at each other across the table. Sofiya said nothing for a moment, perhaps allowing us to cool down. Then, she asked my mother to resume her recollection.

Mother reached for her wine and took a sip. "Well, I was home, in bed, sleeping." To me, she said, "I could scarcely be accused of mind-reading. I didn't have any idea what you were planning."

"And what Simon was planning," I reminded her. "I didn't do this by myself."

"All right, as you wish." She shifted in her chair. "Anyway, I was awakened by someone calling me from the laundry room. I went to see what the matter was, and there you were, lying on the floor, filthy with dirt, your foot and ankle bleeding."

I gritted my teeth. I wanted to shout out everything my mother had omitted: my emotional state, the fact that I was sobbing and upset.

My mother studied her hands resting in her lap and addressed Sofiya. "I brought Olivia into the kitchen, at which point she was kind of mumbling...not making much sense."

"And, unfortunately, I was also messing up your clean floor," I interjected.

My mother ignored my outburst, though one eye twitched. "Finally, Olivia mentioned my son's name. Of course, I thought he was asleep in his room."

"What did she say?" Sofiya asked.

"Something like 'Simon's gone.' I didn't know what she meant. She was rather incoherent."

"Incoherent?" I snorted.

"With good reason," Sofiya said before I could make

another response.

Mother appeared ruffled. She returned her focus on me. "After that, you told me he fell into the river. I was in a panic, as you can imagine."

"Yeah, I can imagine." I felt my face warm with anger. "I think you yelled at me. Like, 'What did you do?'"

"I'm certain I never said that," she snapped. "Anyway, once I realized the situation, I asked you which dock you'd been on. You didn't know the name of the owner, but when we figured it out, I telephoned the police and arranged to meet them there. They called the Coast Guard—there's a base several miles away."

"And what about Olivia?" Sofiya asked.

"I don't recall exactly. I was so frightened about Simon that I wasn't thinking clearly."

"So, if I have the picture correctly...Olivia is in the kitchen, bleeding." Sofiya refilled my mother's glass. "And then?"

Mother fortified herself with more wine. "I quickly bandaged her foot, gave her a coat to wear, and drove to the river as fast as I could. We met the police, and the Coast Guard boat arrived. They searched downriver into the bay and ocean." Tears formed in her eyes. "We never found my son."

"And me?" My voice quavered. I hoped my mother didn't notice.

She didn't. In an offhand tone, as if reciting a movie plot, she replied, "Oh. Naturally, I brought you with me in the car. After the first passes along the shoreline were unsuccessful, we went to the hospital, to the emergency room." Addressing Sofiya again, she explained, "The doctor gave Olivia a tetanus shot and some morphine. Her foot required surgery. Several tendons were torn."

"She must have been in a great deal of pain," Sofiya suggested.

"I suppose she was."

I recalled some of this, but my mother's disinterest in my

condition illustrated exactly how she had behaved. While I understood she was frantic about Simon—we both were—how I felt hadn't registered in her consciousness. Suddenly, the room seemed very hot, the air heavy and hard to breathe. I swallowed some water to keep from crying. When I spoke, I sounded like someone else. Someone far away. "My shoe came off when I fell through the dock, and the nail stuck in my ankle. The only way to free myself was to rip the nail down through my foot."

"Oh, Olivia!" Mother covered her mouth.

"Then, I crawled down the steps onto the beach and climbed up the cliff and through the woods."

"It's over half a mile to the house," my mother said to Sofiya, though she still seemed shocked by what I'd just said.

I struggled to stay in my chair. I wanted to run out the door, to unleash my frustration and hurt. Instead, I forced myself to continue. "I don't remember much about being in the kitchen. Just later, when I was sitting in the car." A shudder passed through me, as I recalled what it was like being there alone. "I was shaking with cold. The blood seeped through the bandage, and I was afraid of getting into trouble because blood was dripping onto the car's carpet. I wanted my mother to come." I turned toward her. "I wanted you to help me. I couldn't stand on my foot to walk, and you were out of sight, with the policemen, looking for Simon. It seemed like forever."

My mother looked at me in disbelief. "It wasn't that long, Olivia."

I couldn't believe how composed she was, especially when I was struggling. I managed to blurt out that we hadn't arrived at the hospital until four thirty in the morning.

"Well, I don't really know. That's possible." Mother fidgeted with her wedding band, rolling it around her finger.

Sofiya frowned. "Evelyn, I understand why you were desperate to find your son and that he was your priority. But imagine this from Olivia's perspective for a moment, as an eight-year-old girl who was traumatized, frightened, cold, and in pain. A girl who felt keenly responsible for her brother. Did you reassure her at the house? Did you hold her?"

"I don't know. The whole thing is a blur." Mother looked at me, her face drawn. "I was upset...about Simon."

"And about me?" I fought back tears.

"You were alive, and my son was somewhere hurt or dead."

This statement left me reeling. While it was honest, I knew what she was really saying. The sentence she never said, the one that haunted me. I looked at Sofiya. She lifted her chin in response, acknowledging my distress.

"Evelyn, were you angry at Olivia?" Sofiya's voice was steady, devoid of accusation. "Are you angry?"

Eyes wide with astonishment, Mother stared at Sofiya. "Angry? No." She seemed to bristle at this idea at first. Then, her demeanor changed. Clutching her glass, she said, "Okay. Perhaps I was a little angry."

Sofiya waited for the tension to lessen. "If you were angry, if in some way you believed Simon's accident was Olivia's fault, this was probably communicated to her and added to the guilt she already felt. That's a huge burden for a child to carry."

I expected Mother to argue, to deny the truth of Sofiya's words, but instead she glanced at me with a distraught expression. Her shoulders drooped, and when she spoke, her voice was almost inaudible.

"Yes, you're right. It is too much." She let go of her glass. Her fingers were trembling.

I remained silent, frozen with fear that my mother would mount an attack, as she usually did whenever sensitive feelings were exposed. Yet, slowly, it became clear she was the one who was defenseless.

"I'm sorry," she said.

Sofiya removed her arms from the table, leaned against her chair, and waited for me to respond. Before I could react, my mother reached to take my hand.

"I'm sorry for that night," she repeated, "and sorry for all the times since. I've been too unhappy, too involved with my own grief and the problems with your father to see how my behavior affected you." Tears formed in her eyes once again and began to slide down her cheeks. She remained motionless, clutching my fingers. "Olivia, can you forgive me?"

I was stunned. Even when Simon died, I'd never witnessed her break down, though she had hidden in her room on and off for days after his death, and her eyes had often been red.

"Please believe me! I didn't mean to punish you for what happened to Simon. Yet that's exactly what I did, didn't I?"

I sat still except to remove my hand, an instinctive reaction because I disliked physical contact with my mother. When I did, I immediately regretted withdrawing because her tears changed into sobs.

"Oh, god! I'm so sorry!" She covered her eyes and lowered her head.

"Mother..."

She continued to cry. Uncertain how I felt, uncertain what to do, I came to my feet and walked to Sofiya, who reached up to squeeze my hand. I continued around the table to my mother, and as I did, she turned in her chair and encircled my waist, holding on tightly. I hesitated and then leaned down and took her in my arms. Over my mother's bowed head, I gazed at Sofiya, who nodded.

—

My mother left a half hour later. Sofiya and I changed into night clothes and sat on our respective beds, facing each other. The small table lamp was the only light in the room.

I drew up my knees and wrapped my arms around them. "I guess Mother will spend a last night with Travis."

"Very likely," she said. "Tomorrow, when your father arrives, I wonder what will happen between your parents. I'm sure you're worried about it."

"I am. But maybe it's time to clean up the mess. We've been in turmoil for too many years. It can't go on, especially after this affair."

"Will you tell your father about Travis?"

I considered. "I'm not sure. I might not have to say anything. Maybe Mother will confess about her relationship with him. She seems ready to move forward." I shrugged. "And Dad might admit he's had affairs, if he hasn't told my mother already. I've heard her accuse him of being unfaithful plenty of times during fights."

"It would be easier if you didn't have to be in the middle."

"Well, my plan is to stay on the sidelines and not favor either parent." I studied Sofiya. "So, what did you think? About dinner tonight?"

"What you think is more important," she replied. "From my perspective, I hope you saw how much your mother loves you. And, given time, I believe you'll realize how much you care about her. I think you do."

"Yes," I agreed, "but I'm not sure I'll ever trust her. Somehow, love seems easier to feel than trust."

Sofiya thought about my comment. "That's probably true. Trust is difficult to achieve, difficult to accept if you've been betrayed or hurt."

"Which is why my feelings for you are so extraordinary."

She smiled, her blue eyes exuding that mysterious inner light. "And you've earned my trust as well, Olivia. And my love."

Day 14

The conversation with my mother provided a glimpse into her private suffering since Simon's death, but it also exposed how she had deflected feelings that she couldn't handle, aiming the heat at me and also at my father. Except for her painting, I wondered what made my mother happy. The affair with Travis did, but their relationship was temporary, a connection that would soon be cut. Would they continue next summer? I supposed this depended on Dad and whether Travis and my mother remained interested in each other. I mentioned these thoughts to Sofiya over morning coffee but didn't reveal my own anxiety, that my relationship with her had been forged from a similar need and our bond might be broken once I left the island.

In her usual uncanny manner, Sofiya said, "I suspect you're worrying, aren't you?"

"Worrying?"

"That I will disappear after you fly home to New Jersey. That our attachment is of great value now, but one that won't survive separation."

"Yes, a little."

"Well, dear Olivia, I promise to do my best to stay connected. That's all we can do. Time and distance are formidable factors to overcome, but let's try to defeat them."

—

We waited for my father to come from the airport. I lay on the chaise by the round table, dressed in shorts and my embroidered shirt; Sofiya sat on a chair next to me, in cream-colored slacks and blouse, reading a newspaper. Her eyes kept darting to the area above the hotel steps as mine did, then we would look at each other and smile at our nervousness. Across the pool, Mother reclined in the shade of the gallery awning, elegantly attired in a pale blue sleeveless dress. She gave the appearance of serenity as she listened to one of Travis's jazz albums, yet she shared apprehensive looks with us and with Travis, whenever he peered from his office. The scene was overtly cheerful—music playing, sun shining, water sparkling—but the tension was obvious.

At last, Dad and his black suitcase arrived. Mother and I rose to kiss and hug him and were greeted in return—a longer embrace for me and a more perfunctory one for her. His face was unusually drawn, with a chalky color to his skin that made me wonder if he hadn't been sleeping well or had been drinking too much. Regardless, he cut an impressive figure in his tan gabardine suit, with his neatly trimmed blond hair and moustache, towering height, and broad shoulders.

"You've grown another couple of inches, Olivia. Haven't you?" he teased.

"I don't think so." My father loved that I was tall like him; I was less enthusiastic.

"Well, you're a knockout!"

I gave my habitual response, "No, I'm not." His praise always made me uncomfortable.

"And, wow! You look like a native with that tan."

This comment seemed mildly offensive to Crucians, though I couldn't say exactly why. He then laughed. I started to do the same but realized he hadn't said anything funny. Observing my reaction and perhaps remembering what had happened, Dad grew more serious. He gave me another kiss and touched a bruise on my neck. "I'm sorry I wasn't here. If

I had been, you would have been safe."

This was similar to what my mother had said about her absence. I then applied his comment to Simon's death, when he had also been gone. Although I was glad to see my father, I realized his arrivals and departures were more memorable than his presence; he was a stranger with a suitcase, a pilot in a hat and a uniform.

Travis emerged from the office to shake hands and welcome Dad to the Pink Fancy. Beside my tall father, Travis looked short, though he exuded a lively energy and humor my father lacked, especially today. When Sofiya walked over, I was proud to introduce her.

"Ah, I see where Olivia gets some of her good looks," she remarked. "Nice to meet you, Mr. Livingston." Of the five of us, Sofiya was the most composed.

Dad smiled and placed an arm around me, pulling me close, as if to showcase the similarities between us. "My daughter outclasses me. And please, call me Steven."

—

My father insisted we book a flight home, but I was adamant about remaining on St. Croix, as was my mother, who hadn't finished working and probably didn't wish to leave Travis. Then, Dad offered to use the porch bed so I could sleep in the bedroom. I told him I wasn't ready to return to the apartment. This was true, yet I also didn't wish to be in the middle of the explosion between my parents when it came. Nor did I explain that I felt more sheltered and cared for by Sofiya, who distracted me with activities like cooking, playing cards, and swimming.

That evening, my parents and I dined at the Stone Balloon, a restaurant my father liked. Both of them drank too much, said little, and seemed uneasy. After we said goodnight, they entered their apartment, and I returned to Sofiya, who suggested a swim. We had been in the water less than fifteen minutes when the shouting began in Fantasy or, as I said to Sofiya, in Fury. We couldn't hear what was being said, but there was little doubt both my parents were broiling mad. Sofiya and I left the pool, toweled off, and rushed inside to shut out the noise.

The Last Days

Sofiya and I spent the next afternoon at Pelican Cove, joined by my father, whose oversized physique reduced the size of the reef to a smaller scale. Dad was very solicitous of Sofiya, thanking her for all she had done on my behalf, though he had no idea of the depth or significance of our relationship. This was just as well. After Mother's insinuations, I didn't want to hear any negative remarks from him, even if close observation was not his strong suit. He was mostly preoccupied with the problems of his marriage, which he referred to but didn't share, saying only that "Evelyn and I are having some issues." I decided not to ask what they were because I still felt raw and emotional. When we went to order a late lunch, Dad made a big deal about ordering a ton of food.

"Hey, how about some fries, Olivia? And maybe two cheeseburgers?"

"One is fine," I said.

Sofiya was unusually quiet and asked for a simple hamburger. Dad insisted she add cheese and a tomato and said lunch was his treat. All afternoon, he laughed a lot and loudly, like he did when he was drunk. He teased me, patted Sofiya on the back as if they were pals, and tried too hard to show us a good time, which we weren't having.

Later, when Sofiya and I were alone, sitting at the kitchen table, she shook her head.

"This must be so difficult for you. I know your father is doing his best to be nice, but it's a strain to pretend everything is fine."

"I know. I wish he would go home—after my parents come to some decisions."

—

Dad might have stayed longer except for Hurricane Faith, which was slowly meandering northward. There was a rumor that the airport might close in three days, so he decided to book a return flight. Also, the storm with Mother intensified when my father discovered where she was during the attack and the truth about her infidelity. Travis, meanwhile, was making himself scarce, anticipating this revelation and my father's response.

The only time I saw the two men interact by themselves was early on the third morning of my father's visit. Sofiya was in the shower, and I was standing by the open window in my bathrobe. Dad had brought out a mug of coffee and was sitting under the awning on a chaise by the pool. He wore a yellow polo shirt, untucked, which wasn't typical, and a pair of blue shorts. A minute later, Travis sauntered down the steps from his apartment, neat in a long-sleeve white Oxford shirt and tan cargo shorts. When he saw my father, he slowed, but then Dad noticed him. Travis nodded and continued to his office, unlocked it, folded back the shutters, entered, and closed the bottom half of the door.

Dad set down his coffee and walked over to Travis. He stood a few feet away, his shoulders square, and his fingers drawn into fists. Offering no greeting, he said, "You destroyed my marriage. I just want you to know that."

I inhaled sharply, scared that my father was about to start a physical fight. Travis approached his side of the door and placed his hands on the shelf. His face was turned slightly away from me, but I saw him shake his head and give Dad a small smile. I listened hard and heard Travis reply, "I didn't destroy your marriage, Steven, but I'm sorry."

My father glared at Travis, returned to the gallery, picked up his coffee mug, and exited into the apartment.

—

Whenever I saw my parents, they argued constantly, their animosity usually inflamed by alcohol, which they were both abusing out of anger and habit. Some of these fights I overheard from the pool; some I witnessed while in their company. The worst was after the morning my father had spoken to Travis. My parents and I had eaten dinner at Café de Paris. They polished off several rum drinks, a bottle of wine, and after-dinner brandies. Anticipating what this fuel might spark, I felt sick, drank nothing, and couldn't finish my meal. Afterward, we walked toward the hotel. In King's Alley, I lagged behind them and watched them stroll a few yards ahead of me.

First, Mother said something. It must have been inflammatory because Dad pivoted toward her and grabbed her wrist. I moved closer.

"If you had been in the apartment instead of screwing Travis, nothing would have happened to Olivia!"

Mother glowered at him. "How dare you, you bastard! And I guess because you were gone the night Simon died that his death was your fault?"

"That's not the same thing."

"Well, maybe what I just said is true. If you'd been home more often—you know, like a father should be—the kids would have asked you to take them fishing, and Simon would still be alive."

"That's the stupidest thing I've ever heard," my father growled. "Lots of men have to travel for work."

"Yeah, but you prefer being anywhere else except home and dealing with your family. No wonder you love being a pilot!"

He shook his head in disbelief. "And how about you, Evelyn? What about your bridge games, book group meetings, garden club lunches, and the hours you stay in your studio?

Huh? And why didn't you notice Simon and Olivia leaving the house?"

"I was asleep, damn it! You know it's impossible to hear the back door opening from our bedroom," she snapped. "And with you gone all the time, I have to make a life for myself in addition to painting—which is *my* work, in case you've forgotten."

Even in the dim light, I could see they were furious with each other. Both of their faces were flushed and taut. It was clear my presence had been erased from their consciousness.

A long pent-up anger rose to the surface, and I stepped forward, pushing them apart. "I've had it! What do you want to hear? That I'm responsible for Simon's death? Okay, fine. Does that make you happy?" I shouted. "But did I deserve years of punishment?"

"Olivia, you know how sorry I am," Mother said quickly.

"Yes, you told me that, but now you're accusing Dad of being at fault because he wasn't there." Facing my father, I added, "And you blame Mother. You believe what happened to Simon and then to me here in St. Croix was because she was negligent. Right? Do I have that correct?" I demanded. "And I assume you think I killed my brother?"

My father's mouth opened in astonishment. "Olivia, no, I don't."

"Yes, you do. You're both so busy blaming each other and blaming me because you can't deal with your own guilt. And in the process, you've ruined your marriage and your relationship with me. Well, I'm fed up with both of you!"

"Everything will be fine," Dad said, taking my arm.

I shook him off. "No, it won't. Mother at least apologized."

"I'm sorry," my father said, reaching for me again, "if—"

I waved him away and swallowed hard, wanting to flee, to leave them standing in the street, and yet I was too angry, too close to my grief and hurt, to run. I'd done enough of that for the last eight years.

"Yes, if only...if only you had talked to me after Simon died—both of you. If you had worried about how I was handling what happened. Then maybe I wouldn't have suffered all those nightmares, over and over. Maybe I wouldn't have walked to the river at night alone, over and over, scared of the dark, hoping to find Simon lying on the beach alive or sitting on the dock. If you had helped me, if you had cared, I wouldn't have been so tortured. Wouldn't have thought the boy I saw here was Simon. Because I did, I followed him, watched from the porch to see if he would return on the street below. If I wasn't so confused and lost, Erich Haller might never have climbed up and attacked me."

My mother came forward and threw her arms around my shoulders. Dad stood there, silent, his eyes darting between us and the buildings beyond. A couple walked by and stared, having witnessed my tirade. Seeing them, Mother disengaged and stepped back, always more concerned about maintaining appearances even at a moment like this.

"We should have done that," my father whispered. "Talked to you."

Though he was saying the right words, they sounded hollow. "I might forgive you one day," I said. "But there's one thing I can never forgive."

"What, dear? Please tell us," Mother said.

I looked from one parent to the other. "That you loved Simon more."

As soon as I uttered this sentence, I ran past them and sprinted down Strand Street.

—

The next day, I was crossing the pool underwater, and as I surfaced, I saw my father disappear into Travis's empty office. I swam nearer and watched him pick up the phone, presumably placing a long-distance call. I hurried out of the water, but he noticed me and held up his hand as a signal to wait. Once he finished, he asked if we could go for a walk. He wasn't smiling.

I changed and we set off toward the harbor, browsing in shop windows, but it was apparent Dad had something of consequence to discuss. Near the fort, he came to an abrupt halt. I expected him to address the issues I'd raised about Simon's death, to apologize for how distant he'd been during the last eight years. I hoped he would finally say he loved me.

"Olivia, you know Evelyn and I have been very unhappy together."

"Yeah."

"For a very long time." He sighed, then said in a hurry, as if he wanted to speed through the unpleasantness, "I'm sorry to say our marriage is over. I just spoke with my attorney and asked him to start divorce proceedings. When I return home, I'll pack and move out of the house before you and Evelyn arrive. A legal separation will start at that point. She'll contact a lawyer, too."

"I see." My father wasn't the kind of man who divulged much except for facts, but I could tell he was discouraged and sad, even though his eyes betrayed anger when he referred to my mother. "I guess it's for the best." Even though I had anticipated this news, had even partly acclimated to the idea, the confirmation of their separation was a jolt.

He spread his thumb and forefinger across his moustache, a habitual gesture. "I'm glad you're being so mature about the situation."

I looked up at him and realized he couldn't see past my self-possession because he didn't want to deal with how I felt. If I held everything in, Dad could go blithely on his way, without worrying about me in the least.

"I assumed this would happen." All the burdens from the last days, the last years, seemed to congeal into a massive weight. I exhaled a long breath, aware of how disappointed I was in my father. "You know, Dad, I've learned something.

About a mistake I've made. One of many."

"What is it?"

"Well, because you were away so much and Mother was home, I thought you were the better parent." I gave him a sad smile. "Now I know you're not. You're no better than my mother, just not as present."

My father started to protest, laying his hand on my arm. I let it rest there without reacting.

"Like I said last night. I don't think either of you cares about me. You and Mother do what you want. Get a divorce. I'll manage."

He took a half step back. Was he upset about what I'd said or that I'd dared to say anything at all?

"It will all work out, I promise." Standing straighter, Dad assumed his captain demeanor. "I'm going to buy a place on Long Island, close to the airport. I'll pick you up on weekends, holidays, whenever I can. And once you have your license, I'll get you a car so you can make the trip yourself. How does that sound?"

I shrugged. "I don't want to drive to Long Island from New Jersey."

Dad's eyebrows flew upward. Obviously, he hadn't expected me to reject his offer.

"I'm sure in a year or so you'll change your mind." He folded his arms around my shoulders. "And don't worry about anything else. Your mother promised me that after the house is sold she'll rent a place in town so you can complete your last two years at school. We'll do everything possible to be fair with you."

Fair but not caring. That's what I told Sofiya.

—

Later in the afternoon, my father and I had one conversation that slightly resurrected my opinion of him. I brought Dad to Sofiya's and showed him my photographs. He said he was really excited by the prints and very proud of me. "Mark my words, Olivia. You have what it takes to be a professional."

Since he was a tough judge, his comments solidified my confidence.

—

The hurricane stalled, but Dad left St. Croix as planned. I felt relieved, as did Sofiya, who had been giving my parents a wide berth because of the tense atmosphere they engendered. Travis was also more present, in his office and the gallery. However, despite the lessening strain, my father's departure marked the end of life as I had known it. When I journeyed home, or rather to the house, because the concept of "home" had been erased, everything would be altered.

—

On the following morning, Sofiya, Mother, and I trekked to the arid eastern end of the island, where agave and acacia trees and prickly-pear and barrel cactus grew in large contrast to the western end's tropical rainforest. My mother sketched the goats grazing, and I photographed them. At the beach, we were delighted to see tracks in the sand made by giant leatherback or hawksbill turtles, who frequented the area and laid eggs above the high-water mark.

"They seem like creatures from the age of dinosaurs," Sofiya said, "a period I know quite well, being so old."

"Me, too," my mother replied. "And walking so much is making my old dinosaur bones hurt."

We enjoyed a picnic, and Mother was pleasant to Sofiya; with me, she was auditioning a new, softer approach, which left me uncertain how to behave and wondering if the transformation was genuine.

Although Travis had already brought my clothes to Sofiya's, I needed to retrieve my journal from behind the dresser so I could write about all that had occurred. Later that day, when Mother was with Travis, I unlocked the door to Fantasy and stepped inside for the first time since the attack. Perspiration popped out on my forehead, and a wave of nausea roiled my stomach. I got in and got out fast.

—

Hurricane Faith had regrouped and was barreling toward St. Croix. Residents nailed shutters and removed anything that could blow away in a high wind. Large boats left port and those that remained were fitted with double anchors. Everything on the porch was brought inside, which made a jumbled mess in the apartment. The outdoor furniture in the gallery and by the pool was gathered and tied in the corner by the laundry; the awnings were rolled up, creating a starkly exposed appearance to the pool area. As the sun was swallowed by thick overcast, the island plunged into an ominous gloom. I helped Travis, while Sofiya drove my mother to the store to fight with frenzied visitors and locals over the remaining food.

Everyone hunkered down, fearing the worst, but a last-minute veer in course steered Faith away from St. Croix. We were pummeled with 65 m.p.h. winds and torrential rain for a day, but afterward, with remarkable speed, the island returned to normal, except for palm tree branches and other debris all over the town and some small boats tossed on the beaches.

The last week of our trip evaporated. Day by day, Sofiya and I became sadder, though she was cheered by a job offer as manager of a beach hotel, which she accepted and would begin two days after our flight. Because money was becoming a serious concern, the job was excellent news, but leaving the Pink Fancy, the temporary home she'd made for herself, disturbed her greatly. I realized that any dislocation, even from the thinnest attachment, would be felt doubly hard by a woman who considered herself permanently displaced.

On the eve of our departure, Mother asked to dine with Travis alone. This suggestion was fine with me because I wished to be with Sofiya. In the afternoon, Mother and I returned to Cavanagh's for a final shopping trip and found another polished cotton dress for me to wear at dinner. This one was similar to the previous dress but featured a hibiscus design. After some deliberation, I selected a purple, blue, and green Thai silk shawl for Sofiya. I wanted to give her a special present, and my mother concurred. We also purchased a small, sturdy straw suitcase for the sea urchins.

Before Sofiya and I left for St. Croix by the Sea, a restaurant and beach hotel she suggested, I presented her with the shawl, which she loved. She promised to wear it on special occasions, each time to remember me. She then placed a velvet pouch in my hand. Inside was a gold box-chain necklace. I felt tears rim my eyes.

"Don't you start or you'll have me crying, too," Sofiya said. "Now, come here." She looped the necklace around my throat, hooked the clasp, and let her fingers remain on my neck. Her gentle touch communicated her feelings far more fluently than words. I stood there, overcome with emotion.

—

St. Croix by the Sea was amazingly beautiful, with an enormous salt water pool surrounded by rock walls and an enclosed cement apron protruding into the sea. Water occasionally overtopped these areas, while tiny crabs scurried there and across the beach. Over the numerous reefs, the waves broke in frilly sets, and as the sun dipped below the horizon and night fell, the white surf contrasted with the dark water. An old sugar mill was spotlighted near the pool.

We dined outside, overlooking this visual splendor, and enjoyed a buffet featuring shrimp, tuna, lobster, barbequed beef, and turkey. Whether the waiter suspected we were unrelated or because the restaurant had an unusually strict policy, I wasn't allowed any alcohol. Sofiya sniffed at this restriction, selected a bottle of white wine, and shared her glass with me, laughing each time she refilled it.

All through the meal, I observed how the breeze caressed the curls that sprang about her temples and forehead; how the candlelight enhanced the smoky blue radiance of her eyes and the sheen of her coral lipstick. I noticed the small lines curving around Sofiya's mouth, lines that deepened when she smiled or laughed; how her face conveyed serenity, sadness, and wisdom. I took dozens of mental photographs because I was too shy to take actual ones. Unusual for us, though much of the conversation was teasing and humorous, we lapsed into several extended silences. I was trying my best to forget my flight home, as Sofiya was, but it loomed large between us. We didn't trust our composure to speak of it.

After the lavish main courses, Sofiya insisted we sample the cheesecake, chocolate cake, and lemon chiffon pie on the dessert table. We did so and immediately decided we should have been more sensible. I paid the check—Mother had given me cash—and, wishing to prolong the evening, we wandered past the pool toward the beach. After removing our sandals, we stepped onto the cool sand and walked shoulder to shoulder away from the hotel, leaving its bright vivacity in our wake. The night's dampness coated our skin; sometimes our bare arms touched. We listened to the palm fronds rustle, the sea grape leaves softly click, and the surf murmur as it swept over the distant reefs, a mixture of sounds that coalesced into a chorus of sighs. Rounding the beach's bend, Sofiya and I remained silent. The moon favored us with its benevolent light, outshining the subtlety of stars. In this exquisitely beautiful place, during this exquisitely poignant moment, if our ages had been closer, our genders different or the times more liberal...if I had been less afraid, we might have kissed.

—

Our last morning was a whirlwind of packing. I stuffed cotton in the sea urchins and stowed them in the straw suitcase. After prying the pickled body out of the conch, I ensconced it and the pottery bowl in my clothes, along with the wind chime. As I did, I thought about Erich Haller, who was in prison. How long would he be there and would he be extradited to Florida? Chief Larsen had explained that my written statements were sufficient for the St. Croix authorities, should they prosecute him, so I had no further responsibilities.

When it was time to leave, Travis carried our suitcases down to his car. Much to my great unhappiness, Sofiya told me she wouldn't accompany us to the airport. It was best to say goodbye now, she said.

Using my camera, Sofiya took a picture of me in my yellow suit, and I composed several of her standing by the pool; I promised to send copies. Travis and my mother descended the steps to his car. When we were alone, Sofiya and I embraced tightly, both of us crying.

"Olivia, I will always…" she began but couldn't finish. Her hand rose to cover her mouth, and she broke away from me. After an intense look, Sofiya ran up the steps to her apartment, turned for a last glimpse, and then disappeared through her door.

I had never felt so bereft in my life, except after Simon fell into the churning, black river.

1966 –1968

Two Years

After I left St. Croix, Sofiya and I exchanged weekly letters and spoke on the phone occasionally. During our two-week reunion the following August, Sofiya had less time to spend with me because of her job. She also seemed changed. Her capacity for humor and kindness was still astonishing, yet she was quieter, more solemn. On the flight home, I worried that profound anguish was overwhelming Sofiya, that her tragic past had become her tragic future. Despite my love and adoration, in my heart I knew our friendship wasn't sufficient to rescue her as she had rescued me. Sofiya remained on an island, hemmed in by a sparkling turquoise sea and unrelentingly terrible memories.

In the following months, I became busy with senior-year activities, some new friends, and thoughts about college. I began to write less often; she, too, wrote less often. I continued to share many things with her, however, and was always excited to receive mail from Sofiya.

In 1968, she promised to visit for my high school graduation in June. I was thrilled about her arrival and eager to see her—it had been ten months since the second trip to St. Croix the previous summer. I realized how important Sofiya was to me and regretted letting my letters and calls drift. I wrote and told her as much but didn't receive a response. Two weeks later, a package arrived from Travis, who had faded from our lives after the second stay on the island. Inside the box was Sofiya's silk shawl, the rooster-tail conch wrapped in tissue, a newspaper clipping, a pale blue envelope addressed to me, and a note from Travis explaining that Sofiya had been drinking heavily during the last year and had been suffering from depression. On the fourth of June, he wrote, she left the enclosed letter on her kitchen table, along with the shell and the shawl, and a few lines to the effect that she couldn't continue living. Sofiya drove her car to Pelican Cove Beach and then, apparently, swam out to sea. Her body was discovered the next day.

I read the brief obituary in a haze of tears, retreated to my room with Sofiya's letter, locked the door, and sobbed uncontrollably. Finally, I opened the envelope.

My dearest Olivia,

This is the most difficult letter I've ever written. When this finds you, it will be sometime after my death. Of all the people I've met over the last years, you are the one who cared about me the most, a great gift that you generously shared, for which I was and am grateful beyond my ability to express. In return, I tried to open my heart, to give you what you needed. In many ways, we were searching for similar things because we were similar: both solitary, hurting, and, yes, lost. Fate brought us together on this small island and transformed our lives for the better, strengthening us through our affinities and our shared laughter and tears. Sadly, Olivia, I could not sustain the happiness. The burden I carry is too heavy.

Your mother once suggested that I was "different." I never really answered that question when you asked. How to honestly respond? I've never had a sexual relationship with a woman, but, as I said then, I couldn't resolve my life's experiences in order to become involved with a man, either. Yes, I did love you, but the passion was pure, composed of only the finest emotions. You will make your own path in your search for love, but if you find that you are different, be brave and true to yourself.

I am very sorry that I must do this as you approach such a joyous moment in your life—your graduation. Forgive me, dear Olivia, but I could not bear for you to see me so depressed, to think less of me.

Remember our time together and please be happy.

My deepest love, always,

Sofiya

Epilogue

I am fifty years older than I was in 1966 when I first visited the island. As I sit here on my bed, I'm holding Sofiya's silk shawl; its purple, blue, and green hues seem to glow in the sunlight streaming through the window. The peppery scent of her perfume still remains on the fabric, but it is so faint that I might be imagining it. Sofiya's handsome face—her large grayish-blue eyes and full lips, her curling silver and black hair—remain clear in my visual memory, separate from the few photographs I took of her.

Much has happened over these years. My parents are long dead—my mother from lung cancer. Toward the end of her life, we achieved the equanimous relationship Sofiya predicted, though even after our first trip in 1966, we were kinder to each other. When I was settling my mother's estate, I found the pictures I had taken of her with Travis, which she must have secretly stolen, thus confirming my suspicion that she was rummaging through my things. After my parents' divorce, Mother made a pragmatic decision to wed a wealthy businessman, a man she didn't love, who died in 1974. Dad remarried when I was a freshman in college, to a much younger woman, and I scarcely saw him after that. He never built the promised darkroom, but I constructed one years later, after studying journalism and photography. Following my teenage ambitions, I was hired to do both for a travel magazine and also exhibited my fine arts images in a gallery in Chelsea and in several European cities.

Over recent months, I've felt compelled to write the story about St. Croix in 1966 and about Sofiya, a woman who was profoundly responsible for my emotional resurrection. In doing so, I recognized we had shared a fixation on the past. Prior to our meeting, the present existed, but it didn't hold either of us in the same strong grasp as compared to what had occurred in our lives previously. When we met, I was sixteen and had been stuck on Simon's death for eight years, and Sofiya was about fifty and had been emotionally mired for over twenty-five years since her experiences during the war. Did it make a difference at what age our traumas occurred?

Yes, as it turned out, it did. If, in our lives, the number of days ahead outnumber the days behind us, then it may be possible to alter the angle of life's seesaw, to switch its orientation from past to future. Thus, I could give more weight to what might happen rather than to what already had. I could fill my life with friends and lovers, go to college, and find a meaningful career. Sofiya had no one, no rewarding work, and far fewer days in her future than those already lived. For her to tilt her life's balance forward was an entirely different proposition than it was for me—not really possible unless she had love and support. Tragically, those inspirations were almost absent, though she may have found companionship with a few colleagues.

For me now, the seesaw is weighted in the past as it was for Sofiya then. I understand more acutely what she felt—the certainty that the future is growing shorter and promises less, the loss of significant people through death or distance, and the mortality of spirit that gradually renders the interior world uninhabitable. Illness is an additional struggle, one Sofiya might have also faced considering the potential long-term deleterious effects of Ravensbrück. Although she fought her uphill battles and tried to flip the seesaw, Sofiya wasn't powerful or loved enough to do so. I'm not sure I can, either. With her astonishing insight, she understood we were very much alike, yet could Sofiya have predicted that fifty years later I would feel as she did then?

I have had long and close relationships, but my time with Sofiya was one of innocence and unique beauty. Reading through my old journal and travel diary written in faded blue ink, looking at my scrapbook of photographs, turning the shells and pottery bowl in my hands, I realize that our graceful circle of loving and being loved could only happen once, upon an island.

When I stayed on St. Croix in 1966, I had recently read William Golding's *Lord of the Flies* and pondered writing a novel set on the island, one that would explore why people are drawn to living surrounded by water and how geographical containment affects residents and visitors. I also wanted to capture the beauty of the island and its magical spirit. The idea of writing such a work stayed with me for decades until I finally made good on my youthful aspiration.

Once, Upon an Island contains some autobiographical details, but the characters' histories and the dramatic plot elements are imaginary. Many of the wonderful area restaurants, hotels, and stores mentioned were real—a few are still in business. The Pink Fancy existed then (now remodeled and called the Sugar Apple Bed and Breakfast). The hotel's charming owner inspired the character of Travis McVay in terms of appearance and manner, yet Travis's life and his behavior are entirely fictional creations.

Sofiya Florián is closely based on a dear friend, Elena Eisenhauer, who shared some of her World War II experiences in the Czech Resistance, though Sofiya's internment in a concentration camp and marriage to a Nazi were invented. Even so, I always suspected Elena's time during the war was more traumatic than she revealed. Elena was a remarkable woman who felt displaced, yet we became very close during my two visits.

My mother, Agnes Ricks Egan, an accomplished artist, brought us to the island so she could create a portfolio of paintings and drawings. These were successfully exhibited at A. H. Riise Gallery on St. Thomas as in the book, but otherwise her personality, background, and marriage bear no resemblance to that of Evelyn Livingston, nor was my father, Richard Patrick Egan, in any way like Steven.

I am not a professional historian, though I did my best to adhere to the primary facts about Czechoslovakia during World War II. I am indebted to Wikipedia for the following articles: "German Occupation of Czechoslovakia," "Sudeten Germans," "Munich Agreement," "Protectorate of Bohemia and Moravia, Slovak Republic, 1939-1945," "Czech Resistance to Nazi Occupation," "Ležáky," "Lidice," "Operation Anthropoid," and "Ravensbrück Concentration Camp;" and for details about the Lesser Antilles Airboats: "Charles F. Blair, Jr." and "Grumman G-21 Goose." An article on the Stone Balloon restaurant by Alan M. Pavlik was very helpful.

It is rare that we can fully immerse ourselves in a long-ago period of our lives, but writers have this unique opportunity. For me, *Once, Upon an Island* evokes nostalgic memories of a bittersweet time and an enchanted place. I dedicate this book to Elena Eisenhauer and to the residents of St. Croix.

ACKNOWLEDGMENTS

I am honored to have Naomi Rosenblatt and Heliotrope Books publish *Once, Upon an Island* and delighted that it will join my 2021 novel, *The Swimmer*, on their distinguished list. Naomi is a wonderful colleague, whose enthusiasm, expertise, and sophistication are rare attributes. Working with her on this, my favorite book, has been a great pleasure.

The initial developmental editing was done by Dr. Helga Schier, who gave her usual brilliant advice, as did Cathie Brettschneider, an early reader. My dear friend, Beverly Jean Harris, provided invaluable suggestions and good humor, as she has for many of my other novels; Jennica Dotson reviewed the manuscript and offered constructive, detailed guidance. Lisa Cantrell, who lived on St. Croix during the period and is the administrator for "St. Croix Memories" on Facebook, caught several errors and helped promote the book through the community of island enthusiasts. Deepest thanks to Karla Linn Merrifield for her last-stage proofreading, sharp eye, and ongoing "writerly" support, and to Jennifer Maguire, the book's publicist, who did a fine job on outreach and marketing. I am so grateful to have these extraordinary women in my life.

When I saw the cover photograph several years ago, I instantly reached out to Jill Dedinsky, who had taken the image at The Palms at Pelican Cove, a significant location in the novel. She sent me the file, but sadly, when I requested formal permission for the photograph's use, I learned Jill had passed away suddenly. After some research, I was able to contact her son, Jay Ridgway, and her friend and executor, Jen Kramer, who gave approval for the picture's publication to serve as a legacy for Jill. Heartfelt thanks to both of them, and to my PhotoShop wizard, Vicki DeVico, who once again demonstrated how adept she is—this time becoming a beach cleaner and removing seaweed and also adding waves to the cover illustration. I am also indebted to Naomi Rosenblatt for her interior design and assistance with the cover's assembly.

Many current and former residents of St. Croix authenticated the historical accuracy of places on the island. Kudos to Carolyn Ehle, Vicki Marsh, Siri Jackman, Judith A. Lordi, Lyn Voytershark, Gary Kilbride, Bruce Dawson, Clifford Charles, Laura Phayre Abbot, Holland Redfield, Kathy Brandenburg, Helen Carnes, Keith Richards, Roy Lawaetz, Marlon Williams, James Curtis Henderson, Joseph Dolloff, Reenie Newsome Niskala, Valerie Resnick Steinberg, Joanna Sedylmayr Bridges, Pat Glassford Laufenberg, Herbert Schoenbolm, and Kobie Nichols at Undercover Books. If any factual details about St. Croix in 1966 are incorrect, the errors are mine.

The book would not be possible without the support of valued friends and readers: Carol Oberle, Betty Harris, Julie and Tom Stewart, Jane Rundell, Lauren Lepow, Mark Conover, Mary McCue, Michael Ungs, Robert Starosciak, Shari Friedman, Cynthia Bonner, and some wonderful Rumson-Fair Haven Regional classmates.

ABOUT THE AUTHOR

Laury A. Egan is the author of nine novels: *Jenny Kidd*, *The Outcast Oracle*, *Fabulous! An Opera Buffa*, *A Bittersweet Tale*, *The Ungodly Hour*, *The Swimmer*, *Turnabout*, *Wave in D Minor*, and *Doublecrossed*; a collection: *Fog and Other Stories*; and four volumes of poetry: *Snow, Shadows, a Stranger*; *Beneath the Lion's Paw*; *The Sea & Beyond*; and *Presence & Absence*. She lives on the northern coast of New Jersey. Website: www.lauryaegan.com

www.ingramcontent.com/pod-product-compliance
Lightning Source LLC
Chambersburg PA
CBHW070851260626
47170CB00007B/2581